PRAISE FOR *LOVE AMONG THIEVES*

"Sexy and smart, *Love Among Thieves* is so much fun it's practically criminal."

Tiana Smith, author of *The Spy and I*

"*Love Among Thieves* is a true romantic comedy! Each page is filled with wonderful tension, wit, and ridiculous amounts of charm. This was such a fun read!"

Hannah Bonam-Young, *New York Times* bestselling author

"Do you love smart, sexy banter between anti-heroes? Long for a man who'll pick the lock on your door, then the lock on your heart? *Love Among Thieves* delivers a heist with benefits—and one of the hottest romantic thrillers I've ever read."

Madge Maril, author of *Slipstream* and *The Paddock Club*

"*Love Among Thieves* gets your pulse pounding in more ways than one! Watch out—this heist romance just might steal your heart."

Carlie Walker, author of *The Takedown* and *Code Word Romance*

"Romance lovers take note: thieves with benefits is my new favourite trope! *Love Among Thieves* is criminally good. West and Adelina stole my heart!"

Noreen Nanja, author of *The Summers Between Us*

"The level ten tension in this slow-burn, opposites attract, forced proximity, heist hijinks romance makes it impossible to put down. I forewent sleep for Katrina Kwan's sparkling banter, simmering chemistry, action-packed scenes, and laugh-out-loud writing, and I have zero regrets. *Love Among Thieves* is a must-read!"

Aurora Palit, author of *Sunshine and Spice* and *Honey and Heat*

"An unputdownable high-stakes, high-spice heist romance, *Love Among Thieves* is just as swoony as it is thrilling. It had me fanning myself while on the edge of my seat the entire time. This book is a masterclass in writing scorching-hot chemistry and jaw-dropping plot twists. I'm going to recommend Katrina Kwan to every reader I know!"

Swati Hegde, author of *Can't Help Faking in Love*

"Action-packed, scorchingly hot, and so clever, *Love Among Thieves* is part heist book and part rom-com with a surprisingly warm heart. Adelina and West are compelling characters with sympathetic motivations behind their lives of crime, and I adored seeing them go from enemies to collaborators to more. The undercurrent of pushing back against familial expectations and the loyal sibling relationships made the story shine even brighter."

Farah Heron, author of *Accidentally Engaged* and *A Little Holiday Fling*

"Smart, sexy, and fun. Adelina and West are a dynamic pairing that readers will be cheering from the jump, both for their Robin Hood-esque thievery and their opposites-attract romance. I would go on a thousand adventures with them and love every one."

Emily Ohanjanians, author of *The Book Tour*

LOVE AMONG THIEVES

BOOKS BY

KATRINA KWAN

Contemporary Romance

Knives, Seasoning, and a Dash of Love

•

Fantasy

The Last Dragon of the East

The Legend of the Nine-Tailed Fox

LOVE AMONG THIEVES

KATRINA KWAN

RANDOM HOUSE CANADA

PUBLISHED BY RANDOM HOUSE CANADA

Random House Canada, an imprint of Penguin Random House Canada Limited
320 Front Street West, Suite 1400
Toronto, Ontario, M5V 3B6, Canada
penguinrandomhouse.ca

Random House Canada and colophon are registered trademarks of Penguin Random House LLC.

The authorized representative in the EU for product safety and compliance is Penguin Random House Ireland, Morrison Chambers, 32 Nassau Street, Dublin D02 YH68, Ireland. https://eu-contact.penguin.ie

Library and Archives Canada Cataloguing in Publication

Title: Love among thieves / Katrina Kwan.
Names: Kwan, Katrina, author.
Identifiers: Canadiana (print) 2025027499X | Canadiana (ebook) 20250275007 | ISBN 9781039014107 (softcover) | ISBN 9781039014114 (EPUB)
Subjects: LCGFT: Romance fiction. | LCGFT: Novels.
Classification: LCC PS8621.W33 L68 2026 | DDC C813/.6—dc23

Text design: Lisa Jager
Cover design: Lisa Jager
Image credits: Copyright © 2026 Jessica Alvarez
Interior images: (laptop) Laura, (sunglasses) leberus / both Adobe Stock
Typesetting: Erin Cooper and Six Red Marbles

Printed in Canada

2 4 6 8 9 7 5 3 1

For Brent, my partner in crime

CHAPTER ONE

Late-Stage Capitalism Would Give Robin Hood an Aneurysm

Adelina

I JUST MADE a quarter of a million dollars—and it isn't even noon.

Of course, when I say *made*, I really mean *stole*, but it's best not to get wrapped up in the semantics.

Today's payload is courtesy of one Mr. Westley Bartholomew Porter. (Talk about stuffy old money, am I right?) I don't know who he is, and I frankly don't care. He's just a name assigned to the bank account information I purchased off the dark web. It's both startling and unsurprising just how much personal information you can find floating out there. In this day and age, data breaches happen more often than you think. All it takes is someone with a can-do attitude and questionable morals to put that data to good use.

Exhibit A: yours truly.

The process is called deetsing, and it's astonishingly simple to pull off. There are entire underground forums dedicated to buying and selling bank account details (that's where the *deets* in *deetsing* comes from), so long as you know where to look and you're willing to pay the price. Account numbers, card expiration dates, CCVs, home addresses, birthdates, social insurance numbers, phone numbers, and passwords . . . It's all right there at your fingertips, and more often than not, the rightful owners of this info have no idea they've been compromised.

Until it's too late.

Now, a well-adjusted, contributing member of society will argue that stealing is bad and morally bankrupt and *blah, blah, blah*. Once upon a time, I would have agreed. But I'm numb to it. I've been numb for a really long time and—forgive my French—I'm out of fucks to give. A part of me wonders if it's an act of rebellion. My way of chasing an exhilarating yet fleeting shot of adrenaline after every job well done. Or maybe it's just a way of getting back at Mom. Whatever the reason, nothing's going to change if someone doesn't get their hands dirty, and I'm both capable and willing.

In my humble opinion, doing bad things for good reasons leaves me net neutral as far as karmic justice goes.

I plug away at my laptop in the back corner of the café, soft jazz playing over the speakers while the barista grinds richly scented coffee beans. I shift funds to and from the handful of mule accounts I've been operating from. I plucked those off a marketplace on the dark web too, but the crucial difference is that these accounts were willingly given. For a fee, of course.

I pay a 1.5 percent kickback to the owners for every transaction that occurs. Given how much I move in a day, that's incredibly generous. I'm still a little paranoid that one of them will squeal, but a) if they're willing to sell their accounts for the use of illicit activities, they're probably desperate for the money, and b) turning on me is basically the same as self-reporting. I haven't run into any problems so far, but caution in my line of work is a must. If they screw me over, I can screw them right back.

My fingers fly over my keyboard. Just because I've got the money doesn't mean the job is done. The tiny voice in the back of my head tells me I should feel bad, but I've seen how much money the mark had with my own eyes. He's got another two million just sitting there collecting dust, so I'm sure Mr. Moneybags will be fine to wipe his tears with a couple of loose hundreds.

Keeping just enough of the funds to pay my bills this month, I split the remainder between three different charities. The receipt emails arrive in my inbox in quick succession, addressing me by my online handle.

Dear QWERTY, thank you for your donation
to the Vancouver Food Drive Society!

Thank you for supporting the Sunshine Children's Hospital,
QWERTY!

Thank you, QWERTY, for donating to Serenity's Women's Shelter!

I sit back with a relieved sigh, flexing my hands. I've done more good in the last two hours than most people will manage in their entire lifetimes. That sounds snarky and condescending, but I don't mean it to be. Honestly, I get it. In this economy, you have to look out for number one—but where does that leave our most vulnerable? Those who need our help but are largely forgotten?

After the Charlie Bower Incident, I figured—why not me? With both the means and the know-how, I can do what many have only ever dreamed about: steal from the rich and give to the poor. Robin Hood was onto something. It's so simple, so elegant.

The precise amount of money I've *made* in the past six years eludes me. Twenty million? Thirty? It's hard to say. I don't keep track because I don't want to risk inflating my ego. The moment I get cocky is the moment I slip up. That's what differentiates me from your run-of-the-mill crook and makes me an A-tier criminal. One careless mistake is all it'll take to land me behind bars. I alleviate *just* enough from my marks that I can help the charities I'm passionate about, but not so much that my targets realize something's wrong off the cuff.

Imagine having so much money you can afford to lose a couple hundred thousand and still not break a sweat. It makes them the perfect targets.

"Addy?"

I look up to find Lily standing on the other side of the café table. We're identical twins, she and I, though I can boast an entire five minutes of additional life experience. The only reason people can tell us apart now is because I've taken to chopping my hair down into some semblance of an uneven pixie cut. Summer is around the corner, and I hate the sensation of hair sticking to the back of my neck. Other than that, we have the same button nose, full cheeks, plump lips and small dark-brown eyes.

We look like Dad.

Lily tries to sneak a peek at my screen. Out of pure instinct, I slap my laptop shut—because that doesn't look suspicious as hell, right?

"What are you doing?" Lily asks with a devious little giggle-snort. I laugh exactly like her, though I haven't had much reason to in a long while.

"I'm committing grand larceny," I tell her flatly. It's not a lie.

My sister rolls her eyes and helps herself to the seat across from me, the chair scraping across the brown tile flooring. "Hilarious. Seriously, what were you doing?"

"Fine, you got me. I'm watching clown porn."

"Why can I never get a straight answer out of you?" She crinkles her nose in disgust. "And please tell me that's not actually a thing."

I shrug, swiping my clammy palms over my jeans. Given the sheer size of the internet, I'm sure there's some small, dark corner where clown porn exists. Out of sight, out of mind.

"How did you find me?" I ask, ignoring her question.

"I stopped by your apartment. The little old lady who lives next door told me I might be able to find you here. Says you come to this spot often."

I click my tongue. "Mrs. Singh ratted me out? That's the last time I'm helping her reset her Wi-Fi router."

Lily pins me with a hard stare. Not quite angry, but certainly exasperated. "I've been worried about you. You don't ever answer your texts."

"I've been busy."

"Still freelancing?"

"Yep."

"You look tired."

"Rude," I scoff without any real heat.

"Are you still seeing that therapist?" Lily asks with a sigh. The way she says it suggests she already knows, but I answer her anyway.

"Oh, yeah," I lie dryly, shifting my laptop off the sticky wooden table and sliding it into my backpack. "I *love* spending a hundred and sixty bucks for her to tell me every week that 'only time heals all wounds.'"

"She's a professional, Addy. You should listen to her."

"I need solutions, not fortune cookie proverbs."

Lily's expression hardens. "Now who's being rude? Therapy is a privilege."

I deflate in my seat. I don't like upsetting my sister, even if it's mildly warranted. She did sort of ambush me, after all. "Sorry," I mumble. "You're right. I just . . . Maybe I just need to try someone else. We weren't a good fit, that's all."

"I understand." Lily nods, casting me a sympathetic look. "Listen, the reason I wanted to see you is because we're having a family get-together. I tried calling you, but you never answer your damn phone."

My eyebrows shoot up. "Is something important happening?"

"I wanted you to be the first to hear this, but . . ." Her whole face lights up, bright and warm like the sun. "I got into law school! I'm shipping out to Dalhousie next year."

A mix of emotions washes over me. Delight—because *wow,* my little sister's finally taking the next big step in pursuing her dreams. Disappointment—because *shit,* Nova Scotia is really far away. Like, *literally-the-other-side-of-Canada* far. And then I follow everything up with a chaser of self-directed resentment because *fuck,* she's moving on with her life and I barely have the energy to get out of bed most days. If it wasn't for my work, I'd probably be worse off.

But then I swallow the feelings down and surprise myself when I don't have to force a smile. This one's genuine. Even though I'm terrible at keeping in touch and we've drifted apart, Lily is still my dearest friend. Probably my only one, if I'm being perfectly honest with myself.

"That's amazing," I tell her. "I'm really proud of you."

"Thank you," she says, reflecting my smile. "Will you come to my celebration dinner? It's this Friday. We can show up together. I'm sure everyone will be excited to see you."

"Even Mom?"

Lily pauses at this, confirming my suspicions. "She . . . doesn't know you're coming yet. Figured it might just be better to—"

"Show up and ask for forgiveness later?" I interject.

My mother and I don't agree on a lot of things, and working myself into an early grave is most certainly one of them. She's a traditionalist. Old-school Hong Kong lower-middle class. Her formula for a comfortable life is *hard work + overtime = financial security*. I could have very easily done my duty as the first-born daughter of two immigrant parents and gone the doctor-lawyer-astronaut route, but I realized there was a better, more fulfilling way to get through life.

Most people live paycheck to paycheck, and that, in and of itself, can be a scary thing. All it takes is one tiny setback: a family emergency, a blown car tire, a violent bout of food poisoning that causes you to miss a week of work. Now you're suddenly scrambling to make ends meet. Having to choose between paying rent and the grocery bills. It's a bitter truth: us regular plebians are closer to financial ruin than we are to being billionaires. It isn't fair.

Life isn't fair, Adelina, my mother liked to tell me whenever she wanted to knock me down a peg. *The only way to get ahead is to work hard.*

Mom would have a cow if she knew what I've been up to lately. She just doesn't understand that sometimes hard work isn't enough. A person can work themselves to the bone and still have nothing to show for it. Dad certainly did, but the one saving grace was that he actually enjoyed what he did for a living.

"I know things have been really rocky, but I want you there," my sister says.

That's putting it mildly. I try not to let my irritation show, but Lily's told me time and time again that I suffer from a deadly case of Resting Bitch Face. (Arguably the *one* thing I inherited from Mom.)

"There's a reason I decided to go no-contact with her," I mumble.

"I know."

"You remember what she said to me?"

"I was there."

"And you said you'd be supportive of my choice."

"I . . . know," she mumbles quietly. "But this is a big deal to me. Plus, I'm going to be leaving in a week."

"Leaving where?"

"I'm backpacking solo across Europe. You know, one last hurrah before I'm stuck in school."

"Solo? That doesn't sound safe."

She waves me off. "It's fine. People do it all the time."

"What if you end up in a *Taken* situation?"

"Oh my fuck, you need to stop watching those movies. You know they make you paranoid."

"I'm just saying shit happens."

"Then I'll put Liam Neeson on speed dial."

"Be sure to get me his autograph."

Lily leans across the table and takes my hand, giving my fingers a light squeeze. "Will you please come to dinner, Addy? I *miss* you."

I take a deep breath. I would be lying if I said I didn't miss her, too. But just the thought of sitting across from Mom at the table sends my heart skittering. I clench my clammy palms and will the tightness in my chest to loosen. There's an invisible hand clamped around my throat, squeezing the air from my lungs, offering just enough give to keep me alive.

Oh, the things I do for family.

"Okay, I'll be there. What restaurant?"

"It's at home, actually."

My chest tightens even more. Great. That means I'll be stepping into the lion's den. I already know she's going to sink her teeth into me the first chance she gets.

"We're having hot pot," Lily says in a singsong tone, as if it's some sort of consolation.

I grit my teeth. I suppose I can suffer through a couple of hours for her sake, but I can already tell it's going to be like getting a root canal without the mercy of anesthesia.

But damn, I really do love good hot pot.

CHAPTER TWO
Just When I Thought I Was Out . . .

West

Fifteen Minutes Ago

`Your withdrawal of $250,000 has been processed.`

I STARE AT my phone with wide-eyed dismay.

What fresh hell is this, and who dipped their grubby little fingers into Berruci's money?

"West! Look!"

Jack waves from the top of the red tube slide. She giggles all the way down, hopping out onto the playground's surface of dry wood chips. I remember to smile when she looks my way. She circles back with a giggle and scrambles up the fake rock-climbing wall to go another round. We regularly come to this playground in particular because it's the only one in East Sacramento with a new built-in waterpark—a perfect place to cool down in the climbing April heat.

While I'm grateful that she's having the time of her life, I'm on the brink of a panic attack seated on the scalding-hot kiddie park bench.

This isn't good. This isn't good at all.

The call comes in not a minute later. My hands shake so hard I nearly make the mistake of hitting decline. I don't have to look at the caller ID to know who's waiting on the other end.

"Val, old friend!" I greet with a strained chuckle, praying he can't detect my unease. "To what do I owe the pleasure?"

He doesn't answer right away, and I know it's a deliberate move on his part to make me sweat. "Went on a little shopping spree, did you?" he asks, his voice raspy from years of heavy smoking.

I haven't had the misfortune of seeing the man in ages, but I'm already about to lose my lunch. Memories of that night come flooding in, leaving no space to think or breathe or remain calm. Months of planning—only for everything to blow up in our faces. Diana, Joseph, Bannock and Henrie . . . all arrested within minutes of each other. I didn't exactly get away unscathed either, forced into this god-awful arrangement. Berruci made it seem like a generous pardon, but I saw it for what was: an ultimatum.

And Michael was the one who paid the price.

I decide to drop the confident act. Knowing Berruci, it'll only piss him off more. "It wasn't me; I swear. I just got the notification too. I know better than to take what's yours."

"Fuckin' right you do," Berruci replies with a dry cough. "I'm sure I don't have to remind you why you're playing the role of a suburban dad. How's your niece doing, by the way? Jacqueline, did I remember that right?"

I grit my teeth. So he wants to throw low blows early, does he? "Leave her name out of your mouth," I snap. "We had a deal."

"A deal that's now been broken. All you had to do was let me use you like a good little mule. Keep my money safe, collect interest and not touch a fucking penny. You seriously think I'm stupid enough to believe you had nothing to do with it?"

"But it's true! I didn't take anything."

It's true that he pays me a 0.3 percent kickback to keep quiet and maintain the account, but I've refused to touch a cent. I've been working nights as a warehouse stocker to make ends meet, which conveniently leaves my days free to look after Jack *and* ensures that Berruci has one less thing to hold over my head.

"Then who did?" he asks gruffly.

My heart plummets. "I . . . I don't know."

"How convenient."

Half a yard away, Jack waves at me again to get my attention before swinging across the monkey bars with impressive agility. I wipe any trace of concern from my face. She doesn't know who I really am—who I *used* to be. She has no idea about the world Michael and I were born into. A world we fought tooth and nail to escape, all so we could keep her safe.

Panic grips my throat, squeezing at my windpipe. I promised Michael I would keep her safe. If something happens to me, what's going to happen to Jack?

"I'll find them," I say into the phone. "I'll find whoever did this and recover the money."

"See that you do," Berruci replies coldly. "And know this: you can either serve the fucker to me on a platter, or I'll kill you in their place. Got it?"

I swallow hard. "Loud and clear."

"Good." And then, after a pause that seems to last an entire decade, Berruci adds, "Isn't it Jacqueline's birthday next month? I'll have to stop by to give her a gift from ol' Uncle Val."

"That won't be necessary," I say firmly.

We both know it's a thinly veiled threat. To think he'd stoop so low as to rope Jack into this . . . She's only six, for God's sake. But I do understand why he's bringing her up. He thinks it's going to light a fire under my ass. An unspoken deadline.

And it's working.

I'd hoped to shield her from all of it. I'd agreed to be one of his mule accounts so that he could launder his illicit funds more easily, and I've never said a damn word, not about his underhanded business deals, about his schemes. About how he made Michael disappear. In return, he was supposed to leave me and Jack alone forever. I should have known better than to make deals with a rat. They're incessant little creatures, capable of squeezing through the tightest of cracks.

"Watch your back," Berruci grunts and hangs up without so much as a *ta-ta for now*. Not that I can imagine a burly tatted crime boss saying something so flamboyant.

At some point, Jack must have hopped down from the monkey bars, because the next thing I see is the blur of her bright-red running shoes—she *begged* me to buy them for her when she saw them at the store—zipping toward me. Her cheeks are flushed, but so is her forehead, a telltale sign that the coconut-scented sunscreen I badgered her into putting on is starting to wear off.

She peers up at me with her big blue eyes, and I can't help but think about how Michael used to pull the exact same face when we were kids. "Does your tummy hurt, Uncle West?" she asks.

I force a smile. "My tummy's fine, sweetie."

"Then why do you look so sick?"

The last thing I want is for her to worry. I ruffle her hair, a much lighter blonde than Michael had. "I think I need a little nap, that's all."

"Aren't you too old for naps?"

"Too old for naps?" I gasp. "But there's no such thing!"

"Tommy from school says I'm too old for naps," Jack mumbles, her face twisting with her obvious disgust. She picks at the edge of her insulin patch on the back of her right arm. She chose tape with bright pink and yellow flowers to keep it securely in place.

I gently pry her hand away. "Don't listen to Tommy. We both agreed that he's a . . . What did you call him the other day?"

"A dickhead."

I throw my head back and laugh, momentarily forgetting my troubles. A few of the other parents standing nearby shoot me disapproving glares, no doubt having overheard her colorful language, but I don't care.

"Remember not to say that behind his back, alright?"

Jack nods. "Right. If you've got something mean to say, you should say it to someone's face."

"*But?*" I prompt.

"But you should always be prepared for the consa . . . the consta . . ."

"Consequences," I say, helping her out.

"Yeah, that."

I nod in approval. "How about we head home? I'll make spaghetti tonight—your favorite."

Jack's smile is the sweetest thing imaginable. For a moment, I almost forget that there's someone breathing down my neck. "With little hot dog pieces?" she asks.

"What do you think, chef? It's a complicated recipe."

She giggles. "We can do it!"

I pick her up and carry her with one arm. My niece is getting a little too heavy for me, which is all the more reason to appreciate the moment. Before I know it, she'll be all grown up and learning to drive. She'll bring home her first boyfriend or girlfriend and I'll have to pretend to be cool about it. Though, if I'm being perfectly honest, I'll probably fail in spectacular fashion. She'll graduate high school and pursue a field of study she's passionate about. And one day, if I've done everything right and kept my promise to Michael, she will grow into a good, sensible young woman.

Provided I can keep Valentino Berruci the hell out of our lives. Therein lies the problem.

Even if I *do* somehow figure out who took the money and turn them in, that doesn't stop Berruci yanking the leash strapped around my neck whenever he feels like it. His very existence is a problem, one that threatens Jack's safety.

I carry Jack home. She makes it a whole three blocks before she falls asleep, drooling a dark patch onto my shoulder. I hold her a little tighter, equally as protective as I am paranoid, all while my mind races to stitch together a plan.

I can do this. I have to. If all goes well, I might be able to take out Berruci once and for all.

Step one: come out of retirement.

Step two: track down the thief.

Step three: find a babysitter.

But before I do any of that, I set Jack down on the couch for her afternoon nap, draping a light knitted throw blanket over her for warmth. I make my way into the kitchen and pull open the cupboards beneath the sink. Feeling around blindly, I locate the small burner phone I have taped to the underside of the counter. I'd tucked it away in a sandwich bag years ago to protect it from the damp. After shoving its battery into place, I boot it up and scroll through my short list of contacts. I don't know if her number is still in service. It's a long shot, but it's the only one I've got.

Thankfully, Diana picks up on the sixth ring.

"*Salut?*" she answers in French.

"It's Mathieu," I reply. The language feels strange on my tongue after all these years. "Mathieu Maunier. Do you remember me?"

It takes her a moment, but she finally says, "How could I forget? I was so sure he made you *disappear*."

"He sort of did. It's a long story."

"Tell it to someone who cares," Diana answers bluntly.

"Wait," I say in a rush. "Please, just . . . wait. I know you're pissed. You have every right to be."

"I served *three* years. And now I find out you're alive and well while I was stuck in the clink. Why wouldn't I be pissed?"

"Diana, listen. I understand you're upset. What happened that night . . . It was a bad night for all of us, but I can make it up to you."

There's a long pause. Somewhere in the background, I can hear traffic and distant chatter. "Go on," she says.

"I have a plan to go after Berruci. Do you want in?"

Another pause, this one so long that I worry the signal's dropped. I don't exactly have a great international calling plan. But if there's anyone I can count on, especially when it comes to putting that son of a bitch away for good, it's going to be her.

"Fine," she says after an eternity. "What do you need me to do?"

CHAPTER THREE From Bad to Worse

Adelina

Friday

CANTONESE. IT'S THE first thing I hear when I step through the front door of our childhood home deep within the Burnaby suburbs, roughly twenty-five minutes by SkyTrain from downtown Vancouver. My aunts, uncles and cousins are a boisterous choir of enthusiastic conversation, chords of rapid-fire syllables accented with staccato intonations floating into my ears like music.

I understand exactly none of it. Well, that's not true. I know the basics:

Ngo tou ngo. *I'm hungry.*

Ci so hai bin aa? *Where's the bathroom?*

Ngo hou gui. *I'm tired.*

And that's about it.

When Lily and I were born, my parents made the executive decision to raise us with English as our first language. My cousins are all a few years older than us. When they went to school and struggled to communicate with their teachers and failed to understand their homework, it made an impression. Mom and Dad were adamant that this would *not* happen to their daughters.

So they spoke English to us everywhere. When we were at home, while we were grocery shopping at Costco. Even when we went out for dim sum, they'd speak to the waiter in Canto and switch back when talking to us. Lily and I thought it was perfectly normal until we were old enough to understand what it was to be left out.

"There she is!" Uncle Tommy calls out as Lily and I slip out of our street shoes and change into indoor slippers Mom bought from T&T a million years ago.

"Hi, everyone!" Lily greets cheerfully. "I'm so glad you're all here."

In the blink of an eye, our family surrounds her. I shrink back, no longer used to the noise and the lack of personal space. Even though it's been years since I saw them all at the funeral, very little has changed. Uncle Tommy still smells of mothballs, Auntie Ying of white flower oil. Cousin Jen has adult braces, so that's new. Cousins Alfie, Richard and George are still the nerdiest manchildren to ever walk the earth. And then there's Auntie June, who isn't actually related to us by blood. She's an old friend of Mom's who has been around long enough that we've basically absorbed her into the Choi family.

While my family pats Lily on the back and offer their congratulations, I am mostly ignored. Not that I mind. Maybe my years alone have exacerbated my natural introversion. I'm not the star of the show tonight, besides, and I'd honestly rather not steal Lily's thunder.

The only person whose attention I have is Mom.

She stands just off to the side, watching me from the corner of the entryway. She's shorter than me (and, by extension, Lily) by roughly two inches, but the overt unpleasantness she radiates makes her feel so much bigger.

"What did you do to your hair?" she asks.

Not *hello*. Not *how are you doing?* I haven't even been home for five minutes, and she's already taking shots at my appearance.

"I needed a change," I reply, my words clipped and restrained. I can sense Lily's eyes on the both of us, gauging our reactions like we're two snarling dogs sizing each other up.

"You look like a boy."

"So? I like it."

Mom curls her nose. She's never been the type to beat around the bush and fake pleasantries, but I'm sure this is just a warm-up. She'll tear me to shreds if given the chance, especially considering how we left things.

"Dinner's ready," she says, not so much to me as to the room at large. "Come sit."

The house is exactly the way I remember it from when I left for college. Save for a new potted money plant here and there, everything's the same. The mahogany furniture with the red silk cushions. The picture frames carrying precious family photos. The large mirrors hung strategically on walls opposite large windows to give the illusion of a larger space. It's supposed to be good feng shui or whatever. I never really understood, but Mom adheres to the concept with an almost religious zeal.

The upright Yamaha piano sits in the den, its lid pulled down. My palms get clammy just looking at it. Mom would make us practice for an hour every single day after we were finished with our homework. We even had a little stopwatch to keep track of the time. Not a moment more, and certainly not a moment less. I used to love playing the piano, I think, but she sucked the fun out of it, and it started to feel more like work than a pastime. No one's played it in ages.

We arrive in the living room, which opens into the dining area and kitchen. The circular table has already been set, with little dishes of vegetables and larger platters of raw beef and pork arranged around the large metal hot pot set over a single-burner stove. It uses gas canisters. I've told Mom that there are electric versions, that she doesn't have to risk burning the house down, but she never listens. I've stopped trying to convince her.

There are ten chairs. The nine of us take our seats.

Everyone digs in, helping themselves to bites of rice while they toss green onions, cubed tofu, clumps of enoki mushrooms and various cuts of meat into the soup. It's been sectioned off by a divider: chicken broth on the right, spicy and sour on the left.

My cousins are deep in conversation, but since it's in Cantonese, I can pick up only bits here and there. It's like putting together a puzzle in the dark, but most of the pieces are missing and I've only got the edges to provide context. And there's no guarantee I've even got *those* in the right order. They mention something about a new movie coming out. Or are they talking about a new video game? On the other side of the table, my aunts and uncle are having their own enthusiastic conversation about the ever-rising price of fresh fruit. Or . . . maybe it's about the price of gas?

Whatever. Having them switch to English for my sake would make me feel too much like an inconvenience.

Lily tries to chime in, throwing a practiced sentence in every now and again, but the table only ends up laughing. If her intonations are off, I can't tell, though it seems highly likely.

"You sound like a gweilou," Richard says with his mouth full.

My ears perk up. Even I know what that means.

A foreigner.

He's only teasing, but it's a backhanded comment all the same. It's almost a little cruel. How are we supposed to improve if all we face is admonishment for simply trying? It's one of the reasons why I stopped trying to learn altogether. When we were kids, Jen once joked that I should have my Asian card revoked. I punched her in the mouth for the comment and wound up grounded for two weeks. (Worth it.)

"So, why'd you choose Dal?" Jen asks. "Not good enough to get into UBC?"

Auntie June titters haughtily. "Lily scored 178 on the LSAT. That's top 99 percent! She could get into any law school she wanted. Even Harvard!"

My sister's cheeks turn pink. "Oh, it's not that big of a deal. I had to take it twice. I didn't perform as well as I wanted to the first time."

"If you could get into Harvard, why didn't you?" asks George. He has a bit of broccolini stuck between his front teeth.

"Because Dalhousie's giving me several scholarships. It's basically a full ride."

Mom huffs. "But it's not."

Just like that, the atmosphere twists into something uncomfortable and sticky. Nobody says anything, nobody moves. Lily's face is as bright as a ruby, and my cousins are all giving each other uneasy glances.

Meanwhile, I fish out two beef balls and dig in, unbothered. This tastes *so* good. If there's one thing I *do* miss about Mom, it's her cooking—not that I'll admit that aloud. There's no need to give her ammunition to use against me.

Lily clears her throat. "I mean, I can always apply for a small loan. I only need a couple thousand and I'll be covered for the whole year. If I keep my grades up, the scholarships renew. I'm sure it'll all work out."

"Didn't Addy get a full-ride scholarship to MIT?" Alfie asks.

All eyes turn toward me. *Now* I'm bothered. I knew there was a reason he was my least favorite cousin. All he had to do was pretend I'm not here. Lord knows *I'm* trying to.

"Uh," I mutter stupidly. "Yeah, I did."

"Oh, yes," says Jen. "Computer stuff, right?"

"Computer science," I correct, though I don't know why. The more I engage, the longer the spotlight is going to be on me. I'm already sweating buckets as it is, though I'm sure the sour and spicy soup is partially to blame. I keep filling my bowl (a bit of marinated beef skirt this time), silently praying that the table will move on to a new topic.

"Oh, that's . . . *cute,*" Jen says, saccharine as can be. "It must suck, though. Isn't the job market *super* oversaturated? My old college buddy has been struggling to find work for ages."

That's rich, coming from her. I'm tempted to ask her if she's finally put her artsy-fartsy MFA from the University of Toronto to good use and written anything significant, but I won't stoop that low because I know for a fact she hasn't.

"I'm managing, thank you," I mumble, holding my rice bowl to my lips to scarf down a few bites. I'd forgotten how small my social battery is. My brain is already foggy, the tiny voice in the back of my head politely suggesting we take a four-hour nap. At what point is it considered socially acceptable for me to leave without it coming across as rude?

"Not that any of it matters," Mom butts in, bitterness dripping off every word.

I look up at her from across the table and hold her pointed scrutiny.

Here we go.

Family dinners are supposed to be fun, a great way to catch up with those closest to us. But let's be perfectly honest, shall we? They're dick-measuring contests, designed to flaunt your latest achievements in a constant game of one-up. I'm more than aware that the reason Mom is so bitter is because she can no longer use me as a trophy, can no longer live vicariously through my success. She makes it no secret that I'm a failure in her eyes—and therefore her greatest shame.

Sometimes, when I'm feeling particularly angry with her, I try to remind myself that she was a young woman once too. It's a trick my therapist suggested I try before I stopped going to see her.

Once upon a time, Mom must have had dreams, aspirations, hopes. She must have experienced first love and heartbreaks. There was likely a time when she made silly mistakes, or even egregious ones. And for a moment, it helps me remember my compassion. My empathy. Words spoken in anger are not always the result of a single moment, but a slow culmination of many.

"I'd rather not talk about this here," I say firmly. "We're here to celebrate Lily's achievement."

"Achievement? What achievement? She isn't a lawyer yet." She's getting louder and louder as she speaks. Mom's never had any volume control. "Do you have any idea how hard your father worked to provide for you two? Getting into law school is the *bare minimum*."

I take a deep breath and count back from three. Just because I went no-contact doesn't mean I hate her. Hate is a waste of energy. She's in no way a bad person . . . she's just not a good parent. It's an important distinction that I've worked hard to keep in mind, but *boy* is she good at blurring the lines. She's a lot to handle, but so am I. When two like sides of a magnet meet, the laws of physics dictate they'll push one another apart.

"I don't think it's polite to diminish Lily's hard work."

God, could I sound more clinical? It's like my ex-therapist is using me as a sock puppet and I'm just mouthing along to her words.

"Hard work," Mom says with a scoff. "What do you know about hard work? Four years at MIT only to drop out in the last semester!"

Lily visibly squirms in her seat. "A-Ma, let's not do this, okay?"

I wave my sister off. "No, no. Let her talk. She's clearly got some things she wants to get off her chest."

When Mom sits back in her chair, her head tilted up so she can sneer down her nose at me, I mimic her posture. I've made my boundaries clear, but since she won't accept them, I show that I can give as good as I can take.

"You threw away a good thing," she says. "All that, and for what?"

"You know precisely what happened," I snap back.

"Young people today are so lazy. When I was your age, we worked hard and never complained."

"Oh, yes. Let's conveniently leave out the impact that's had on your entire generation's mental health, shall we?"

"Do you have any idea how many people want the opportunities you had? How can you be so ungrateful?"

"I never said I was ungrateful, Mom."

"Your father and I sacrificed a lot for you."

"I *know*, but—"

"Clearly that wasn't the case!"

"You never stopped to try to understand what I was going through—"

"And now you walk in here, come eat *my* food . . . It's shameful."

"*Mom*," Lily cries. "You promised!"

Fuck it. Coming here was such a bad idea.

There's a reason why I haven't made an effort to keep in touch with my family, and tonight has reaffirmed it. Between my family's toxically competitive nature and Mom's outright hostility, there's only so much that I'm willing to put up with. I stand up from the table and glance down at my wristwatch—a gift from Dad the day I got my acceptance letter to MIT. I lasted a whole half an hour. Impressive.

But now I've had enough.

"It's fine," I say calmly. "I think I've overstayed my welcome."

Lily stands up too. "Addy, I'm so sorry, please don't go."

I grab the last remaining fish ball in my bowl, stuff it in my mouth and turn to leave. "Congrats on getting into law school. Text me pictures of your trip."

"Mou gwai jung," Mom mutters under her breath.

I freeze, her words cutting through me like a blade.

I lied before. That's not all the Cantonese I know.

Mou gwai jung. *Useless.*

I take the train home. It's mostly empty, so I'm able to snag a seat by one of the doors. It's after 9 p.m., but because the spring days are longer, the sun's still out. Come wintertime, it'll be pitch-black by five, so I'll enjoy it while I can. Contrary to popular belief, it doesn't rain in Vancouver 24/7. Sometimes we're capable of decent weather.

I hop off at Stadium-Chinatown and walk the rest of the way. My apartment building is only a few blocks from the station. I pass by not one, not two, but five unhoused individuals on my way. Some ask if I have any spare change while most keep quietly to themselves. Robert happens to be a familiar face, standing on his corner at West Pender and Homer Street.

"Good evening, Ms. Choi," he says, chipper as always. His cart is full of empty plastic bottles.

"Good haul today?" I ask, digging into my pockets for that five I was saving just for him.

"Better than good. I hit the jackpot down on Main. Some sort of street festival. People were tossing their bottles left and right. I'm on my way to the depot now."

"Nice," I reply with a smile.

Dad was the one who introduced me to Robert at the food drive. He's a good man who fell on hard times, not unlike so many whom Dad helped. From what Robert's told me, he's been on and off the streets for quite a while, but bless him, I see how hard he's trying. He broke his leg after a tumble down some stairs, and because he couldn't work his construction job, he was let go. One thing led to another, a downward spiral with no help in sight. He couldn't make rent payments and wound up living out of his car. The only reason I know this is because I took the time to treat him like an actual human being. Most people look at Robert and assume the worst. Drugs. Alcohol. Gambling. But that's not always the case. And even if it were, that wouldn't mean he doesn't deserve respect like every other person.

"Is there anything I can help you with?" I ask. "Toiletries, blankets . . ."

"Oh, that's alright. The jacket you got me last month was more than kind."

I smile. "Well, if there's ever anything you need, just let me know."

"You're a real one, Ms. Choi," he says, pushing his cart. "Edwin would be proud."

I ignore the lump that sticks to the back of my throat at the mention of my father's name. It's always hard to talk about him. I wave goodbye as I carry on my way. "I'll see you soon."

A part of me wishes I could help everyone in Robert's position, but things have gotten bad in recent years. With rent and the general cost of living through the roof, it's frankly no wonder Vancouver's seen a spike in the unhoused population. I make a mental note to donate to a local soup kitchen the next time I manage a sizeable take. As tempting as it is to go on a thieving spree, I have to be careful. Too much heat will only bring unwanted attention. Besides, it'll take some time to find a fresh set of account numbers to target.

Mrs. Singh stands just outside the building's entrance with her black Labrador, Pepper. Pepper's getting up there in years, the fur around her muzzle and eyes turning grayer by the day. It's rare for me to see these two apart; they're usually out and about together for a bit of fresh air regardless of rain or shine.

"Hello, Adelina," Mrs. Singh says as I bend over to pat her dog on the head. "Did your sister end up finding you? Goodness, when I saw her the other day I could have sworn she was you."

I manage a tired smile. I was admittedly a little peeved that she gave away my favorite hiding spot, but I'm over it now. Arguments with my mother tend to put everything else into perspective. I don't want to hold on to my anger like Mom does. "Yeah, she found me. Thanks for pointing her my way."

We enter the building and ride the elevator together in blissful silence. Mrs. Singh isn't the chatty type, and since I'm not either, we make the perfect neighbors. She gives me a polite smile and heads into her apartment, Pepper following dutifully behind. I have to fish my keys out from the bottom of my backpack before heading into my own apartment, ready to put this sordid day behind me. Days like today deserve a nice hot soak in the tub.

Only, I never make it to the bathroom.

Sitting on my secondhand leather couch in my too-tiny living room is a man I've never seen before. He lounges, an arm slung over the back while one of his legs is crossed over the other. He has short blond hair and piercing green eyes, and is dressed in a casual white button-down and black slacks. He doesn't look like a violent home invader, but looks can be deceiving. I, of all people, would know.

"Be not afraid," he says with a light chuckle, like he's some sort of biblically accurate angel trying not to freak out humankind. His voice is low and smooth. "As you can see, I'm unarmed. I just want to talk."

I should run. I should *scream*. But for some reason, I'm frozen in place. Fight or flight is a real bitch, because I do precisely neither.

"Who the fuck are you?" I snap, my heart trying to thud its way out of my chest.

The cocky son of a gun has the audacity to smile. "My name is West Porter, and you're Adelina Choi—the woman who stole my money."

CHAPTER FOUR
. . . They Pull Me Back in.

West

SHE THROWS THINGS. They hit me.

All in all, I'd say our first meeting is going really well.

"Get out!" she shrieks. "Get out, or I'll call the cops!"

I duck out of the way of a flying plate. The only thing separating us now is the small kitchen island built into the floor of her one-bedroom apartment. Adelina's managed to slip into the kitchen, an arsenal of knives and forks and heavy bowls she can use for ammunition at her fingertips. A critical error on my part. She has an impressive arm.

"We both know you're not going to do that," I reply quickly, dodging a Tupperware lid that she throws like a discus. She nearly takes the top of my skull off with that one.

"Try me, asshole!" She grabs a cleaver next. The shiny glint of the metal makes my stomach flip. There was probably a better way to introduce myself, but it's much too late for that. I've got one foot in the grave, and she's got the shovel ready to bury me alive.

I raise a hand like I'm trying to tame a clever velociraptor. "Take it easy, alright? I don't want tonight to end in murder."

"You should have thought of that before you broke into my apartment!"

Three sharp knocks sound at the front door. She turns, her face pale and her eyes wide in mortification.

"Adelina, dear?" comes the voice of an elderly woman. "Is everything alright?"

I move before Adelina has a chance, racing for the door. "One second!" I call out.

"Don't you dare!" Adelina hisses.

But it's too late. I pry the door open wide and lean casually against the doorframe. Adelina has no choice but to hide the cleaver she's wielding, tossing it away and out of view. More importantly, out of reach.

"Oh," the lady says, blinking up at me. "Is everything alright in there? I thought I heard shouting."

"Sorry about that," I say, with one of the most charming smiles I can muster. I may be out of the game, but there are some tricks that come as naturally to me as breathing. "Adelina and I were trying to figure out where we wanted to go for dinner. She can be very enthusiastic."

"Is this true?" the woman asks. "I've never known you to have guests."

"We met on a dating app." Adelina lies with much more fluidity than I was expecting. She shoots me a hard glare. "I have a feeling this might be our first and last date."

So she can think on her feet. That bodes well for me.

"The night's still young," I reply with a wink.

When she turns her nose up at me, I'm almost offended. Damn, I must be rustier than I thought. It used to be I could charm my way into anyone's heart with a simple compliment and an honest smile—the con man's favorite tool. Although, in hindsight, I wasn't a very successful one.

"Well, as long as everything's alright," Adelina's neighbor says. "If you're looking to try something new, there's a lovely kebab place not too far from here."

"We'll keep that in mind, thanks," I say as I close the door gently, leaning my back against it so I can keep an eye on Adelina. Better to not let her catch me unaware. "There. Happy?"

She frowns. "What?"

"Your neighbor's seen my face. If I try anything fishy—which I wasn't planning to, calm down—she can give my description to the police."

"Mrs. Singh is eighty-nine and forgets to put in her dentures most mornings, so that's hardly reassuring."

"Look, I'm sorry about the breaking and entering, but it's not like I could have knocked on your door and asked to come in. If I really wanted to—"

"Murder me and chop me up into little bits?" she interjects.

"If I really wanted to do that, I could have hidden behind your curtains and caught you by surprise." I take a deep breath and place a hand over my heart. "Well, *more* by surprise."

"How *did* you get in?"

I slip the small pin I had tucked beneath my tongue out, pinching it between my teeth. "Picked your lock."

"Do me a favor and choke on it."

Ooh. She's feisty, this one.

I slip the pin back under my tongue. A pocket is probably less of a hazard, but Michael was the one who taught me this little trick. Cops check pockets, after all, and necessity begets creativity. The tools I use must not only be discreet but accessible at all times.

"Aren't you curious?" I ask her.

"Curious about what?"

I grin even wider, loving the anger in her dark eyes. "How I found you. I bet it's burning you up inside."

This is a gambit on my part. She was probably too busy throwing things at me to wonder, but now that I've planted the seed, I can see her mind at work. It's in the twitch of her left eye and the tight line of her jaw.

She appears to be a woman of simple tastes. The type to dress for comfort rather than style. Her black hoodie is a size too big, and her acid-washed blue jeans are baggy as well. I wouldn't be surprised if she chose a pixie cut out of convenience rather than as a fashion statement, and apart from the three small hoops in both her earlobes and the watch wrapped around her wrist, she doesn't have any flashy jewelry. Odd. Given the plainness of her apartment—scuffed secondhand furniture and sparse white walls—I figured she would at least splurge on herself.

What does she do with all the money she steals? Does she really give it all to charity? That doesn't sound like fun at all.

Like a feral cat backed into a corner, Adelina studies me with a level of intensity that sends a shot of adrenaline racing through my veins. It's her gaze, as studious as it is sharp. She isn't just angry, I realize, but furious.

And for some reason, I find that absolutely *thrilling*.

Our standoff lasts another moment, the air around us so heavy that I can feel it bearing down on my shoulders. I've placed the ball in her court, but I don't know if she'd rather play or throw the basketball directly at my nose. Given her propensity for using me for target practice, I'd argue the latter.

It isn't until her shoulders loosen that I know I've won this round. Marks like her have their intellect, which is often wrapped up in their pride. She wants to know. *Needs* to. Which is why I'm not at all surprised when she says, "Fine. But we're not talking here."

"What do you suggest?"

"A restaurant."

I chuckle. "Because you want witnesses around?"

"Why else?"

"Works for me," I reply. "That kebab place your neighbor suggested sounds nice."

"Whatever. You go first."

"So you can stab me while my back is turned? Nice try. We'll leave side by side; how does that sound?"

Her left eye twitches again. “Fine.”

I gesture toward the door with a sweep of my arm. And although she flips me the bird, we do end up leaving the apartment together.

Look at that. We’re getting along already.

CHAPTER FIVE

(Surprisingly) Not the Worst Date I've Ever Been On

Adelina

I SHOULD BE freaking out right now, but I'm unexpectedly calm. Maybe it's a coping mechanism. Like my brain knows to release an excess of serotonin to keep from going into a total destructive meltdown. Or maybe I'm delusional enough to believe that I have everything under control.

Denial can be such a beautiful thing.

Despite being called Kebab *Town*, the restaurant isn't even big enough to host five two-seater tables. It's a cramped space with sticky black linoleum flooring, grease-covered walls and a bathroom the size of a broom closet. In fact, I'm fairly certain it *is* the broom closet, and they somehow squeezed a toilet and sink in there to meet health code requirements.

West sits across from me, a large lamb kebab platter set out before him on a paper plate. They only offer plastic forks and knives here, too. Not exactly great for the environment, but at least the food smells great and the portions are generous. He eats like I'm not even here, eyes closed as he savors every bite.

Either he's incredibly stupid, or he doesn't think I'm a threat.

I'll make him regret it either way.

"This is so *good*," he groans dramatically. "I should join a food tour while I'm here. Vancouver's got food tours, right?"

I strum my fingers along the table's surface, staring him down while I mentally put on my detective's cap. If he's not from around here, where is he from and how on earth did he manage to track me down?

He opens his eyes and grins, his smile somewhat crooked. "Your head looks like it's about to burst."

"How did you know it was me?" I whisper, casting a cautious glance over my shoulder. There's a young couple in one corner of the restaurant, as well as a lone businessman who looks like he's had a really rough day, but they don't seem like they're paying us any mind.

"I'll admit you nearly gave me a heart attack when I noticed the money missing," he says. "But, as I'm sure you know, there's nothing money can't buy—and that includes information. It took me all week to find you. Had to do some thorough digging on the forums, but someone eventually let your name slip."

My heart leaps up and lodges in my throat. "But I've been careful."

"Not your real name. 'QWERTY.' That's all I had to go off of for a while. You're very well-known in certain circles. Always have lots of work, apparently." West takes a bite out of his skewer. "But then I found someone wanting to sell a mule account. He'd apparently sold one to you a few years ago but wasn't happy with the piddly kickback. All I had to do was pay him triple your normal rate and he sang like a bird."

"Piddly?" I echo with a frown. I don't know why I'm so offended. That's really not what I should be focusing on right now.

West shrugs. "What can I say? Criminals are a greedy sort."

"I'm not like them. I only do this because—"

"Are you referring to your little charity spree?" he interjects. "Yes, I'm well aware. It's actually what wound up getting you caught."

I listen intently, teetering between irritation and genuine intrigue. "Explain."

"Ms. Choi, you donated exclusively to local charities. It was no small feat untangling your money trail, but in the end, it led me to Vancouver. Had you given to more international organizations, it would have been much more difficult."

I sit there, stewing in my own stupidity. I'd been so confident that nobody would take the time to follow the mess of transactions I left behind. It turns out I'm not the only one with a can-do attitude and questionable morals.

This guy is trouble.

"That's when things got really tricky," he continues. "I had a location and a handle, but not an identity. It wasn't until an extensive internet search that I found an article."

He reaches for something in his back pocket and I move on instinct, my muscles a wound-up spring. I snatch up my plastic fork, fully prepared to jab, but he counters with just as much speed, placing his hand over mine to pin it there on the table. The other customers glance at us, startled by the commotion.

"Relax," he says. "It's just my phone."

As promised, he produces the device, opens up a pre-saved link in a browser tab, and sets it between us. I give it a quick read. It's a local newspaper announcement—the one that Dad paid for when Lily and I graduated from high school.

Congratulations to Adelina and Lily Choi!

Lily Choi will be attending Simon Fraser University to study political science. Pictured left: Lily winning first place at the regional spelling bee.

Adelina Choi will be attending the Massachusetts Institute of Technology to study computer science. Pictured right: Adelina with her provincially ranked junior robotics team, Team QWERTY.

Beneath the announcement is one last picture of Mom, Dad, Lily and me on graduation day. Lily and I are dressed in our blue gowns, caps adorning our heads. We're all smiling at the camera.

West sits back. "I don't believe in coincidences," he says. "An MIT computer scientist from Vancouver involved with a robotics team with the same name as my thief's handle. There was a chance I was connecting unrelated dots. Grasping at straws, really, but I had a feeling. Finding your address after that was a cinch."

"How?" I ask.

"Your twin," he answers vaguely. "She tagged you in a photo on her Instagram page."

A chill runs through me. He has to be bringing her up for some reason. If he plans on using her as blackmail, I'm going to stab his eyes out with my fork. "She wouldn't be stupid enough to tag my location too."

"It was a picture of you two at a restaurant a year ago. Caption said something about moving into your new apartment. Figured I'd check out the area, ask around. Came across a lovely gentleman named Robert only a few blocks from here. Showed him this picture and he pointed me in your general direction."

My stomach twists. I'm sure Robert didn't mean anything by it. West clearly tricked him, that's all.

"So you're a creep, is what you're telling me."

"Trust me, I take no pleasure in any of this. Although I one thousand percent agree that geotagging is a tool for evil."

"If you came here to get your money back," I say through gritted teeth, "it's already gone. And don't you dare ask me to steal it back from those charities, because that's just plain wrong."

"Interesting," he muses.

"What is?"

"You don't look like much of a thief."

"Good. God forbid I be mistaken for a landlord."

West laughs at this, bright and loud. The low bass of his voice vibrates through the air. "I don't want the money back."

I strum my fingers impatiently against the table, surprised and confused and exasperated in equal measure. "Then what are you doing here? Why go through all the trouble?"

"I would like to propose a deal," he says slowly, carefully. I wouldn't be surprised if he practiced his lines in front of a mirror, they're *that* rehearsed. "I want you to work with me."

I stare at him blankly. Did I hear that right, or have I finally snapped? The pieces slowly begin to click into place. His ability to navigate the dark web, to ask the right questions. The massive amount of money just sitting there in his bank account.

I was wrong before. He isn't some rich elite living a life of luxury.

"You're a thief too," I realize aloud. It feels strange to say it, like an admission of guilt, though there's no denying that's what I am. "The money I took from you . . . it wasn't even yours to begin with."

"Birds of a feather." He shrugs casually, his gaze somewhere distant. "Though I'm not an active practitioner."

"Oh?"

"In another life, I made bad choices. Ran with the wrong crowd. Thought that their way of doing things was the only way to get ahead in life. That isn't who I am anymore."

"So you're . . . retired?"

"Sure, we can put it that way."

Irritation licks at the nape of my neck. I suddenly understand how annoyed Lily gets whenever I don't give her a straight answer.

"Who's the target?" I ask.

"I can't tell you until you agree to join me."

"Then that's going to be a problem, because I don't steal from just anybody. I only take from the rich."

"Naturally. They're the ones with money to take. I can tell you how much we stand to gain, though."

He pauses to take a slow bite of his kebab.

"Oh, come *on*," I hiss.

"Fifty," he says after an infuriatingly long while.

"Thousand?" I attempt to clarify, unimpressed. When he doesn't respond, I try again. "Million?" My voice comes out squeaky. He raises his eyebrows, as if to suggest I try even *higher*. "Billion!?" I croak in disbelief.

"A big ol' capital B."

I deal with numbers all day, lines of code tucked between pretty semicolons and brackets, but nothing could have prepared me for this. A five followed by ten zeroes. I can visualize it, but I have difficulty wrapping my head around a sum of that size. Is it even possible? The takes I've been scoring look like chump change in comparison. I'm pretty sure that's enough to buy roughly five hundred high-end private jets.

"You're lying," I say.

"Am I?"

The sinking feeling in my gut tells me not to get ahead of myself, but my pulse is already racing. What could I do with that kind of money? Think of all the people I could *help*.

"What happens if I say no? Are you going to blackmail me?"

He clicks his tongue and shakes his head. "That's such an awful word."

Neither a *yes* nor a *no*. It's Schrödinger's cat, but I'm the one trapped inside the box. The more I think about it, the more I realize I don't have much of a choice. If I decline to work with him, he could easily turn me in to the cops. But if I agree to carry out the job and it goes sideways, I could end up behind bars regardless. Maybe even dead.

And if Mom ever found out . . . Honestly, just pull the trigger at that point. I'd rather die than suffocate beneath her avalanche of disappointment.

"Why me?" I ask. "Can't you find someone else?"

He takes a moment to think before he says, "Because I'm on a deadline, and I believe in seizing opportunities as they come."

I glare at him, swallowing the string of not-so-polite names I desperately want to call him. "You want me to work for you—"

"*With*," he corrects. "I believe in lateral work relationships. It encourages productivity."

"You want me to work *with* you, but you're not exactly being forthcoming. How am I supposed to trust you won't stab me in the back? How do I know you're not leading me straight into danger?"

"Don't be so dramatic. I always keep my tech support away from the main event. I'll be the one doing the heavy lifting."

"So you can run off with the take?"

"So I can minimize *risk*," he says firmly. "You won't be in harm's way, I assure you."

"You expect me to believe your word, Mr. Porter?"

"Please, call me West. And yes. It's a little-known concept called honor among thieves."

I take a deep breath and exhale slowly. This is a fine little mess I'm in. Things might be different if I had more information, if I could glance at the cards in his hands. But I don't know the first thing about who West truly is. What are his motivations? Where did he come from? And how the hell can I get out of this hole I've accidentally dug myself into?

"Can I at least have some time to think about it?" I ask. "Since you're not going to give me details until I agree."

West *beams*, flashing his pearly whites as the corners of his eyes crinkle with his smile. I bet he thinks he's handsome. It would surprise him to know just how badly I want to break his nose.

"I can give you twenty-four hours," he says. He reaches into his pocket, and this time pulls out a business card for one of the fancier hotels by the Vancouver waterfront. He hasn't provided a room number, but the hotel address is really all I need. "Time is of the essence, Adelina."

I stand and swipe up the card. "That's *Ms. Choi* to you," I grumble before turning on my heels to make a hasty exit.

West

SHE'S JUST SO *angry*.

I'm kinda into it.

CHAPTER SEVEN

Better Reluctant Allies Than Outright Enemies

Adelina

IN THE WORDS of Admiral Ackbar: *It's a trap*.

No matter what I do, no matter the different scenarios I play out in my head, I'm going to lose either way. If I decline his *oh-so* generous offer to work *with* him, West will turn me over to the police. I don't know exactly what evidence he's managed to collect, and there's a chance it's all circumstantial, but the last thing I want is for the cops to start poking around and asking unnecessary questions. A glaringly obvious one would be: How have I been able to afford rent in one of Canada's most egregiously expensive cities without a job?

But if I agree . . .

He could be a serial killer for all I know. Or a cannibal. Or, God forbid, a cannibal serial killer. He's given me next to nothing, just an empty promise of fifty billion dollars and no apparent plan whatsoever. The less I know, the more danger I'm in.

There's really one way to fix this problem, and that's to get to work.

I stay up all night, click-clacking away at my desktop computer. I triple-checked my apartment door's lock when I returned from the restaurant. No signs of forced entry. West really must have picked it open. (It doesn't surprise me that my landlord decided to go with the cheapest lock on the market, the stingy bastard.) Regardless, I've created a makeshift barricade out of dining table chairs to keep it sealed—just in case West really *is* a serial killer. I've got a small can of pepper spray in my pocket too, because a woman can never be too careful. It's technically illegal to own pepper spray in Canada, but you can sneak anything into the country if you know where to look and who to ask.

The next time I check the clock, it's pushing 4:30 a.m. The pale morning sun filters through the crack in the curtains roughly an hour later, and all I've got for my efforts is eyestrain compounded by a terrible headache. The third energy drink I knocked back definitely isn't helping things.

Nothing. Zilch.

Even though I already have his banking information, the address on file, even his social insurance number, I can't find a *crumb* of info on the guy. No social media presence, no record of employment, not even so much as a parking infraction. While the money in his account is most certainly real, the man who supposedly owns it is nothing more than a ghost.

It can only mean one thing: West Porter is a fake.

Identity theft isn't my area of expertise. I've obtained personal information, yes, but I've never gone so far as to actively masquerade as someone else. Back in ye olden times before the dawn of the internet, all you really had to do was keep an eye on the obituaries and use the name of the recently deceased as your own. There wasn't a database to raise any red flags. But now, it's a matter of forging IDs: driver's licenses, passports, and so on. Not impossible, but definitely not as easy as it used to be. It's also entirely possible that West is more of a DIY kind of thief. He's already proven resourceful enough to pull something like that off.

Rubbing my fingers against my eyes, I take a deep breath. This is . . . not ideal. And with my twenty-four hours slowly counting down, I'm nowhere closer to deciding than I was last night.

On a whim, I check my phone. There are several texts from Lily waiting for me. A quick look at the timestamps suggests she messaged me shortly after I left dinner at Mom's. My sister's right. I'm terrible at answering my phone.

Lily: I'm so sorry, Addy. Mom was being a total bitch.

Lily: I really thought she'd be nice. Please text me back?

Lily: Can you at least let me know when you get home?

God, I'm such an asshole. Lily's always been a worrywart, and here I am constantly ignoring her messages. I send her a quick response that everything's fine (it's not) and that I made it home safely (home invader aside). She doesn't get back to me right away, and I don't expect her to. Not only do we share the same genetic code, but my sister and I also share a burning hatred for early mornings.

I reach into my pocket and fish out the hotel business card West gave me, running my fingers along the rounded corners. I like to think I'm a good judge of character, but when it comes to West, I genuinely can't tell. A part of me wishes he'd been some tatted-up criminal with a mean mug. At least then I could have written him off as an outright threat. The fact that he was all smiles and teasing leaves me . . . unsettled. Walking on eggshells. He could be a wolf in sheep's clothing, tricking me into stepping into his jaws.

But what choice do I have?

"Fifty billion dollars," I mumble, my whisper somehow too loud in the space of my lonely little apartment. Turning the number over and over again in my head, I try to formulate a contingency plan.

If I'm going to do this, I need to stay one step ahead.

Sneaking into a hotel is surprisingly simple. All it takes is an empty pizza box pilfered from my own fridge and a general expression of fatigue. It may be cheap as far as disguises go, but it's incredibly effective. I need to even the playing field with West, and I'm most definitely not above a little fraud and a skosh of impersonation.

I stride up to the front desk and pretend to look out of sorts. "I've got a delivery for a Mr. West Porter?"

The receptionist doesn't really look at me so much as she looks *through* me. The phones are ringing off the hook, and it seems like she's struggling to respond to all the emails piling up in her inbox. The lobby is busy, full of irritable hotel guests that I've unapologetically budged in front of. For whatever reason, she's the only one on duty. "Just leave it here. We can bring it up."

I take a measured breath. That won't do.

"Instructions say to deliver it to him in person." I talk quickly on purpose, allowing my words to run into one another to give the illusion of urgency. It definitely helps that I've got a trustworthy-looking face. *Unassuming* might be a more accurate term. "He probably doesn't want a whole bunch of people touching his food. Could you tell me his room number? I can't remember what it was. I can just pop up and get out of your hair."

The receptionist, flustered and probably considering handing in her two weeks' notice, nods distractedly and types something into her computer. "Room 501. The elevator's around the corner."

"Thanks," I say, and scurry off before she can think twice about all the privacy laws she's just breached.

When I locate West's door, I promptly pull out my phone and hold it near the electronic card reader. All modern hotel chains use RFID readers to lock their doors. It's more secure than a run-of-the-mill key, and the average person doesn't have the technical know-how to hack into one.

At the risk of sounding like a complete ass, I'm a bit more than average.

There's no need to bridge wires, no need to break the lock into tiny bits. All I need to do is confuse the chip reader into believing I'm in possession of a legitimate key. Before I came, I spent a couple of hours writing a mimicking software and downloaded it onto my phone. I was stumped for a bit on a particular line of code, but there's nothing I can't achieve with the power of a helpful YouTube tutorial. (Who knew there were entire channels made by lock-picking aficionados?)

When I bring the phone up to the reader, the little light blinks green; this is followed by the metallic *click-thunk* of the mechanism's release. How James Bond manages to do all the cool shit he does and *not* act like a giddy schoolgirl is beyond me, because holy crap I feel like a total badass right now.

The room is empty when I arrive. West's small black suitcase is tucked away neatly by the end of the bed, which tells me he hasn't left yet. There's still three hours before his deadline is up. He must have figured I'd run out the clock and took the chance to sightsee. Maybe he's on that food tour he mentioned earlier.

That's his mistake.

I toss my empty pizza box and high-vis vest aside and casually make my way over to the mini fridge. I pry the door open and survey the absurdly expensive snacks and drinks within, helping myself to a bag of M&M's, a Toblerone bar, a can of pistachios and a bottle of Diet Coke before grabbing his suitcase by the handle and tossing it onto the bed. It's unlocked. He probably didn't expect me to arrive early and snoop through his things.

There's little of interest. A couple shirts, a knitted sweater, a few pairs of pants, socks and boxer briefs. I take special care not to touch his underwear because that would push me over the line into Creepyville. No rope or handcuffs or weapons, so it's safe to assume he truly has no plans to hack me to bits. No wallet or phone, though. He must have taken those with him. What I *do* find, however, is his passport inside one of the small inner pockets.

It has a burgundy cover with a golden emblem embossed onto the front. At the top it reads: Union européenne République française.

I raise my eyebrows. He's French? I never would have guessed. His American accent is immaculate.

Flipping it open to the personal information page, my interest is immediately drawn to his photo. He looks a little younger, but more intense. His dirty-blond hair was shorter back then, buzzed down to the scalp at the sides. His eyes are more or less the same, a vibrant green—only the picture fails to capture their spark. But what interests me most is his real name.

Mathieu Guillaume Maunier. If his listed birth date is to be believed, he's only a year older than me at a rather sharp twenty-nine.

I take a seat in the solitary chair in the room, kick up my feet, turn on the TV and enjoy my snacks while I wait for West/Mathieu/whatever his real name is. Before I get too absorbed in the rerun episode of *The Big Bang Theory*, I take a picture of his passport with my phone and draft up a message.

The door's electronic lock beeps, signaling his arrival roughly twenty minutes later. He jolts when he sees me, and I can't help but feel a sliver of satisfaction. Now he knows how I felt.

Payback's a bitch.

"You look constipated," I say, holding up his passport.

"I was going for 'blue steel,' actually."

"Did you have this forged?"

"Does it *look* forged?"

I frown steeply. "You need to stop answering questions with questions. It's one of my conditions if I'm going to agree to work with you."

He crosses his arms and leans casually against the nearest wall, looking far too amused for my liking. "Conditions, plural?"

I chuck a pistachio shell into the plastic garbage bin I'd dragged over. "One: You must always be honest with me. No vague wording, no omissions, no answering questions with questions. Don't worry, I'm not going to pry into your personal life. In fact, I'd rather get through this without knowing a single thing about you. Because the sooner we're finished with this job, the sooner we can have a clean break."

"Planning to break up with me already?" he asks with a chuckle. "That's cold."

I continue to glare at him, chucking another pistachio shell into the bin. "Two: The moment you give me reason to doubt you, that's it. I'd rather take my chances with the cops."

West shrugs. "Suit yourself."

"Three: When this is all over, I want to return home like nothing ever happened. No witnesses, no one hitting me up for future jobs. I enjoy my anonymity. Done and dusted, are we clear?"

I can practically hear the gears in his head turning as he weighs the pros and cons. Eventually, he nods. "Alright. I guess I can work with that."

I want to breathe a sigh of relief, but unfortunately for him, I'm not done. "Are there going to be others? As confident as I may be, stealing fifty billion isn't a two-person job."

West cracks a smile. "Yes. I've got a crew."

"Who are they?"

"Old friends."

I shake my head. "You need to give me their names, their aliases . . . I want to know who I'm working with. You're also to refer to me as *Qwerty*, not by my real name. I don't need them all up in my business."

"So you get to know them, but not the other way around?"

"If you have a problem with that, I'll walk."

"You're a very thorough thief, Ms. Choi."

"Better safe than sorry."

"Fine. Anything else?"

"Yes," I say as I stand. I brush the crumbs off my lap and step forward, holding out his passport between my middle and index fingers. "Is this a forged passport?"

There's a devious twinkle in his deep-green eyes. "Do you have a thing for French guys?"

"What did I say about answering questions with questions?"

He sighs. "It's real. Westley Porter is just the name I go by in the States."

"Why?"

"Because I, too, enjoy my anonymity."

I press my lips into a thin line. Infuriating bastard. That was a vague answer, but we have more important matters to discuss. "Oh, and in case you get any ideas," I say, "I've helped myself to some insurance." I present my phone and show him the text I've drafted. Attached is the picture I took of his ID.

"What's this?" he asks.

"I've programmed a text to send every night unless I override it with a password that, naturally, only I know. If anything happens to me, your identity will be sent to a contact I trust, who will turn it over to the authorities along with my last-known location. Screw me over, and it's mutually assured destruction."

For the first time since I met him, it seems West is at a loss for words. The muscles in his jaw twitch, and his gaze turns cold. I've gotten under his skin, and I can't for the life of me think of anything more electrifying. I half expect him to get angry. Start yelling. Whenever I mouthed off or did something Mom didn't like, she'd erupt. I'm primed to be on the defensive, to prepare for a fight.

Imagine my surprise when West simply smiles. It makes me want to grab him by the shoulders and throttle him. Can't he act normal for *one* second?

"What?" I demand uncomfortably.

"Nothing. Just thinking . . ." He sticks his hand out to shake. "You've got yourself a deal, Ms. Choi."

I hesitantly slip my hand into his, noting the length of his fingers and the width of his calloused palm. His grip is firm but not overbearing—the handshake of a proper businessman. I'm the one to pull away, unsure what to make of my skittering pulse. I feel like I've made a deal with the devil. That, at any moment, this will all go terribly wrong.

Clearing my throat, I ask, "Who's the target?"

"His name is Valentino Berruci, a disgraced former member of the Italian mob."

The smallest gasp escapes my lips.

I haven't been in the game long, but even *I* know who the guy is. I've seen his name pop up from time to time on the forums, whispers of his exploits, often bloody and merciless, cropping up here and there. I don't know the precise details, but from what I've heard, Berruci stepped on one too many toes. Too aggressive to control and too wild to predict, he'd become too much of an inconvenience for those in charge.

My heart thunders. "You mean the underboss who was too greedy even for the Mafia?"

West nods. "The account you stole from . . . It's under my name, yes, but it was his money. I was instructed to move to America under a new identity with the sole purpose of opening accounts for his use."

"You're his mule," I realize aloud. "To launder his money."

West nods again, this time with a grim look in his eyes. "You didn't steal from me, Ms. Choi. You stole from one of the most dangerous men in Europe."

A shudder slams its way down my spine as my mind spins with confusion. "But . . . if you work for him, why would you double-cross him? Shouldn't you just turn me in?"

"Do you *want* me to turn you in?"

"Of course not. I just don't understand why you'd rather betray him."

"I'm afraid that's personal, Ms. Choi," he says in a teasing tone.

"Oh, come on, that's—"

"I believe *you* were the one who said you didn't want to know anything about me. Don't worry. My motivations won't impact our objective in any way."

I swallow my irritation. We're only thirty seconds into our reluctant partnership, and he's already figuring out ways to dance around the terms I set. "Whatever," I grumble. "Now, please tell me you have some sort of plan. This isn't going to be a walk in the park."

West's charming smile returns, bringing brightness to his face. Most might find it breathtakingly handsome, but I'm starting to see the truth. It's a smile that comes with practice, something to mask what I'm realizing is his unease.

"I'll tell you on our way to the airport," he says. "Assuming you haven't accidentally landed yourself on a no-fly list."

I frown. "Where are we going?"

"If I say it's a surprise—"

"I don't like surprises."

"You're no fun, Ms. Choi. Learn to laugh a little." West relents with an exaggerated sigh before he says, "Ever been to France?"

CHAPTER EIGHT

Kindness Costs Nothing

West

Unknown: Did you find the guy you were looking for?

West: It's a woman, actually.

West: I think she might be my soulmate.

Unknown: Quit joking around.

Unknown: Our whole plan hinges on them.

Unknown: What if they choke?

West: Relax. I've got everything under control.

"Twenty dollars for a chicken wrap the size of my fist," Adelina mutters bitterly as she sits next to me on the bench, foodstuffs in hand. "Prices like this should be illegal."

"What do you expect?" I ask, shoving my phone into my pocket. I feel it buzz, but Diana will just have to wait. "It's the airport. Everything is overpriced."

We're among the first at the gate, so we have our choice of seats and enough privacy to converse without fear of being overheard. For now, at least.

Adelina slouches as she eats. “Tell me the plan again. Go over every possible detail. I want to really nail them down.”

“I could write it down for you if you’re having that much trouble remembering.”

“And leave evidence behind? Absolutely not. I’m just trying to be thorough.”

I throw her a wink. “Are you sure it’s not because you love hearing the sound of my voice?”

She sneers, but I’m positive it’s because her sad excuse for a chicken wrap is as tasteless as it looks. I’m a considerate guy, though, so I start at the very beginning.

“After being run out of Italy by his own family, Valentino Berruci managed to make quite a name for himself in France. He quickly gained influence over local gangs in Paris and worked his way up to controlling the entire territory. He now has a private villa located on the outskirts of Nice where he not only resides but also runs his operations.”

Adelina snorts. “Shitting where he eats isn’t exactly a good idea.”

“An oversight that we’re going to take advantage of,” I say with a shrug. “Berruci primarily specializes in racketeering, but it’s gotten to the point that he even has some major politicians under his thumb. Using their influence and connections, he’s been able to break into the arms market with little to no pushback.”

“Filthy rich *and* a villain,” Adelina muses dryly. “A match made in heaven.”

“Don’t sound so pleased. Berruci may be a megalomaniac, but he still has to maintain some level of order. He keeps track of every euro earned and spent. His ledger is kept in an encrypted file on his computer server. That’s where you come in.”

She nods, polishing off her chicken wrap. “Sounds simple enough.”

“Right, except his servers are protected by a specialized firewall modeled after the one they use at INTERPOL. Any attempts to break through security protocols from the outside will result in the immediate wiping of all data—and his ledger along with it. That's where *I* come in.

"Since it isn't connected to the internet, hacking in will be impossible, but if I can locate the physical domain controller and connect you directly with remote-access software, you'll be able to open a VNC backdoor without ever stepping into harm's way. Once we have his financial records, you'll locate his mule accounts and drain them into your own through the SWIFT banking system. Berruci will be left with nothing, and his operation will crumble overnight without proper funding."

Adelina studies me with a healthy dose of skepticism, her lips pressed into a thin line. "How do you know all this stuff?"

Oh, the things I could tell her. I wonder how she'd react if I told her I'd already tried this job once. I was so desperate to get out that I did every ounce of research possible, bribed every source I could to get information on Berruci's setup. Knowledge is the only thing that gives a thief their edge, and I had diligently worked to gather as much as I could. But even with everything I knew, I realized that it wasn't a job I could do on my own. I understood what to do in concept, but I lacked the technical know-how, in the same way that I understand the importance of the human circulatory system but am by no means qualified to perform open-heart surgery. I needed help, and none had been available at the time. I was stuck, and I certainly wasn't going to risk leaving Jack behind.

But Ms. Choi changes all that. She doesn't know it yet, but she's going to be the ace up my sleeve.

"It's my job to know," I say, despite knowing how much she hates my vague explanations.

Adelina has the good graces not to continue pushing, though I can sense the irritation washing off her in waves. "Fine, so that's the end goal. Steal his money and destroy his criminal empire."

"Two birds, one stone," I agree. "Provided you're actually as good as you think you are."

She glares at me, and I hold back a laugh. She's just so *serious*, her brow knitted together in a permanent scowl, her eyes dark with never-ending concentration. I'm tempted to make her smile, if only to see how painfully awkward it'd make her look. Like the Grinch discovering he does, in fact, have a heart.

"Anything linked to the internet is hackable," she explains. "Once you connect me, it's just a matter of time and skill."

"Show me."

Adelina glares. "What?"

"I want to make sure I'm in good hands, Ms. Choi. I'd like a demonstration."

"Stealing two-fifty wasn't good enough for you?"

"Could have been a fluke."

"You're one to talk. You say you're going to carry out the job, but I haven't seen you do anything remotely impressive."

My ears perk up. I know she's baiting me, but I've never been one to back down from a challenge. I look her over and spot the glint of her wristwatch, its strap made of precious white gold. It's the fanciest thing on her—and it'll have to do. I may be rusty, but I can use this as a warm-up, at the very least.

"Do me a favor and stand," I say.

"Why?"

"Just do it."

With a reluctant huff, Adelina does so. "Now what?"

"Hand me your backpack."

She squints at me. "What are you playing at?"

"Nothing," I reply innocently.

Adelina gives me her bag, holding it out by the top strap. "If you run off with my shit, I'll kill you."

I take it with a chuckle, trapping her hand beneath mine. I step forward and crowd her space, treating her like I would any other mark, dipping in close to ensure she keeps her eyes on me. Her eyes go wide, full of distrust and suspicion.

"That's all I needed," I say, stepping back. "You can sit down again."

She gives me a murderous glare. "Was there a point to all this?"

I hold her watch up by the strap, savoring the way realization creeps its way across her face. It was easy enough to lift. Using her own bag as shade to hide my handiwork was Pickpocketing 101. Having her follow all of my commands was simply a tactic to over-stimulate her senses, drawing her attention elsewhere while I worked.

"You motherf—" She swipes it out of my hand, quickly securing it around her wrist.

"That's not all," I say, producing her passport and boarding pass that I pinched from the front pocket of her sweatshirt. I'll confess that I only wanted her watch, but what can I say? It feels good to show off.

Her jaw drops. "How did you do that?"

"A little sleight of hand, a bit of misdirection. You were so distracted that you didn't even notice."

"Great. I teamed up with a magician."

"Are you not impressed?"

"Pull a rabbit out of your ass and then we'll see."

"Tough crowd," I say with a grin. "It's your turn, Ms. Choi. Fair's fair."

This time, she *does* roll her eyes, but she moves to pull her laptop out of her backpack. She boots up the device and looks around, no doubt cooking up some elaborate scheme. Getting to see her in action brings with it its own sort of giddy fascination.

Her gaze falls upon a small group seated a few feet away at our neighboring gate—a flight out to Miami, Florida. An exasperated mother of three struggles to tend to her little ones, the eldest being no older than five. The poor woman is clearly out of sorts, her messy red hair pulled up in a lopsided bun, the rims of her eyes red and watery. She tries to soothe her youngest, who's bawling in his stroller, while the other two treat the area like their own personal playground. Sympathy tugs at my chest as I think about Jack back home in Sacramento. I wonder where the woman's partner is. Maybe she's a single parent, like me.

Given her prickly nature, I fully expect Adelina to scoff at the children running amok. I wouldn't be surprised if she was the type of grouch to make underhanded comments about the woman's lack of organization or some cheap shot about poor parenting. But then she surprises me by standing up and handing me her laptop.

"Hold this," she says before making her way over.

I take it and look down in surprise. It's nothing special. Password protected, so I have no hope in hell of snooping around her files. What catches my interest, though, is the solitary sticker she's placed next to the power button. A sunflower, its edges worn and colors faded with age. I find it strangely amusing. Adelina doesn't seem like the type to enjoy flowers, or stickers . . . or act like the world hasn't been sapped of sunshine and color.

When I look up again, I find Adelina speaking to the frazzled woman out of earshot. Even if I strain to listen, the airport is a cacophony of distractions. Announcements play over the speakers in both English and French. Suitcase wheels rumble over YVR's floors of blue carpet. The man sitting directly behind me has decided now is the best time to rip into his bag of particularly crunchy vending machine chips. Those were probably overpriced too.

Adelina remains with the woman and her kids—even lets one of them sit on her lap. She's . . . surprisingly sweet with them. At ease. Even cracks a small smile or two, which admittedly throws me for a loop. I thought for sure the effort would kill her. Adelina doesn't return to my side until roughly twenty minutes later, the children now seated quietly at their mother's side as she pulls out an iPad for them to watch cartoons.

"What were you talking about over there?" I ask her.

She takes her laptop back and plugs in her password, her fingers a fluid blur. Adelina simply shrugs as she works. "Nothing."

"You were gone for a while."

"Aw, did you miss me that much?"

"Like the stars miss the night sky."

"Are you a poet now too?"

"What can I say? I'm a man of many talents."

"Endless chatting isn't a talent."

"*Ow*." I try to peek at her screen, but she rotates her body so that I can only see the back of her laptop.

"Do you mind?" she grumbles.

I give her some space. I suppose I wouldn't be able to work with someone breathing down my neck either. Adelina types what I assume is the equivalent of a short novel, totally focused on the task at hand. Her frown has returned, the softness I thought I saw complement her features now hardened steel.

She shuts her laptop abruptly and returns it to her backpack.

"Well?" I ask. "What did you do?"

"Hmm? Oh, I was just drafting an email."

"What about—"

"The demonstration?" she interjects sharply. "Oh, please. I know what I'm capable of, and I know I have what it takes to see this job through. If you expect me to bend over backward and jump through hoops just to satisfy your need for a power trip, you can go ahead and suck my dick."

I burst into a fit of laughter, partially out of nervousness and mostly because her bluntness startles me. "You're very mean, Ms. Choi."

"Cry me a river, pretty boy. I'm not going to tone it down just to make you comfortable."

There's a lot I could say to this: that I wouldn't expect her to, or maybe that I'd think less of her if she did. Not that Adelina would care about my opinion. Instead, I gasp dramatically. "You think I'm pretty?"

She pulls out a pair of wireless headphones and an e-reader from her backpack, blocking me out completely. I wonder what she likes to read. Books about coding seem a bit boring, even for her. Maybe she enjoys spicy romances. If things are getting raunchy on the page, her dead-eyed poker face gives nothing away. Then again, it could be a gruesome horror. She seems like the type to indulge in a good slasher.

While I'm busy musing, an announcement plays over the airport speakers. "Will a Ms. Julia Anderson please come up to the service desk?"

The mother of three whom Adelina was speaking to earlier looks up, clearly taken aback at hearing her name. She manages to corral her children together and makes her way up to the gate's service desk.

"First class?" the mother of three gawks loud enough for me to hear. "I don't understand. This has to be some kind of mistake."

"It seems we have a very full flight," the service attendant says with a smile. "You and your little ones were randomly selected for an upgrade. Congratulations!"

"Oh, gosh, I . . ." The woman laughs, breathless. "Thank you so much."

I can't help but smile. She clearly needed this break; her joy is downright infectious. Out of the corner of my eye, I notice Adelina thoroughly invested in her book. Something tells me that their fortuitous upgrade wasn't random at all.

She takes no credit, makes no fuss. Unlike me, Adelina doesn't have an ounce of showmanship. But I suppose at the end of the day, that's exactly what I need.

No bullshit. All skill.

I don't think I've ever met anyone more fascinating.

CHAPTER NINE

I Don't Care That It's Statistically Safer Than Driving

Adelina

I HAVE A confession to make: Planes and I do *not* a happy couple make.

There's plenty to complain about. The food, the cramped quarters, the fact that flying is an incredibly carbon-intensive mode of transportation. And let's not forget the fact that we're thousands of miles above ground in a flying metal tube. Logically, I understand the physics that backs this up (a combination of lift, weight, drag and thrust), but that doesn't stop the little voice in the back of my head from screaming at me: *GROUND GOOD. FALL BAD. WHO'S EVEN DRIVING THIS THING?*

"Should I call the flight attendant to give you some Sleep-eze?" West asks with a light chuckle. He'd spent the last hour flipping through the list of provided movies but ultimately settled on watching the flight map like some sort of psychopath. Right now, the little plane symbol is hovering just over Calgary.

"Quit hogging the armrest," I grumble, doing my best not to focus on the slight tremor that passes through the cabin. The flight has been mostly smooth so far, but even the smallest of bumps and jolts is enough to make my stomach clench. I think the chicken wrap I had at the airport might have been a little funky.

"May I remind you that you called dibs on the window seat?" he asks.

"So?"

"You can't have the window *and* the armrest. It's called etiquette."

I pin him with a glare. "Just be glad I'm not one of those assholes who takes their shoes off on planes."

He grimaces. "That *would* be awful, but the issue still stands."

With an exasperated huff, I concede the armrest in favor of reaching for my backpack, which I've shoved beneath the seat in front of me. I pull out my laptop, lower my flimsy seat tray and set to work. If nothing else, it will be a good distraction from thoughts of plummeting to our deaths.

I've always enjoyed the process of coding. It started with my very first computer science class in ninth grade where Mr. Harker taught us basic HTML. My classmates thought it was as confusing as it was boring. But for me, it was as if someone flipped a switch inside my brain, or like one of those sappy old romance movies where a man spots a woman from across the room and instantly knows she's The One™. I was overcome with the need to learn everything there was to learn with an almost frightening fervor. It wasn't long before I graduated from front-end development learning HTML and CCS to back-end development with Python, C#, C++, Java and JavaScript (and yes, they're all different). I even studied COBOL and FORTRAN, since many banking systems tend to use these older languages, though I've had little excuse to use them with how I run my operation.

Talking to Mom had always been an impossible task, but talking to computers . . . it felt like there was a mutual understanding between us. Not to mention the added bonus that if I got something wrong, the code didn't yell at me until I cried. I'd take an error message any day.

Mou gwai jung.

Something soft tickles my cheek. At first, I think it might be the air blowing in from the vent above, but a quick glance to my left and I find West leaning in close enough so I can feel his breath. He leans over, studying the lines of code I've written as if he's discovered an alien language.

"Whatchya workin' on?" he asks, sounding deliberately obtuse.

This is the guy I agreed to work with on one of the most dangerous jobs of my criminal career?

Great.

I'm suddenly caught between laughing and slapping him, so I settle for lightly checking him with my shoulder, shoving him back over the invisible border running down the middle of our shared armrest. "I'm building a program to use against Berruci. A virus."

"How does it work?"

"It's complicated. You wouldn't understand."

"That's why I'm asking, Ms. Choi."

I look at him then. Really, truly look at him. He's . . . not hard on the eyes, I guess. Handsome in a classic sort of way, with an air of Old Hollywood charm. If we were strangers who had passed each other on the street, I probably wouldn't have been able to pick him out of a lineup or give a helpful description to the cops, though I suppose I wouldn't have been above helping myself to an appreciative second look. He doesn't appear intimidating or suspicious. No visible tattoos or piercings or the kind of bulky, threatening physique that would make a woman uncomfortable if she found herself trapped with him in a confined space (like on an airplane, for example). Very *guy-next-door*. The type to help a little old lady cross the street, spend his Sundays hiking out in the woods or something as swoonworthy as saving kittens from a tree.

When I take too long to respond, West smiles and I suddenly find myself staring directly at the sun—warm and brilliant enough that my cheeks start to burn. I wonder if he knows just how disarming he can be, if he uses his breeziness to get through a person's defenses as his weapon of choice. It's almost . . . hypnotizing, that smile of his.

For a moment, and only a moment, it makes me feel like everything will be okay.

"If you wanted a staring contest, you could have just asked me," he says, breaking me out of my thoughts. "Or are you looking for an excuse to stare into my beautiful eyes?"

I look back at my laptop screen. "Your eyes are okay at best."

"But you *were* looking."

I groan and try to pray away the migraine knocking against the inside of my skull. "How long is this flight?"

"Four more hours until we land in Toronto, and then another seven and a half or so to Paris."

"Yay," I grumble dryly.

"You could have made this easier on us, you know."

"What do you mean?"

"If it was so easy for you to give that nice lady a seat upgrade, you could have done the same for us." West shrugs his shoulders. "Unlimited champagne plus generous legroom and it wouldn't have cost you a thing. Hell, I'd bet you probably could have figured out a way to charter us a private jet."

"No."

"No?" he echoes.

"I don't do this for personal gain," I clarify. "There's no need to go overboard."

I'm not sure how it's possible, but I swear West grins even wider. "You must be fun at parties."

"I don't go to parties."

"Of course you don't. Too busy dwelling in your parents' basement, right?"

"I resent that stereotype, and you know for a fact I have an apartment."

"Ah, yes. The one with the flimsy locks and no doorman. You should really consider moving to a more secure building."

"You're the last person I want advice from."

West shakes his head. "I understand. Common sense isn't a flower that grows in every garden."

"Did you read that off a bumper sticker?"

"A fortune cookie, actually."

"A man of culture, I see—"

The plane jolts. It's so sudden and violent that a passenger somewhere up front yelps. The seat-belt sign lights up, followed by a few quick clicks as people fasten their seat belts. (They should have been wearing them the whole time. Did they not pay attention to the safety demonstration?) I hold my breath and wait for the rumbling to pass.

It doesn't.

The entire plane shakes with a vengeance, rattling around like we're somehow traveling over a bumpy gravel road rather than several thousand feet up in the air.

"Ladies and gentlemen," the pilot's muffled voice sounds over the speakers. "It seems we're hitting a bit of a rough patch." *Yeah, no kidding*. "Please fasten your seat belts, stow your trays and remain seated."

Several thoughts cross my mind as I hurriedly put my laptop away and tighten my seat belt like a seventeenth-century corset: 1) What are the odds of a plane dropping out of the sky? 2) Does turbulence normally last this long? 3) Could I have avoided all of this and just stayed home?

Something warm caresses my palm. I force my eyes open and find that West has taken my hand. Or maybe I took his? Either way, I've got him trapped in a white-knuckled vise. He doesn't throw me off. Doesn't ask me what the hell I'm doing. Instead, he patiently holds on and makes no effort to let go.

"One in eleven million," he tells me calmly. "You have a much better chance of being struck by lightning. I'm not sure how long turbulence lasts, but we'll get through it. And yes, you absolutely could have avoided all this, but then you'd be missing out on an adventure of a lifetime."

I blink up at him, shivering from either nerves or the cold or both. It occurs to me, then, that I must have had my meltdown out loud. I should be grateful for his comfort. It's a nice gesture. Sweet, even. The polite thing would be to thank him for being so understanding—

"You better not use this against me," I say like the emotionally constipated asshole I am.

West simply smiles. That infuriatingly dashing, wonderful, disarming smile.

I'm really starting to fucking hate it.

"And where's the fun in that?" he asks.

I'm usually well-equipped with a snappy comeback, but whatever I have to say dies on my tongue when the plane takes an all-too-sudden drop. We're in free fall for only a millisecond, but it's enough to send my heart flying up into my throat.

What will Lily think, I wonder, if she learns that I died in a fiery crash? She'll want to know why I was on my way to Paris and will undoubtedly sift through my things for some trace of an answer—and that poses a certain kind of danger. What would she be able to glean from my search history? Would she discover the truth about who I was and what I chose to do? Would she be proud or horrified?

By some miracle of aviation, the plane levels out. The roar of the engines is a low hum in my ears as an uneasy quiet falls over the cabin. I release West's hand only once I'm convinced we aren't going to plummet out of the sky.

"See?" he says, sounding much too chipper for my liking. "Not so bad. It's like a roller-coaster ride."

"I hate roller coasters."

West laughs. "Color me surprised."

I chew on the inside of my cheek. Either he has nerves of steel, or he's full of it.

The rest of the flight to Toronto is smooth sailing, but I don't mind the way West keeps his hand on our shared armrest.

Within reach, just in case.

CHAPTER TEN
She Could Make a Killing as a Boxer

West

Paris, France

IT'S BEEN SIX years since I was last home, and I'm relieved that very little has changed. The Eiffel Tower is still towering. The Champs-Élysées is still as song-worthy as ever. Notre-Dame has been renovated and reopened to the public, as glorious and awe-inducing as it always was. The skies are cloudy, sporadic moments of sunshine peeking through. It's nowhere near as romantic as the movies make it seem, but that's probably because I was born and raised here. I never had the luxury of rose-tinted glasses, though there's something to be said about the city's beautiful architecture and rich history. I missed strolling alongside the Seine, the smell of fresh bread wafting from the boulangeries and the hard-to-miss tinge of cigarette smoke in the air.

We're nine hours ahead of Vancouver. Adelina snores lightly beside me in the back of the taxi. She conked out the moment she slid into her seat at the airport pickup. Between traveling, jet lag and the fact that I didn't catch Adelina rest a wink while on the plane, it's no wonder she's out cold. She hugs her backpack close to her chest, defensive and prickly even in sleep. It's a shame she's missing the view. We won't have any time to spare for sightseeing once the rest of the crew arrives, not that this is exactly my idea of a vacation.

It takes us another thirty minutes to get to our hotel in the fourth arrondissement—one of twenty boroughs that make up the city—the traffic growing heavier and more congested the closer we draw to Paris's core. The taxi driver stops along the curb, and I pay him the handful of euros he's due over his shoulder. Adelina doesn't stir.

"Ms. Choi?" No response. She's out like a light, so I try again. "Ms. Choi?"

It's then that I pause, taking the opportunity to study her face. She has a cute button nose, full lips, and lashes that don't so much curl as they grow straight down and out. There is a small mole just above her right eyebrow and a splash of faded freckles sprawled over her cheeks. But what I find the most intriguing is the tiny tattoo just behind her ear.

A sunflower.

First the sticker on her laptop, and now this. I feel a bit like a Victorian man catching a glimpse of ankle for the first time, utterly enthralled. I'm starting to wonder if it's her favorite flower, though she doesn't strike me as the type of person to have a favorite *anything*. More of a doom-and-gloom kind of gal. I can't help but feel like I'm intruding on her secrets, glimpsing at facets of her life that I was never meant to see.

As I place a hand on her shoulder and give her a gentle shake, I notice the edge of her phone sticking out of her jacket pocket. My heart thuds. The pictures she took of my passport . . . She was smart to collect blackmail against me, but I really can't afford to have that kind of ammunition pointed my way. It puts me in a tough spot, but more importantly, it could put Jack in danger. I don't need the police sniffing around and digging up things from my past. For a moment, I consider swiping her phone and deleting everything she has on me, but Adelina's bright. She'll notice sooner or later, and then she really *will* turn on me.

"Adelina," I whisper, her name rolling off the tip of my tongue.

Her eyes flutter open—

And then she yelps and throws her fist, a purely instinctual reaction, her knuckles cracking against the bridge of my nose. I reel back with a grunt while she screams, "What the fuck are you doing?"

"What the hell was that for?" I groan, pinching my bloody nose. "I was trying to wake you up!"

"Si tu bousilles mes sièges, tu me payes le nettoyage!" the taxi driver snaps, exasperated. *If you mess up my seats, you're paying for the cleaning!*

Great. Now we're *all* yelling.

"You startled me!" she protests.

"What? Did you think I was going to kill you?"

"Yes!"

"You think I would endure a fourteen-hour flight seated next to your mouth-breathing just to kill you now?"

"Who are you calling a mouth-breather?!" she asks, incredulous.

"Sérieux, dégagez avant de foutre le bordel dans ma caisse," cries the driver. *Seriously, get out before you mess up my car.*

Adelina and I rush out of the cab together, the cool morning air sticking to my skin. When we manage to make it to the front reception area, the man in a suit standing behind the counter looks understandably troubled.

"Oh, goodness!" he says when he notices the state of my poor nose. I really didn't want to start this job off by making a scene, yet here we are. "Are you alright, sir? Let me get you some ice."

I wave him off. "Just a little accident," I tell him. "We'd like to check in. Reservation should be under my sister's name, Natalya Petrova."

It's a fake name, of course. There's no telling how far or deep Berruci's network extends, so I'd rather proceed with caution. I don't know if Diana has arrived yet, but she promised to take care of the arrangements by the time Adelina and I touched down.

The receptionist checks his computer. "Yes, it seems she's already arrived. Your suite is on the top floor."

Adelina appears at my elbow with a handful of napkins. She must have nabbed them from the continental breakfast tables set up on the other side of the lobby. When she offers them to me, I spot something close to guilt in her eyes.

That can't be right. Adelina—the woman who pulled a cleaver on me without hesitation—feeling sorry? I think she's given me a concussion.

We take the elevator up to the sixth floor, making our way toward the suite at the very end of the hall. It comes with four separate rooms, a spacious living room area and kitchenette, all the while boasting a charming view of the Seine, the Eiffel Tower poking out over the rooftops.

I take a seat on the loveseat and inspect my nose. Despite the wallop behind her fist, I don't think it's broken. "My beautiful face," I groan.

Adelina moves swiftly, retreating to the bathroom only to return a few moments later with a damp hand towel. She sits beside me and shoos my hand away, inspecting the damage done. "You'll live."

I huff. "Would it kill you to say sorry?"

"I already apologized."

"Actually, you didn't."

She blinks, her cheeks turning the lightest shade of pink. In all the mayhem, it's entirely possible that it slipped her mind. Adelina looks almost . . . ashamed. "I'm sorry," she mumbles, unable to hold my gaze. The earnestness in her tone catches me by surprise. "It was a gut reaction."

Whatever snappy remark I had queued up withers in the back of my throat.

Honestly? I get it. She's alone in a foreign country with a guy she hardly knows, working a job well outside her comfort zone. A partnership built on mutually assured destruction isn't exactly an ideal foundation for building trust. If I were in her shoes, I'd throw hands first and ask questions later too. Hell, if some jerk kid at school ever gave Jack a hard time and disrespected her space, I'd be the first to give her the all-clear to reinforce her boundaries. Ideally through words, of course, but sometimes a good knock on the head is the only way to get your point across.

"It's alright," I say gently. "I'm sorry I startled you."

Adelina glances at me then with almost bashful surprise. It's like watching a robot trying to decipher the sensation of forgiveness, or a stray determining whether the hand I've offered will be used to praise or scold.

Try as I might, I can't seem to get a read on her. She's clearly intelligent, quick on her feet, cautious. A good childhood, from what I've been able to glean off her twin sister's public Instagram account, though social media can be deceiving. Everyone knows that it's all curated junk to show a person's highlights and little else. Curiosity simmers beneath the surface of my skin. Even after all the work I did to track her down, Adelina is very much a mystery.

How did she go from studying at a prestigious school—no doubt with a bright future ahead of her—to *this*?

"I think the bleeding's stopped," she whispers.

"Oh, good. I was starting to feel faint."

Adelina shakes her head, lingering. She smells faintly of flowers, though I can't exactly put a name to what kind. She dabs at my nose with the towel, her touch surprisingly gentle.

I guess she isn't a robot after all.

But then our eyes lock for the briefest moment, and this somehow signals to her that she needs to reboot her system, because she quickly rises and steps away. She takes in the suite. It's opulent, bordering on ostentatious, what with its cream-white walls and gold-painted molding.

"Who exactly is paying for all of this?" she asks.

"That would be me," comes a woman's smoky voice.

A tall woman in her mid-thirties steps in from the front door, her severe gray power suit contrasting sharply against her dark-brown complexion. She wears a mischievous grin, her hazel eyes observing Adelina intensely.

I can't help but chuckle. "Still with the dramatic entrances, I see."

"Dramatic?" she huffs. "You're the one coming back from the dead."

"Ad—Qwerty, this is Diana Nadkarni. She's the backer behind our operation."

CHAPTER ELEVEN Meet the Skeleton Crew

Adelina

"I PREFER THE term 'investor,'" Diana says wryly, opening her arms to capture West in a hug. They laugh merrily as they kiss each other's cheeks, long-lost friends reunited at last. The undeniable warmth between them practically takes up all the space in the room.

But then her attention turns to me and my stomach flips. She reminds me so much of a shark. Circling, waiting; trying to determine if I'm worth taking a bite out of.

"'Qwerty,' is it?" she says, only the faintest trace of an accent in her English. "What's this codename nonsense?"

"It's for my security," I answer, unwavering. "Please respect that."

"But you get to know my identity? That's hardly fair."

I look to West for . . . well, I'm not sure what for. Support, maybe? I understand the hypocrisy, but it's too much of a risk letting her know who I am. What if they learn about my family? It isn't that far-fetched a scenario where they might be used against me.

West waves a dismissive hand. "It's fine, Diana. You have my word. This is just how Qwerty works."

Diana crosses her arms over her chest, her lips pressed into a thin, unimpressed line. "So, you're the hacker," she says. "I've heard so much about you."

I frown at West. I'd been keeping a careful eye on him, though clearly not careful enough. When did he manage to sneak off and spill my life story? "Is that so?" I murmur.

"He tells me you went to MIT."

I set my jaw. This is already turning out to be way more information than I'm comfortable sharing. Should I mention that I dropped out, or should I keep that little tidbit to myself? Not that it really affected my understanding of computers and coding. There are extensive resources online—for *free,* I might add—that supplemented my education. And with only a semester left to complete my degree, I felt like I'd soaked up enough information to be self-sufficient. But Diana is clearly trying to appraise me, surveying where my weak points are.

I, for one, am too jet-lagged to play ball.

"He talks a lot," I reply evenly.

Diana arches her brow. "So it's not true?"

"Who's to say?"

"Are you normally so roundabout?"

"Only when I feel like I'm being interrogated."

"There are risks to this job. I need to make sure you'll take this seriously."

"I think you'll find she takes *everything* seriously," West pipes up. "A real buzzkill, if I do say so myself." I pin him with a glare, but he shrugs it off with ease. "Don't worry. I've seen what she's capable of. We can trust her."

Diana clicks her tongue. "*Trust* isn't a word you should take lightly."

A tense beat passes between us, the temperature in the hotel suite dropping a few degrees below comfortable. West is the one who breaks the tension, sighing like the drama queen he is.

"Let's not get off on the wrong foot, ladies. I'll force you to hold hands and sing 'Kumbaya' if I have to."

"I'd like to see you try," I grumble.

Ignoring me, he continues, "Where's Henrie?"

"Prison," Diana answers. "Twenty years for armed robbery in Monaco."

"Bannock?"

"Dead."

West frowns. "What happened?"

"Old age."

"Damn."

I cross my arms. "I thought you said you had a crew."

"I do have a crew. I just . . . haven't kept the best tabs on them," West says, making a face that means either he's stressed or he has a stomachache. He takes a step back and holds a hand over his nose, watching me warily. "You're going to punch me again, aren't you?"

I grit my teeth. "Thinking about it."

"What about Joseph?" West asks Diana. "Please tell me we at least got—"

The doors to the suite burst open with such force that it rattles the walls. A man with curly brown hair dressed in a painfully bright yellow Hawaiian shirt rushes in. Geometric tattoos spiral around both of his arms, a triangular pattern working its way up the side of his neck. Everything about him is loud and flashy, like a bird with bright feathers trying to attract a mate.

"Holy shit!" the man exclaims, practically throwing himself at West with enough speed to break his neck. "I'm so happy to see you I could kiss you! Everyone told me you were dead!"

West chuckles. "Not dead. Just hibernating."

"Fashionably late, as always, Joseph," Diana says without any real heat. It seems that her earlier hostility is reserved just for me. "I hope you aren't this tardy when the job is underway."

"A thousand humble pardons, princess. I was in the middle of a high-stakes online poker game. You know there's nothing I crave more than the thrill of going all in."

"Did you win?" I ask sardonically.

Joseph finally notices me, his jaw dropping in what I can only describe as dumbstruck amazement. "Who is this goddess among mortals?" he asks, moving to take my hand. He makes a flamboyant show of kissing the back of my knuckles. "I knew there was a reason I felt so lucky when I woke up this morning. What's your name, my dear?"

"Qwerty," I mumble, shifting uncomfortably.

He regards me with an amused quirk of his lip. "Oh? I didn't realize we were using codenames," he says. "If that's the case, you may call me 'Agent Handsome.'"

I cringe. "Um . . ."

"Not to your liking? Yes, a bit of a mouthful. How about—"

"We aren't using codenames," Diana interrupts. The bitterness in her tone is undeniable. "Just her, apparently."

Joseph shrugs, taking nowhere near the same level of offense. "Well, Qwerty, what are your dinner plans tonight? First time in Paris, yes? Let me buy you a drink. Then I'll take you on a tour of a lifetime—"

"Give her some space to breathe," West says. He casually makes his way over, wearing that disarming smile of his as he places himself between me and his friend, and I . . . I strangely appreciate it. Joseph is *a lot* to take in all at once. Nice, but certainly more energetic than I was expecting. I think it's sweet of West to use himself as a buffer, but then he points at his nose and says, "I'd be careful around her. You think a door did this?"

Ah. Just when I was starting to tolerate the guy.

"This is Joseph Demarr," West continues, tossing me a wink over his shoulder. "Fixer extraordinaire and our getaway driver. Anything we need, he'll deliver."

"Anything?" I ask skeptically.

"All you have to do is name it, my dear," Joseph says with an unmistakable tone of pride. "I'm the guy who knows a guy. My network is as impressive as they come."

"I assume your network primarily consists of poker buddies?"

Joseph laughs. "You're not entirely wrong."

"Enough," Diana snaps, clapping her hands together twice like a frustrated primary school teacher gathering her students' attention. "I know this is not the team you were hoping for, but it's all I could manage on such short notice."

"Not a problem," West replies with a cool nod. "We'll make do."

I don't understand his confidence. This is as bare bones as it gets, and I'm frankly feeling more and more apprehensive by the second. Maybe I should try my luck with the cops back home. I would much rather deal with prison than a half-cooked heist that's already short one too many ingredients.

Joseph hooks his fingers together behind his head. "So what are we stealing, exactly? Please tell me it's gold. Or an entire vault full of bonds. *Ooh,* please tell me there's a long-lost Old Master involved. Those could go for millions."

"We're not stealing anything," West explains. "Well, nothing physical. Consider it a reverse heist, if you will. We need to break in and *leave* something behind. Something that will take care of the work for us."

Diana and Joseph exchange a confused glance. "What is that supposed to mean?" they ask at the exact same time.

"Gather around, kids," West says. "Here's the plan."

CHAPTER TWELVE
First, Arrive Undetected

Adelina

"THIS IS FOR you," Joseph says chipperly as he slides an old black flip phone toward me.

I eye it suspiciously. It's as clunky as it is an eyesore. "What is it?"

"Your new burner. Each of us has one, and I've already programmed our numbers onto them. We'll communicate using these, and if anything happens, just toss it." He winks at me. "Keeps the pigs off our tails."

I take the phone and stuff it into my pocket. That makes sense. In the unfortunate event that we're caught by the authorities, the last thing I need is to link myself to the others on my personal device.

"Is there a reason West isn't traveling with us?" I ask over the rush of wind past the train windows. The French countryside is breathtaking, wide swaths of golden farmland beneath a crisp blue sky, the landscape speckled with rustic homes and a wash of luscious trees. It's a stark contrast to the city. Don't get me wrong—they're both equally lovely, but in their own way. One is a gorgeous scenic painting, while the other is a bustling center of vibrant culture. If I had to choose, it would probably come down to a coin toss.

We boarded at the Gare de Lyon to Marseille Saint-Charles, where we'll catch a connecting train to Nice (which I learned is pronounced like *niece* and not *nice*). I wasn't even aware that there were high-speed trains in France, but I'll fully confess to North American ignorance on my part. I'm not exactly a world traveler. The farthest I've ever managed was Massachusetts, never mind Europe.

"He's in another car somewhere," Diana says coolly, not bothering to peek over the edge of her newspaper. She sits across from me next to Joseph, a bolted-down table dividing us, her impeccable posture making me look like a curled-up shrimp in desperate need of a chiropractor. "Berruci has eyes all over Nice who may be able to identify him. It'll be more inconspicuous for us if we arrive separately."

"Blackjack!" Joseph exclaims, his attention glued to his phone screen. A passenger somewhere farther down the aisle shushes him. "Pardon," he replies sheepishly.

So much for being inconspicuous.

My laptop sits open before me on the table, my code only a third of the way written. It's not something I can magically throw together overnight, though I'm certainly trying. It's nothing like the movies, where the actor slams his hands over the keyboard and—*bam! I'm in.* God, I *wish*. I'm so tired and travel-weary that I find myself missing functions left, right and center. Staring at the screen for extended periods of time has my eyes going a bit crossed. With any luck, I'll have time to do a few test runs and work out any bugs, but the stakes are high and the clock is ticking. While I'm confident in my abilities, the consequences aren't lost on me.

What happens if I fail? Will West turn me in to the cops? It's entirely possible that he would hand me over to Berruci just to save his own neck instead.

I wipe my clammy palms on my jeans. "How do you two know West? Or . . . Mathieu, I mean."

Diana sets her newspaper down, her lips pursed. "Why should we tell you?"

I frown deeply. "Did I do something to piss you off?"

"You are an outsider," she replies simply. "One who hasn't even given us her name. The playing field isn't even, so excuse me for being cautious. I don't know what you're capable of, what connections you might have, or what your reason for joining us even is."

"I'm in it for the money," I reply fluidly. Not technically a lie, but not the whole truth either.

Her eyes flit over my face as though memorizing my features. "I don't believe you," she says, the corner of her lip tugging up into a grin. There's nothing friendly about it. It's cool and calm and self-satisfied in a way that makes me squirm. "I'll be the first to say it, since Mathieu—or West, as he goes by now—seems adamant about keeping you on the team: I don't trust you. He seems to have a lot of faith in your capabilities, but faith doesn't get the job done. For all I know, you may end up being useless."

Useless.

The word ricochets around the inside of my skull and sends my heart stuttering. Do I somehow have the word tattooed onto my forehead, but I'm the only one who can't see it?

I might have been able to forgive Diana for her combative nature. She's just trying to keep herself safe, same as me. But this is a slap across the face, one hard enough to knock the air from my lungs and superheat my blood past the boiling point. I gave West shit for wanting a demonstration back in Vancouver, but now my pride has been thoroughly bruised. I want nothing more than the chance to prove her wrong, to show Diana and all her doubts that I am, in fact, more than enough.

I don't need to be everyone's best friend, but the least I require is a sliver of respect.

"Joseph, what casino website are you using?" I ask him.

He looks up from his phone. "It's called Triple Golden Jackpot."

Diana huffs at him. "Don't you have anything better to do with your time?"

"What can I say? I'm a hustler, my darling. There's always money to be made."

"Do they have slot games?" I ask him.

"They do, but the odds are always shit. I prefer live tables."

Returning my attention to my laptop, I pull up the site in question and am immediately bombarded by all manner of flashing ads and bright colors. Good Lord. It's a good thing I know how to protect myself digitally. One misplaced click could probably overload my laptop with malware.

"What's your username?" I ask him.

"JoeLeManGeeOh."

I frown. "Seriously?"

Joseph shrugs and chuckles. "What? I thought it was funny."

"Enter a game," I instruct, squinting at the tiny font that floats onto my screen.

Diana snorts, crossing her arms over her chest with an impatient click of her tongue. "What's the point of all this?"

"Give me a minute and you'll see."

Hacking into a website is easy enough. There are several possible routes I can take (a brute force attack, clickjacking, SQL injection, spoofing the DNS, cross-site scripting, etc.), but a quick glance at the code tells me I don't have to put in nearly that much effort. There are holes in the security *everywhere*. It's frankly a miracle that Joseph hasn't had his personal information stolen, or infected his phone with a plethora of viruses.

Now, I would normally hesitate to mess around with someone's website, but these big online casinos are predatory as hell. (And I sincerely doubt some sweet old grandma is the one running it.) Much like in a real casino, the odds are stacked in favor of the house, preying upon those foolish enough to think they have Lady Luck on their side. Some people are desperate for the money, for a quick solution. Others may be predisposed toward compulsive gambling. It isn't right to take advantage of people like that.

It takes me a few minutes to sort through all the junk code, but when I finally find the specific algorithm in charge of setting the digital slot machine's odds, a shot of electricity bolts through me. It's set to 1 in 5,000 for minor prizes (a couple bucks here, a bonus pull there) and 1 in 35,000,000 for the major jackpot. Unbelievable. It's no fucking wonder some people lose their life savings to the slots, all while some greedy hotshot takes and takes and *takes.* I'm sure they have their twisted justifications—that they didn't *force* anybody to bet their money—but that's a straw man's argument. I draw the line at designing a system meant to bleed a person dry.

Once I trick the website into believing I'm logging in as admin, I inject a few lines of custom code and change the odds in Joseph's favor. "Go ahead and play," I tell him.

Joseph arches a brow but taps his screen with a shrug of his shoulders. The flashy numbers spin around and around, slowly coming to a stop on—

"Triple sevens!" Joseph gasps.

"Play again."

He does so, this time landing on the images of three red cherries. "I can't believe it," he says with a laugh.

While I'm glad Joseph is impressed, Diana looks the furthest from it. "It's all luck," she says.

"Is it?" I reply, dipping back in to delete my work. It's important that I don't leave a trace. West being able to sniff me out was a terrible oversight on my part, and I'm determined never to let it happen again. "Go ahead and make another bet," I tell Joseph.

He does so with an almost fiendish glint in his eye, but his joy swiftly drains away when he loses all the money he just earned. "You turned it off?"

"That's what I can do in ten minutes. Imagine what I can accomplish with a dedicated couple of days." I close my laptop and rise from my seat. "Now if you'll excuse me, I'm going to the food car for some breakfast."

I make my way down the aisle without so much as a backward glance, the train jostling slightly underfoot. My face is warm, my heartbeat erratic. I shouldn't have let Diana get under my skin like that, but if there's one thing I hate, it's when people doubt my work. I was one of the only girls in my computer science class in high school. In college, I had to endure an entire classroom full of boys with massive egos, always the first to laugh when I made a mistake or sling dirty looks my way when I outperformed them.

Maybe I have an ego of my own. My pride simply couldn't stand Diana's skepticism. God forbid a woman have talent, drive and a thirst for knowledge only to have her efforts diminished as little more than luck. To be written off as some Mary Sue. Diana wasn't there to see all the hours I put in to get to where I am. She doesn't know what I sacrificed.

You have to work twice as hard for half the recognition, Mom used to say.

She was right, but that doesn't make it any less exhausting.

I step through the sliding doors between train cars and spot a familiar tuft of blond hair sticking out from beneath a navy-blue baseball cap. West is on his phone, leaning against the wall for stability, his back to me. He looks unassuming in a pair of gray slacks and a black sweatshirt, wearing sunglasses over his eyes even though it's nowhere near sunny enough to warrant them. I guess this is what he thinks it means to go incognito.

"I miss you too," he says warmly. "I'll be home as soon as I can. No, you should really go to bed . . . I love you, too, sweetie."

Well, this is awkward. I didn't mean to intrude on a private conversation. I wasn't even aware that West might have a partner waiting for him back home. My imagination gets the better of me as I wonder what they're like. Do they know who he really is? Are they aware of what precisely he's here in France to do? If I have to hide the truth from the rest of my family, does West need to do the same?

He hangs up and nearly jumps back five feet when he sees me. West throws a hand over his heart. "How long were you standing there?"

"Not long."

His momentary surprise melts away, quickly replaced by his signature smile. "Did you leave the comforts of first class just to come visit me? You're too sweet."

"Don't flatter yourself. I was looking for something to eat."

He tilts his head to the side, contemplative. "Did something happen?"

I cross my arms. "I don't know what you're talking about."

"Don't play with me. I can hear it in your tone."

"I don't have a tone."

"*Riiiiight,*" he says. "And I'm eight foot nine."

A heavy sigh escapes my chest. "It's not important. Diana's just . . ."

West frowns. "What did she do?"

"I don't think she likes me very much."

"Don't take it too personally. This job is a lot of pressure. She has her reasons for wanting to go after Berruci."

"Why?" I ask, instantly jumping at the opportunity. I worry I'm being too transparent, that West might shut me down the same way Diana did, but the nagging voice in the back of my head burns to know. Who are these people? What's in it for them?

West chews on the inside of his cheek. I can practically see the gears turning in his head, mentally debating whether or not it's wise to let me in.

"A lot of money on the line," he says, but I know he isn't being forthright.

"Is that why she's coming with us?"

"I don't understand."

"She's the investor," I say, as though it were a perfunctory fact like *water is wet* and *the Earth isn't fucking flat*.

"She's a cautious woman."

"So she's babysitting us."

"Supervising," he corrects.

I glare at him. "Oh, yeah. That's *way* better. Can't wait to have her constantly breathing down my neck."

"Diana probably just wants to make sure she gets her cut."

"Make sure? I have no plans of double-crossing her. Do you?"

"Of course not."

"Then what's her problem?"

West sighs. "Look, she's a hands-on kind of investor. She's honestly not that bad. Give her some time to warm up to you."

I tap my foot impatiently. "Where did she even get all this money anyway?"

He scratches behind his ear. "Her family owns a successful chain of bakeries back in New Delhi, I think. When she came to France, she opened her own chain. Took the profits and made smart investments. I don't know the details. Rich people are always a little dodgy about how they left everyone else in the dust."

I snort. Truer words have never been spoken.

"Well, it's a good thing the train ride is six hours long. We'll *really* get to know each other. A flight to Nice would have taken an hour, you know."

West grins. "I know, but you hate flying."

My heart stutters. Wait, did he do this for *my* sake? It's a simple kindness, yet one I'm incredibly grateful for. Before I have a chance to think too hard on it, my personal phone rings in my pocket. It's the alarm I set—programmed to go off ten minutes before my scheduled text to Lily, arguably the only person in my contacts list whom I trust to raise hell in the event something should happen to me.

West looks at me, and then at the phone as I cancel the alarm and reschedule the message to send in twenty-four hours' time. The air around us suddenly grows thick.

"The food car is just up ahead," he informs me, easily slipping on his mask of casual ease. "Do you remember the next part of the plan?"

I nod, stuffing my phone back into my jacket pocket. "Joseph is going to secure a warehouse for our base of operations. Diana is in charge of securing lodging. And we're heading out immediately once the train arrives to begin reconnaissance."

"Prepare yourself, Ms. Choi. There's no turning back now."

CHAPTER THIRTEEN: Safety First

West

Nice, France

I BLAME HOLLYWOOD for a lot of things. Unrealistic beauty standards for both men and women, unhealthy celebrity worship, the fact that studios would rather throw their money at sequels and IP remakes rather than try to give us anything fresh.

But tonight, my main gripe with Hollywood is the fact that heist films make heists seem a million times more thrilling than they really are. The hard cuts, the big explosions, the car chases, the breathtaking soundtracks . . . I'd take all of it over *this*.

Adelina and I have been cooped up in the rental car for five hours now, parked atop a hill a good distance away from the seaside villa in question. I have a hard time believing someone actually lives in there. It looks more like a franchised resort than a home, what with its beautiful cream walls, sunburnt-orange tiled roofs and gorgeous archway accents. There's even a crystalline infinity pool in the back, which makes no sense to me considering the ocean is *right* there, but I guess I'm not filthy rich enough to understand.

Adelina is in the passenger seat of our rented black Renault Clio, her feet up on the dashboard. She's got her laptop balanced on her knees, an HDMI cable running from its side to the DSLR camera in my hands. I'm in the driver's seat, a massive lens stuck out the window.

Every picture I snap is automatically transferred to her computer for analysis—though I'm really starting to worry about storage.

"Did you need to take a picture of that guard's butt?" she asks dryly.

"I was *trying* to get a closer look at his ID," I reply, mildly distracted as I hold the viewfinder up to my eye. The shutter goes off again, and this time I get the photo I'm looking for. I should be able to print off a convincing fake if we need one. Hopefully it doesn't come to that.

We've counted a patrol team consisting of roughly fifteen men so far. All armed, all twice my size. They conduct their rounds at regular intervals, and they have to present their ID badges for scanning regardless of whether they're entering or exiting the premises. Berruci has at least twenty different cameras placed strategically around the perimeter of the property, leaving virtually no blind spots, and there's only going to be more inside.

This place is more of a fortress than a home. Getting in and out unseen won't be simple.

"Do you think you'd be able to access them remotely?" I ask her.

"They're probably closed-circuit. Same as Berruci's computer. Someone would have to let me in from the inside."

"Do you see anything that you *can* tap into remotely? Anything we can use to our advantage?"

Adelina hums, deep in thought, observing the villa from afar. "His cars, maybe?"

"You can do that?"

She shrugs. "Cars are just computers on wheels attached to a motor. I can piggyback off the cellular connection needed for its entertainment system. If I wanted to, I could take control of the vehicle's transmission, steering and brakes. Everything, really. I don't know how you'd incorporate it into your plan, but the option's there."

I stare at her, caught between awe and horror. "There's no way."

Adelina smirks, opening the command prompt on her laptop. She types hastily, lines upon lines of code branching out across the screen. When she hits Enter—

Our car engine rumbles to life. She presses the button again and turns it off. The fine hairs on the back of my neck stand on end.

"Holy shit," I say, utterly amazed. "Good thing you're on my team."

"And don't you forget it."

"Uh-oh," I mumble under my breath.

Adelina sits up, instantly alert. "What's wrong? Did someone see us?"

"Nothing. My camera battery just died."

She throws her head back and sighs. "Don't scare me like that. I thought we'd been made."

I can't help but chuckle. "Made? What is this—a 1940s old-timey gangster movie?" I bring my fingers up to my lips like I'm holding an invisible cigar, pantomiming a puff. "See here, little lady," I say in my best impression of a transatlantic accent. "We gotta handle this here sitch real smooth-like. I've got me a damn good crew, so you can bet your bottom dollar we'll be countin' those clams in no time, see?"

What she does next surprises me. Her shoulders start to shake as she fights a giggle, and then gives way to outright laughter. It's a bright sound, so light and sweet that I almost can't believe my own ears.

But most bewildering is her smile. Carefree and warm and . . . pretty. She looks like an entirely different person. And I know this is ironic, since she has an identical twin and all, but the sentiment stands.

What happened to her that made her so dour? And while we're at it, how did she come to find herself in this line of work? She clearly has an impressive skill set. Why isn't she working for some big tech company? Hell, after her stunt with the car, I'm sure the military sector would be right up her alley. How does someone so amazing end up playing Robin Hood instead?

I know I've been staring too long when Adelina's laughter fades back into silence. She glances at me, no doubt taking note of my quizzical expression.

"What?" she asks.

I clear my throat, returning my attention to the villa. I need to focus. There's too much on the line to be sidetracked. "Nothing."

"Why are your ears all red?"

"It's warm in here."

"*Oh*," she says slowly, watching me with far too much amusement. "Did I catch you off guard?"

I don't understand why I take it as a challenge, but now I'm curious to see if I can make her smile again. Adelina might be allergic to fun, but she's already proven that she isn't immune to it.

"I'm a man, not a robot. Beautiful women happen to be a weakness of mine."

Her cheeks turn pink, but I'm pretty sure I can turn them crimson. "You're shameless."

I turn in my seat to get a better look at her, setting my camera aside on the dash. "What's wrong, Ms. Choi? Feeling warm?"

She opens a new browser tab only to close it again. She's cute when she's flustered. "I don't think it's appropriate," she says firmly.

"What is?"

"Your . . . Your flirting."

"Because we're colleagues?"

Adelina scoffs. "Like hell we are."

"Friends?"

"Friends don't blackmail each other."

"You've got me there."

"Look, are we done here? I want to head back to the hotel."

I gasp as if scandalized. "You're so forward, Ms. Choi. At least buy me dinner first."

"I'm going to strangle you."

"Please be gentle. My safe word is 'umbrella.'"

She drags her hands over her face. "Jesus Christ."

"My name's West, actually."

"It's inappropriate because you have a *partner*!"

I still at this. I'm fairly certain my jaw would hit the car floor if it could. "What?"

"I heard you on the train." Adelina shifts in her seat. "You were talking to them on the phone when I found you."

"Oh, that wasn't—" Out of the corner of my eye, movement. "Shut up," I snap hastily.

Adelina frowns deeply. "Excuse me?"

Tilting my chin toward the windshield, I draw her line of sight to the large black SUV pulling up at the villa's front gates. It's an entire procession, in fact, a line of ants on their way to do some very important business. The guards we've been watching for the past couple of hours flit around with an almost frantic energy, as if caught unprepared for the fleet's arrival.

"Who is it?" she asks.

Before I have a chance to answer, someone steps out of the vehicle closest to the gate. A man in his late fifties, dressed in a pair of white linen pants, a pale-yellow polo shirt and wicker sandals. His greasy black hair is thinning on top, but out of sheer stubbornness, he's elected for a comb-over rather than shaving his head outright. We're too far away to hear what he's saying, but his body language is plenty loud. He gesticulates angrily, pointing at the closed gates while yelling at the guard in the adjacent control booth. His aggression makes my pulse race. I haven't seen him in years, but I'd know that man anywhere.

Valentino Berruci.

Things escalate with alarming speed. I can see the guard struggling with what I assume is the control panel inside the booth. When the gate still doesn't open, Berruci roughly grabs the smaller man by the front of his shirt and winds his arm back.

I move instantaneously, reaching across the center console to press my hand over Adelina's eyes. I don't know why I do it. It's instinctive. She's her own woman and I'm sure she can handle herself, but . . . I know what Berruci is capable of. I've seen his cruelty firsthand. If I can spare her from seeing what's about to happen, I'll gladly do it.

"Don't look," I order.

"What—"

"Trust me, Adelina. Please."

Her breathing thins, but she doesn't push me away. She nods slowly, her clenched hands resting on her lap.

It's not a pretty picture. The guard doesn't fight back. He can't. If he raises a hand to Berruci, he's as good as dead. All he can do is defend himself against Berruci's unjustified anger. It's over within a few seconds, but it feels like an eternity has passed. Someone finally gets the gate open and Berruci stuffs himself back into his vehicle. The guard is on the ground, curled up in a ball. I'm thankful there's so much distance between us because I don't know that I'd be able to handle seeing his injuries up close. When one of his buddies goes to check on him, I decide I've seen more than enough.

"I'm going to drive us out of here," I whisper. The air inside the car is unbelievably still. "But I need you to keep your eyes closed."

"Why?" she asks. "Oh, God. Please tell me that guy's still alive."

"He is, but . . ." I take a deep breath. "Just promise me you won't look until I say it's okay, alright? You don't want to see this."

"O-okay," she replies with a shiver.

I slowly remove my hand from over her eyes and pause—just to make sure she's being true to her word—before I reach for the keys. The engine rumbles to life. Air rushes over the hood of the vehicle and past the windows, eventually mingling with the sound of traffic as we return to the city center.

I knew Berruci was dangerous, but now my belly is especially queasy. If he's willing to punish his own employees over something as uncontrollable as a faulty gate, what horrendous things is he willing to do to his enemies? There's a reason why his own family wanted him out of the picture. Such vile, erratic and unhinged behavior . . . I wouldn't want to be anywhere near it either.

The car comes to a full stop. I kill the engine.

"Okay," I murmur, my voice suddenly too loud in the quiet that surrounds us.

Adelina opens her eyes slowly and looks around. We're parked on the side of the road near a long stretch of beach. There are still a lot of people out despite the late hour. My grip on the steering wheel is punishing, the leather creaking in protest beneath my hands.

"West?" Adelina whispers, reaching out slowly to place a hand on my forearm.

"I'm fine." I don't think she believes me, but I do my best to keep my voice level. "Has Diana texted us the hotel address yet?"

She checks her burner phone. "Yeah. Looks like she found one twenty minutes away. Berruci apparently has eyes on all the big chains by the waterfront. Joseph's back with the blueprints you asked for too."

"Good. That's good. We should meet up with them and—"

"I think you should let me drive."

"There's no need for that."

"West, you're *shaking*."

It's hard to think past the blood rushing through my ears and the adrenaline coursing through my veins, but I finally manage to release the steering wheel. I can feel it now, the slight tremor of my hands and shoulders. I didn't realize how badly I'd been affected.

It all comes rushing back to me. How our Paris heist went up in smoke. There's even more on the line this time. I couldn't protect Michael, but I *have* to protect Jack. No matter what happens, I can't let Berruci win.

"You don't know the area," I mumble.

"Then give me directions."

Even if I wanted to argue, she's already slipping out through the passenger-side door. Maybe she's right. It's probably safer for everyone if she drives. Once we've changed spots, Adelina hands me her laptop for safekeeping. She pulls into traffic without issue. At some point, she rolls down the windows, allowing the warm ocean breeze to wash over us.

The ride is silent, for the most part, save for the occasional direction. We arrive in front of the hotel—a smaller three-star chain—and pull into an empty stall in the adjacent parking lot. Even though she turns the engine off, Adelina doesn't exit the vehicle right away. Instead, she turns to me, her dark eyes questioning.

"I want you to tell me the truth," she says, her tone surprisingly gentle. "This is clearly about more than just money for you. That man *scares* you. Why do you want to go after him so badly? Why risk turning against him?"

I take a slow, deep breath in through my nose. Adelina's too sharp. She was bound to ask sooner or later—but can I trust her? If I tell her about Jack, will she use that information to help me or hurt me? I don't think she realizes just how dangerous she is.

"My niece," I reply after some thought. "I'm doing this for my niece."

CHAPTER FOURTEEN Phase One, Complete

Adelina

"SHE'S ADORABLE," I say as I scroll through his camera roll.

We're seated across from each other at a small table in the hotel's breakfast area. Diana and Joseph have yet to arrive, so we decided to treat ourselves to a few complimentary pastries while we wait. They're cold and a bit stale, given that they've been out since the morning, but they're a welcome rush of sugar. The hotel doesn't seem particularly busy, and I have to wonder if Diana chose this place for that exact reason. It's a far cry from the fancy hotel we met up at in Paris, but it's certainly comfortable enough. Without a lot of foot traffic, we'll minimize the chances of being recognized.

"Jack's the one I was talking to on the train," he says. "She's been a handful for her babysitter. Keeps staying up way past her bedtime."

"How old is she? Jack, not the babysitter."

West laughs softly. "She's almost seven."

I swipe to the next picture and pause, unable to fight my smile. It's a picture of West and Jack for what I can only assume is Halloween. West is dressed up as a giant chocolate chip cookie while Jack is dressed as the Cookie Monster.

"We scored a ton of candy that year," West says with pride. "Though she was very upset when I wouldn't let her eat most of it."

"Fear of cavities?"

He shakes his head. "Diabetic. It was hard trying to explain why too much sugar was bad for her. She refused to talk to me for a whole day and it nearly killed me. She came around eventually."

"You must love her a lot."

West grins, an undeniable warmth in his green eyes. "That kid's my whole world. There's nothing I wouldn't do for her."

"And that includes toppling a maniacal crime boss with anger issues?"

West sighs, stacking his mini croissants into a wobbly pyramid on his plate. It's almost jarring to see him so . . . quiet. Unnatural. I'm used to his loud smiles and blinding cheer. I know shit's real when West is *serious.*

"Berruci promised me a long time ago that he'd let Jack and me live in peace," he says. "All I had to do was monitor his mule account. Move money around from time to time. Give him a heads-up if the cops ever came sniffing around."

"But then I took from it," I mumble, guilt twisting my guts into tight knots.

"Don't feel bad. You didn't know."

"Did he threaten you? When he realized the money was gone?"

When he nods, I shrink into myself a little. I've spent the last few years stealing from the rich to give to the poor, but at no point have I really stopped to consider who I was hurting. I try justifying it to myself, of course. If the people I target have millions to their name, where's the harm in taking a couple hundred thousand here and there? Never in my wildest dreams would I have taken West's money had I known I'd be putting him and his niece at risk. What are the odds that I wound up taking from him, of all people? How many others might I have accidentally harmed with my twisted logic?

"Don't look so sad," he says gently. "If anything, you did me a favor."

I look at him, confused. "How so?"

"I've been living with an ax over my head for years. Berruci could have come after me for literally anything at any time. He's always had the power to do so. But when I realized what you'd done . . . saw what you were capable of . . . I realized I might finally have a shot at putting him away for good."

"So you sought me out."

"Yeah."

"Why didn't you just tell me?"

"You were a little busy throwing dishes at me. And you said you didn't want things to get personal."

"Actually, I believe what I said was that I wasn't going to pry."

He shrugs. "Tomato, to-*mah*-to."

I keep scrolling through his collection of pictures, the pecan tart I swiped from the food display sitting ignored. The next picture I land on is one of Jack blowing bubbles at the camera, all smiles with the noonday sun giving her hair an almost angelic golden glow. As I admire her toothy grin, burning questions rattle around inside my head. What happened to Jack's parents? And how did West come to work for Berruci in the first place?

"Thank you, by the way," I mutter under my breath.

"For what?"

"For covering my eyes."

West regards me warmly and my chest suddenly feels . . . tingly. "Don't mention it," he says.

"Oh, good, you're both here!" comes the sound of a familiarly low voice, cutting through the delightful haze that's settled in the air.

Joseph strolls in through the lobby and joins us at our table, plopping himself down in the vacant chair next to West. He helps himself to the snacks we scrounged up for ourselves.

"How did it go?" West asks.

"Didn't even break a sweat." He reaches into the inner pocket of his jacket to produce a folded-up piece of paper, tossing it casually onto the table like a discarded hand of cards. "My second cousin's wife's dogwalker works as a temp clerk at city hall. Had to bribe the guy double his monthly pay, but it all worked out."

"You can invoice Diana later," West says distractedly, already unfolding the blueprints to get a better look at Berruci's villa. Is it strange that I kind of like the notch between his brows when he's deep in thought?

"You said you managed to secure a warehouse?" I ask Joseph, remembering Diana's text from earlier.

"Not yet. Ran into a bit of a snag."

"What kind of snag?" West asks.

"Nothing serious, old friend. There aren't very many places that meet your specifications. I've still got plenty of feelers out."

My stomach flips as I look to West, studying his stern expression. "How badly does that mess with our timeline?"

Joseph waves a hand dismissively. "No more than a week, I promise. I might have something. Less of a warehouse and more of a decommissioned airplane hangar, but it's got plenty of space for us to work with. Once I track down and bribe the owner for the keys, we'll be golden. In the meantime, you can tell me what kind of equipment you need."

"Equipment?" I echo.

"You weren't going to run this whole operation off your cute little laptop, were you?"

I press my lips into a thin line. "It's always gotten the job done."

He winks. "Give me a list. I'll throw everything together for you."

"Are you sure that's okay?"

"Why wouldn't it be?" comes a sultry voice. Diana approaches with several hotel key cards in hand, the sharp click of her stiletto heels accompanying her graceful strides. "For the sake of the job, you better not spare any expense."

Joseph puts his hands on his hips. "Nice of you to finally join us. Now who's fashionably late, princess?"

Diana ignores him, setting the key cards down on the table. "Everything went well with reconnaissance, I hope?"

West nods. "We've got plenty of pictures, but we're going to need to get a good idea of his security's routine. If we keep an eye on him over the next week, we'll be able to get a sense of his itinerary."

I observe West carefully, surprised that he didn't mention anything about Berruci showing up or the altercation he had with his own guard. Does he not think it's relevant? Is he still too shaken to talk about it? He wears the illusion of confidence well enough. Better than most, in fact. But those few minutes allowed me a glimpse of the man beneath it all. I had never seen West look so ill before. Now that I know about Jack, I can understand why.

"Let's get some rest," West says, returning to his usual chipper self. "We'll reconvene in the morning. I want everyone well rested before we move on to phase two."

I check the time on my phone. It may be just after 10 p.m. here in France, but it's only around one in Vancouver. I haven't adjusted to the time zone change yet, so I'm wide awake and itching for something to do. The more time that passes is time wasted; we can't risk Berruci finding out that we're moving against him. It could throw our entire plan out the window. Right now, we're working with the element of surprise, so it's imperative that we strike as hard and as fast as possible.

But maybe West is right. We can't afford to burn out before the finish line.

CHAPTER FIFTEEN Hello, Neighbor

Adelina

FINDING MY HOTEL room is easy enough. We all load into the elevator together. Joseph gets off on the second floor, Diana on the fourth, and West and I step off on the fifth. I stop in front of the door that reads 501, at the very end of the hall. West ends up in front of 502.

"You better not throw any loud parties," he teases. "I need my beauty sleep."

"I hate to be the one to tell you this, but I don't think it's working."

West places a hand over his heart like I've just shot him. "Who are you kidding? We both know I'm the most gorgeous man you've ever laid eyes on."

"*Goodnight*, West."

"You didn't deny it!"

I enter my room and close the door on him, the sound of his laughter making the butterflies in my belly flutter. He's just so . . . so . . .

"Annoying," I mumble, because I can't find the perfect adjective. I have to remind myself that it's just an act. West has all the markings of a class clown, whereas I'm a former high school vice president. We couldn't make a more clashing pair.

The room is nice, though certainly nothing to write home about. It comes complete with an empty writing desk, a spacious queen-sized bed with an unnecessarily large pile of pillows, and that strange singular chair in the corner that all hotel rooms seem to have for some reason. (Seriously, what is that about?) The wall art is generic and impersonal, abstracts in a wash of different shades of blue. The only thing that strikes me as odd about the room is the door just to my left. It's a bit out of place, a little too central to be a closet.

Since I'm not ready to sleep, I decide to investigate.

Tossing my backpack onto the bed, I start toward the door and pull on the handle. I find myself staring at yet another door (like one of those Matryoshka nesting dolls), this one locked from the other side. These two rooms must have been built as a suite, the doors used to separate it into two different rooms depending on hotel vacancy. I'm admittedly a little underwhelmed until—

The other door swings open. I'm suddenly face-to-face with West.

A very *shirtless* West.

"Oh," he says in surprise. "Sorry. I thought this led out onto a balcony or something."

My brain struggles to form a proper sentence. I'm pretty sure all that manages to come out of my mouth is a stupid little "*Umm . . .*"

I just didn't expect West to look so *good*. It flies in the face of his *friendly-neighborhood-accountant* aesthetic. (Maybe that isn't fair of me to say. Accountants can be conscious about their health too.) As he stands there in nothing but his dark jeans, my eyes have ample opportunity to roam. He's . . . unexpectedly well-built. Lean and strong like a swimmer. I'm not sure why I never noticed the impressive definition of his arms and wide chest. Can anyone really blame me? I've been so concerned about this whole Berruci situation that I didn't even stop to consider that maybe, just maybe, he's our mastermind *and* primary for a reason.

What leaves me absolutely flabbergasted, however, are his tattoos.

I'd mistakenly believed that West didn't have any. Considering his Steve Rogers Boy Scout impression, I never would have guessed he was the type to be into ink. They're strategically placed, the designs on his arms cutting off just above his elbows, with enough of a gap that a T-shirt's sleeve can easily cover them. Even the ones on his chest dip below his collarbones, out of sight even with a deep V-neck.

I stare at the details of each piece—splices from famous paintings working together to form a glorious collage—marveling at the intricate shading and expert lines in black and white made to imitate the look of carved marble. *The Fallen Angel* by Alexandre Cabanel sweeps across his left pec and down the side of his ribs; the near-touching hands found in *The Creation of Adam* by Michelangelo rest over his right shoulder and arm; and one last one that I can't put a name to, though it's clearly some depiction of the Virgin Mary holding her child, set upon a bed of flowers.

"Stare any harder and you'll go cross-eyed, Choi."

Every inch of my skin is on fire, all that heat rising out of the top of my head as if it were a fucking steamed dumpling. I need to get a damn grip, or, at the very least, *close the damn door*. What the hell am I doing ogling him like a piece of meat? Then again, he's a walking art museum. I'd bet my cut of the fifty billion to the first person who manages *not* to stare.

"Sorry," I mumble.

"Are you drooling?"

"What? *No.*"

West grins. "I'll take your word for it."

"Do you normally make a habit of walking around without a shirt on?"

"I was about to hop into the shower."

"What's—" I clear my throat, daring to reach out. I hold my breath when my fingers hover over the lines of the painting I can't name. And although our skin never makes contact, I can feel the heat of his chest radiating against my palm. "What's this one?"

"*La Vierge au lys,*" he says. "By William-Adolphe Bouguereau."

"I don't think I've ever seen it before."

"That's because it's in a private collection."

"And you know this how?"

West shrugs. "Let's just say I might have wanted to liberate it once. Never got around to it, lucky for them."

"You were an art thief?"

"Art *liberator*."

I snort. "Semantics."

"Semantics," he agrees. "I didn't stick to it very long. The crew decided there were faster ways of getting rich. It was nice, in a way. I finally got to go to museums to appreciate the work, not just case the joint."

"Well, it's beautiful," I murmur, hypnotized by the beauty of the composition. I'm not sure what impresses me more: West's impeccable taste in art or his tattoo artist's skill.

Our eyes finally meet. There's a glimmer of amusement in his gaze, tinged with curiosity. We're standing close. *Much* too close.

I take my hand back, surprised he allowed me to indulge for so long. Talk about embarrassing. "I'll, uh . . . I'll just go."

"You mean we're not going to stay up and have a movie marathon?"

"This isn't a slumber party."

"But it *could* be. You fail to see my vision."

I shake my head. If the stress of this mission doesn't kill me, dealing with West certainly will. "I'm closing the door now."

He leans against the shared doorframe, and I kind of hate him for it because he smells really good. He's wearing a light cologne, a mix of pine and fresh laundry, that doesn't overwhelm my usually sensitive nose.

"Don't you want a kiss goodnight?" he asks, too suave for his own good.

I won't dignify that with a response, but *damn*. He's planted the thought and it's concerning just how quickly the idea takes root inside my head. How *does* a man like West, retired thief and international man of mystery, kiss someone goodnight?

With his aptitude for teasing, I wouldn't be surprised if he's the type to relish going slow and gentle, spoiling a partner with soft caresses and sweet words murmured against their ear until they beg him for more. Or maybe he's an animal. The type to pull their hair and leave marks on their neck, every ounce possessive and commanding and greedy. I can imagine the hard press of his body, the grip of his strong hands on my waist, all while he bites down on my bottom lip and—

Wait. Shit. What the hell am I doing? I need to push these cursed thoughts from my mind and blame it on the jet lag.

"You're thinking about it," West says lowly, a dark glint in his eyes. "Aren't you?"

This bastard is toying with me on purpose. "Screw you," I grumble.

"Only if you ask—"

"If you finish that sentence, I'll kick you in the balls."

I roll my eyes and shut the door in his face. West's laughter booms from the other side.

CHAPTER SIXTEEN

It's the Little Things

West

Monday, 6:15 a.m.

"GOOD MORNING, SUNSHINE."

"Shut up."

I suppress a smile as I hand her a cup of coffee. My own tastes like absolute crap—burnt, with bitter grinds swimming around the bottom—but they come complimentary with the hotel, so who cares? If there's one thing a thief loves more than anything in the world, it's free stuff.

Adelina takes a hefty swig. If she doesn't like it, she certainly doesn't have the energy to complain. The combination of her flat hair and wrinkled hoodie, and the dark circles under her eyes, delights me to no end. She reminds me so much of a grumpy Doberman. I'm not scared of her, though. Every Doberman I've ever met was as sweet as can be. They just have a bad rap and intimidating presence—not unlike my dear hacker.

"You're not a morning person, huh?" I ask as I reach for the car keys in my jacket pocket.

"No."

"You know, banter's a lot more fun when you put a little effort in. I'm trying to build team rapport."

"Sorry, let me try again," she says before clearing her throat. "*Fuck* no."

I bump her arm with my elbow. "That's the spirit."

Adelina grumbles under her breath. I don't catch what she says, but I have a sneaking suspicion that it's something that could make even the most foul-mouthed of sailors blush. "Are we going to stand around all day, or are we getting to work?"

"Are you that excited to spend the whole day in a confined space with me?"

She presses her lips into a thin line. "Remind me again why you can't do recon by yourself?"

"Safety in numbers."

"Then take Joseph. Or, better yet, Diana, since she's so keen on making sure we're doing our jobs."

"Joseph and Diana are teaming up to cover the night shifts. That way, we'll be able to learn about their movements around the clock."

"Wouldn't it be easier to set up cameras?" Adelina asks. "Plug them into a couple of power banks and you're all set. Hell, you heard Diana. I'm sure she'd be happy to buy us a small drone. We could do a lot with an aerial shot."

"Sure, but you have to take into account blind spots, camouflaging the cameras . . . and if Berruci spots a drone overhead, it's game over. Not to mention you'd have to scrub through hours of footage." I tap my temple. "A good thief is a patient one. No shortcuts allowed."

"Seems inefficient."

I offer her a warm smile. "You can't put all of your faith in technology. Sometimes the old-fashioned way is best."

"Can't put your faith in technology?" she echoes, incredulous. "How dare you say that to my face and live."

"I said you can't put *all* of it." I laugh. "Trust me, Adelina."

Adelina tilts her head back and takes a big gulp of coffee. A weary sigh bubbles past her lips. "Fine. The boring way it is."

Tuesday, 6 p.m.

Her notes are immaculate. They're typed—so of course they are.

```
Shift change @ 6 a.m. → Night crew relieved.
Shift change @ 6 p.m. → Day crew relieved. (Do
they get a lunch break? Info TBD.)
10 guards working patrol, always in pairs. Armed.
Total time to walk perimeter = 20 minutes.
5-minute gap between pairs.
3 guards working booth at front gate.
They've got trained guard dogs housed in back-
yard. Sharp teeth. Big yikes.
```

"Don't you think that last part is a little unnecessary?" I ask her as I read her screen. She's crammed her open laptop between the windshield and the dashboard.

Adelina leans back in her seat and tilts her head toward me. "I'm trying to be thorough. Wouldn't want you to mistake them for a basket of kittens."

"Funnily enough, I'm deathly allergic to cats."

"Ha."

"Seriously. I could die. Someone should probably know that."

She makes a sound. Not quite a laugh, but more than an exhale. I catch the barest glimpse of her smile before she replies, "Duly noted."

"Are *you* deathly allergic to anything?" I ask.

"I fail to see how that's relevant."

"I thought we were bonding."

"Over allergies?"

"You give me so little, Ms. Choi. Work with me here."

She's quiet for a long time. I'm convinced she's going to spend the rest of the evening ignoring me when she says, "Bananas."

My eyebrows shoot up. "Really?"

"No. I hate them, though. Growing up, it was easier to tell people I had a banana allergy than to try to explain why I didn't like them. People get weirdly defensive over their favorite fruit."

"Honestly? I get it. It's the texture."

Adelina's eyes shimmer. "Right? It's *gross*."

In the grand scheme of things, learning about someone's food preferences is the furthest thing from exciting, but a thrill rushes through me all the same. Adelina is a treasure trove of secrets, and I've accidentally stumbled upon a gem. I tuck this rare, shiny fact away—not to use but to admire. It feels like a privilege to hold, to keep for myself. What other jewels is she willing to share with me?

There hasn't been any new movement in ages. Adelina glances at her wristwatch. She looks like she'd rather watch paint dry. I take the opportunity to get a good look at it. It's nice. A mid-to-high-end model cast in rose gold. Worth a couple thousand, if I had to venture a guess. A bit flashy for someone like her, but I've never seen her take it off. A light laugh escapes me.

"What?" she demands.

"All that grief you gave me yesterday about being old-fashioned, but you wear an analog watch."

The corner of her lip pulls up into a grin. "It was a gift," she says with much more warmth than I was anticipating. "From my father."

For a moment, I feel a pang of guilt for pinching it at the airport. No wonder she was pissed. If I'd known, I probably would have gone for something less sentimental for my demonstration.

"Great taste," I murmur.

"Yeah," she replies softly, thoughtfully running a thumb over the strap. "Will you teach me how you did it? Lift it, I mean."

"But a magician never reveals his tricks."

Adelina huffs. "Never mind."

"I'm *kidding*. Give me your hand, Grumpy."

I'm surprised when she does so without argument. No comeback for the nickname, apparently. Maybe she's too distracted by the way I take her wrist, easily encircling it beneath my fingers. Her skin is wonderfully soft and cool. For a brief, fleeting moment, I wonder if she's this soft all over.

"The first step," I tell her, my voice strangely hoarse, "is to condition your mark to your touch." I trace the pad of my thumb over her pulse point, studying the subtle lines and creases of her palm and the way her long, elegant fingers naturally curl. She lets me press my hand flat against hers but doesn't take her eyes off me as I interlace our fingers. We look good together.

"Why, um—" Adelina takes a breath. "Why?"

"If I go straight for the steal, it's too obvious. It's all about misdirection."

"Are you sure it's not just an excuse to hold hands?"

I can't help but grin. "Would you like me to stop?"

Adelina's ears turn a glorious shade of pink. "What's the next step?" she asks quietly.

"Now you have to manipulate your mark's attention," I say. "You know how a magician has a pretty assistant to use as a distraction? Pickpockets work much the same way. When you're out in crowded tourist areas, you'll find that most work in teams. The goal is to overwhelm, to split focus. They'll crowd you on the train or push petitions in your face for you to sign. Everything is done to cover their true intentions."

"Is that why you had me stand up and pick up my backpack at the airport?" she asks. "To split my attention?"

I nod. "You're a fast learner."

"Then how are you going to do this? I know your tricks now. You can't distract me."

"Can't I?" I ask as I lean forward, closing the already minimal space between us.

I place my free hand on her knee, sliding my palm slowly up her thigh. Adelina's gaze falls to my lips, her own parting just so as she inhales, breathless. Even though it's starting to get dark out, with little more than the orange glow of the setting sun illuminating the car's interior, I can see the way her pupils are blown wide.

"You're probably right," I murmur. "You're far too clever for me, Adelina." I hold her wristwatch up by the strap, swinging it gently from side to side like a pendulum.

"Show-off," she grumbles without heat, quick to take what's hers. Adelina turns away, but there's no denying the bashful grin that stretches across her face.

Wednesday, 12:45 p.m.

"I spy with my little eye . . ."

"West, I swear to *God*."

She turns away from me to observe out the passenger-side window. Despite her best efforts, I can make out the slight shake of her shoulders as she holds back a laugh.

Thursday, 7:15 a.m.

"Good morning, sunshine," I say as I hold out a cup of hot coffee. This has become our daily routine.

"Mornin'," Adelina says as she takes the offering. She doesn't even pin me with a death glare today.

I think she's warming up to me. "Ready to get going?"

"Wait just a moment," a sultry voice calls.

I turn to find Diana sauntering toward us. She's in an off-white button-down and jeans dyed a deep burgundy that complements her dark skin tone. Her hair is curled, and her eyeliner is sharp. How she's managed to look so put together before eight in the morning is beyond me.

"I'll be joining you today," she says. "If I have to spend another evening trapped in a confined space with Joseph, I'm going to lose my mind."

I don't understand the pang of disappointment that settles in my chest. I like Diana. We go way back. And I'm sure that as our investor she wants to make sure we're upholding our half of the surveillance operation. But for some reason, the thought of her joining us today feels . . . intrusive.

I glance at Adelina, only to find her already looking at me. Her gaze darts away, her lips pressed into a fine line. I'd like to indulge the idea that she doesn't want Diana cutting into our quality time either, but I know better. She probably doesn't want someone breathing down our necks while we do . . . whatever it is that we've been doing.

"Shall we?" I ask her.

Adelina nods. "After you."

We get through our shift in awkward and excruciating silence. Diana playing third wheel doesn't help at all, and the problem is that I don't think she even realizes how much of a damper she's put on things. I'm a shameless flirt—that much is true. I like putting Adelina on the spot for the simple pleasure of seeing her face turn red. But it's a different matter entirely with our guest sitting in the back seat. I don't want to embarrass Adelina.

Every now and then, I catch Adelina watching me. It feels like a game, one where we don't have to say anything to play. The next time I catch her eye, I shoot her a wink. Again, she's quick to look away, sheepish and oddly adorable. She tries to hide her smile, but I make out her reflection in the window. I can't help but chuckle.

"What's so funny?" Diana asks from the back seat.

"Nothing," I say innocently. "Nothing at all."

CHAPTER SEVENTEEN

A Taste of His Own Medicine

Adelina

Sunday

THE GOOD NEWS is that the guards' schedule doesn't change at all. They're very punctual. Clock in, clock out. Shift changes occur with surgical precision.

The bad news is that Berruci comes and goes on a whim, which makes it impossible for us to determine our window of opportunity. The last thing we want is to be in the middle of breaking in only for him to catch us as he's coming home.

West stretches his arms, hands pressed to the roof of the car. He looks squished and uncomfortable behind the wheel. We've spent the whole week cooped up in here, but I'm proud to say that I haven't murdered him out of sheer irritation. (An impressive feat of self-control, let me tell you.)

He yawns and rubs the back of his neck. "Movement by the west wing," he says, his eyes trained on the villa. "Chip and Dale just hit their check-in point."

I nod, confirming with my notes. It was *his* idea to give all the patrol guards codenames to help keep better track of everyone. "Which means Peanut and Butter will be up next," I say.

"Excellent." West rolls his right shoulder.

"What's wrong with you?" I ask.

"Well, some say I'm so handsome that it's dangerous. People have broken their necks trying to get a second look at me."

I roll my eyes. "I meant your neck, Narcissus."

He shrugs. "Hotel pillows. Slept kind of funny last night."

I'm not sure what convinces me to do it, but I set my laptop down on the dash and reach out. "Here," I say. I run my thumb down the back of his neck, applying a hint of pressure. His muscles are tight and stiff.

West seems surprised when I begin to massage in earnest. He's so surprised, in fact, that he's fallen completely silent. No cheeky comment, no crude innuendos. He simply turns in his seat so I can see his full back and sinks into my touch. I knead a knot I find around his middle trapezius. He groans, low and rich, the sound igniting something in my belly. I should be alarmed by the feeling, but I find it strangely enjoyable.

I like the solidness of his shoulders beneath my fingers. I like that I can help him in this small way.

"Oh," he groans. "Right there."

I swallow, my throat suddenly dry. I don't think he meant to sound so sexual, but *damn*. He could ruin a woman with a voice like that.

I move to massage his other shoulder. "How about this?"

"Fuck, Adelina, just like that."

"Yeah?"

"Yeah, baby. Give it to me good and hard."

I lean over to catch his eye, squinting at him with suspicion. I'm not at all surprised when I find his smug grin. The son of a bitch is doing this on purpose. "A bit much, don't you think?" I ask, failing to mask the amusement in my tone.

"It's not my fault," he says as he turns back toward me. "You make it too easy."

I give him a gentle shove and laugh. "Asshole."

"Who are you kidding? You know you love it."

"Keep telling yourself that."

"Oh, please. You think I haven't noticed?"

I frown. "Noticed what?"

"How you *so* obviously want to kiss me."

I take a deep breath and force myself not to take the bait. All this teasing is starting to get on my last nerve. What I really want is to give him a taste of his own medicine. Knock him off balance. I think I would enjoy the challenge. Without breaking eye contact, I lean forward and trail the tips of my fingers down his chest. It's the barest of touches, the slightest ghost of a graze.

"Go on, then."

His smile falters, slipping into something akin to surprise. "Oh?"

Before he has a chance to react, I climb over the center console and place myself on his lap, straddling him between my thighs. His hands instinctively fly up to my hips to keep me from losing my balance.

"It better be *really* good," I continue, tilting my chin down to offer him the perfect angle. There's barely an inch between us, my body pressed flush against his. "If you kiss me, I want to see stars."

"That's, um . . . a lot of pressure."

"Not up to the task?"

His Adam's apple bobs up and down, the cracks in his composure rising to the surface. A laugh escapes me, a giddy and light sound from deep within my core. It's no wonder he's always trying to tease me. This is *fun*. But all good things come to an end, and I'm going to have to stop tormenting him at some point. Besides, if this is a game he's determined to play, I'd rather have the upper hand. There's nothing quite like leaving your audience wanting more. He's apparently part magician, after all. He should know.

"Our shift is over," I say, climbing off his lap to retake my seat. "We should head back."

His eyes linger, a bewildered grin tugging at the corner of his lips. It takes him a moment to collect himself before he finally clears his throat and twists the key in the ignition.

CHAPTER EIGHTEEN

No Plan Is Without a Little Hiccup

West

IT TAKES JOSEPH a whole week to secure the location, but the hangar is honestly perfect. I never had any doubt that he'd pull through. There's no one in all of France—maybe even all of Europe—with as impressive a network. He once landed a last-minute table at The Lunchbox, some impressive Michelin-starred restaurant in Seattle, despite a three-month waitlist, simply because he had an old schoolmate whose wife's best friend's daughter happened to know one of the chefs. As Michael always used to tell me, getting through life isn't about what you know but *who* you know.

We've spent the better part of the morning setting up the labyrinth of metal box trusses, which Joseph (once again) procured for us through his great-aunt's gardener's brother. We've followed the blueprints to Berruci's villa to a T, mimicking every doorway, hall, room and window to create a skeletal one-to-one replica.

I should concentrate. Focus on the task at hand. But there's only one thing on my mind right now.

If you kiss me, I want to see stars.

Well, shit. I didn't know Adelina had it in her.

I would be lying if I said I wasn't tempted. I can still feel the impression of her touch against my skin, her thighs impossibly soft and warm when she sat on my lap, but . . . she probably wasn't being serious. This is just a little game we're playing, needling each other to see who folds under the pressure first. She's gotten a good couple of hits in—one quite literal—and in a strange way, I'm curious to see where this all leads.

But the answer is obvious: it's going nowhere.

Adelina said it herself. Once this job is over, that's it. A clean break. She wants to go home and go back to playing hero.

And maybe that's *why* we're playing this game. It's harmless, unserious. What's a little light flirting to pass the time, to ease some of the tension now that we're entering the next phase of my plan? It's far better than spending my every waking hour worrying about how it could all go wrong.

"A little to the left," Adelina instructs from her corner, the sound of her voice snapping me from my thoughts.

"Your *other* left, Joseph," Diana clarifies beside her, blueprint in hand.

Adelina's got a brand-new setup, courtesy of Joseph's connections and Diana's wallet. She's got three wide monitors, one of which has been oriented vertically to better display her lines of code while she rapidly clicks through all the reconnaissance pictures we took on the other two. I can tell she's happy with her new equipment even if she won't admit it aloud. There's a glint in her eyes, a lightness in her posture. As giddy as a kid on Christmas morning. Despite all the money she's liberated for the sake of others, it makes me wonder when she last took the occasion to treat herself.

The sound of my phone's ringtone startles me out of my thoughts. It's my own device, not the burner squirreled away in my pocket. Thinking that it might be Jack's babysitter calling with an emergency, I fish it out, only for a cold wave to crash over me.

Berruci's name fills the screen.

I hastily step as far away from the crew as possible. Only once I'm sure I'm out of earshot do I grumble, "Hello?"

"Have you made any progress?" comes his rough, gravelly response.

I glance at Adelina, barely able to concentrate over the rush of blood past my ears. *She's right here*, the voice in the back of my head screams. *Tell him and save yourself. Save Jack.*

Guilt lances through me. I can't do that. I can't turn Adelina in. I refuse to be Berruci's puppet any longer, and I would never dream of putting someone else in harm's way just to save my own neck. Besides, she may be the only one capable of getting me out for good.

"Not yet," I reply evenly. "But I'm getting close. I've tracked a person of interest all the way to Australia."

"Australia?" he echoes.

"I know. Random, right? It's going to take me a bit longer."

"How disappointing," he says, hanging up abruptly.

For a moment, I fear he might be on to me. Did I sound convincing enough? Hackers can work from all over the world, so my story isn't improbable.

At least I can rest knowing that I've got my bases covered. I'm so paranoid that Berruci might use my phone to keep tabs on me that I never go anywhere without a VPN. If he checks on me right now, it'll look like I'm back in California, and the entire time I was taking Jack to a babysitter far from the city, I made sure my GPS signal indicated I hadn't left home at all. Even if Berruci dared to make a move behind my back, my niece's location is a secret that I'll take to my grave.

"Eh, t'es dans la lune ou quoi?" Joseph grunts, his arms visibly shaking beneath the weight of the truss he's carrying. *Eh, why are you daydreaming?* "Help me move this damn thing. I'm about to get a hernia."

I shove my phone back into my pocket and rush over to help him set it down on top of a makeshift wall we've crafted, representing the southernmost wall of Berruci's villa. "Not bad," I say as I observe the maze we've created. "Should we grab lunch?"

Joseph tuts in exaggerated disapproval. "Not so fast, old friend. What's got your head in the clouds?"

I make the mistake of glancing in Adelina's direction. It's a snap reaction that I correct by sliding into a casual shrug, but Joseph's much too bright to be fooled. He follows my line of sight and smiles.

"Mixing business and pleasure?" he asks.

"It's not like that."

"So she's available, is what I'm hearing."

I set my jaw. "Leave her alone."

A mischievous grin stretches across his lips. "Because you called dibs?"

"Don't be crass. She's a woman, not a car seat."

"Such a gentleman." Joseph throws his head back and laughs. "I'm only joking. We used to rib each other all the time, remember?"

The tension in my shoulders slowly melts away. Why the hell am I getting so riled up?

"Where did you even find her?" Joseph asks. "We could use her skills on future jobs. I've heard whispers that there's this casino in Monaco that—"

"No," I say in a rush. "This is a one-time thing. We're both out for good once Berruci's dealt with."

Joseph looks at me as if I've suddenly grown a second head. "You've really changed. What the hell happened these last six years? You really expect me to believe that you disappeared off the face of the planet and came back as an angel?"

I'm not sure how to respond. If I even *want* to respond. Berruci forcing me out of France was as much a blessing as it was a curse. I didn't realize it at the time, but cutting out this part of my life was one of the best things that ever happened to me. It gave me a fresh start. Let me become a new man—a *better* man. And if we play our cards right, things can stay that way.

For Jack's sake.

Hell, maybe even for my own.

"My priorities have shifted," I reply. "That's all."

"Um, West?" Adelina calls from behind her shield of screens. "I think we've got a problem."

My stomach flips. Maybe I spoke too soon.

I make my way over and join her, my eyes scanning over her work. She's drafted lines upon lines of code for the virus, a complicated language in and of itself, but what Adelina seems most concerned with is a particular picture I snapped of Berruci's villa yesterday. "What's wrong?"

Adelina taps the screen. "See this guard?"

The picture quality is decent despite the dim lighting. I can clearly make out one of Berruci's patrolmen. "What about him?"

She cycles through the next few frames, the patrolman's movements spliced like a stop-motion animation. The man starts to descend, dropping out of sight behind what I initially believed to be a decorative rock wall, before disappearing altogether.

"I thought it was weird, so I pulled up satellite footage," Adelina explains. She clicks to a new window and offers a top-down view of Berruci's villa. There's a noticeable patch of discolored grass near the rock wall in question. "It's a hidden door. Some sort of alternate entrance leading beneath the villa."

"Beneath?" I repeat in disbelief, picking up the blueprints spread out over her workstation. I scrutinize them carefully. She's right. "I guess Berruci has been keeping himself busy with a home reno project."

"How big of a wrench does this throw in our plans?"

"It could be nothing," Joseph says. "Maybe Berruci put in an indoor pool or a bowling alley or something."

"Or it could be a huge problem," I grumble. "There's no way to tell unless we get a look inside. He could have his ledger tucked away somewhere in the basement behind a bunch of high-powered lasers and moat piranhas for all we know."

Adelina arches a brow. "Moat piranhas? He's a crime boss, not a Bond villain."

"You're right. Bond villains would be much more imaginative."

"What are we going to do? We can't start test runs until we know the precise location of Berruci's servers."

"Can't you hack into his security cameras?" Diana suggests. "That'll give us a good look at what we're dealing with."

Adelina shakes her head. "I already told West that it's a closed circuit. I'd have to be physically on the premises to tap in."

A tense silence falls over us. I knew this job wouldn't be without its challenges, and in a way, I'm glad we've come up against a wall early. It's better if we eliminate any last-minute surprises. My mind races while the rest of the crew throw ideas at the wall to see what sticks, though nothing practical comes to mind. We can't afford any unnecessary risks. If Berruci catches us, he'll likely put us through far worse than that gate guard.

"Is it really that big of a deal?" Joseph asks. "We can try to wing it like we did last time."

Adelina frowns deeply. "Last time? What do you mean *last time*?"

"We . . . tried before," I murmur. "To steal from Berruci."

"And judging by your enthusiastic tone, I'm assuming it went great?"

Diana crosses her arms, and Joseph shifts his weight uncomfortably from foot to foot. My silence is the cherry on top.

"Fuck," Adelina mutters.

"Look, just because it didn't go our way last time—"

"You didn't think to mention this to me *before* you had me sign on?" She rises from her seat. "I would have liked to know I was put on a losing team."

"This time is going to be different. It's going to work."

"Why?"

"Because this time we have *you*," I say hastily.

Adelina holds me beneath her intense glare. I wish I knew what she was thinking. What if she bails? If that happens, this entire plan of mine is dead in the water.

Diana is the one to break the silence. "Come on, *Qwerty*." She says Adelina's codename with a derisive curl of her nose. "West clearly needs some time to re-evaluate. Let's get out of here."

Adelina's glare turns suspicious when Diana loops her arm through Adelina's own and steers her toward the door. "Where are we going?"

"To get some air."

CHAPTER NINETEEN
A Walking Fashion Faux Pas

Adelina

AS FAR AS sightseeing goes, this wasn't exactly what I had in mind.

"I hope you take this the wrong way," Diana says, "but you look like an absolute delinquent." She drags me down the narrow aisle of the store, clothing racks bracketing us on either side.

"Don't you mean 'I hope you *don't* take this the wrong way'?" I ask, fearing we might have gotten lost in translation somewhere.

She gives me a once-over from head to toe before resuming her search for a shirt she deems suitable. "Not at all," she says.

"I really don't think this is necessary."

"You're in a heavy hooded sweatshirt. In the south of France. In the middle of April." Diana tosses me a shirt to try on. The fabric is soft, but it's light pink and paisley. I make no effort to hide my grimace

"I mean . . . I *am* a tourist."

"Tourists come here to sunbathe and dip their toes in the Mediterranean. You're going to attract the wrong kind of attention, and attention is the bane of a thief's existence."

I cast a cautious glance over my shoulder. The boutique Diana has brought me to is small, boasting only a handful of other customers and a store clerk who looks bored out of her mind. No one pays us any attention, continuing with their leisurely browsing.

Maybe Diana has a point. I'm dressed for North Pacific weather, not the beach. Intentionally or not, I stick out like a sore thumb. Not to mention that with the climbing temperatures and plentiful sun, I'm at risk for heat stroke, which is why I don't turn my nose up at the next shirt Diana plucks off the rack and shoves into my hands. (It's a deep burgundy, which is a dark enough shade that I can make peace with it.)

"Why are you doing this?" I ask her quietly. "I appreciate it, but you don't have to go through the trouble."

She shuffles through a selection of shorts, holding her silence like a shield against me. It's a strategy Diana uses often, I realize, and it gives off the illusion of graceful control. Difficult to master, powerful once perfected. I'm sure a businesswoman like her makes great use of such a tool.

"I wanted to make up for my behavior," she says after a while. "I was . . . unnecessarily harsh toward you the other day. I'm sorry."

This takes me by surprise. Of all the things I thought she could have said, an apology wasn't one of them.

"Oh," I mumble dumbly.

"What we do is dangerous," she continues. "It's hard to know who to trust. Women in our line of business have to work twice as hard for half of the take."

I laugh softly, a curt little huff. "My mother used to say something similar."

Diana looks up then and slips into an amicable smile, as though offering a truce. "It comes from a place of love, but God, sometimes the *pressure* is just . . ."

"First-born daughter?"

"Yes. You?"

I nod. "My sister says I suffer from 'eldest daughter syndrome.' Whatever that means."

Diana hands me a dress to try on. Not really my style, but I'm enjoying our conversation enough to at least hold on to it. "Are you close?" she asks. "You and your sister."

"Sure."

"That didn't sound very confident."

I bite my tongue, shrugging as nonchalantly as I can manage. "We've . . . been drifting apart."

"Ah, it happens."

"What about you?" I ask, testing the waters. "Are you close with your family?"

"They moved back to India after my father passed away a few years ago."

Her answer punches me in the gut. I understand all too well what it's like to not only lose a parent but be isolated from your family. Granted, I *choose* to be alone for sanity's sake, but I'm beginning to see that Diana and I have a lot more in common than I first believed.

"I'm sorry to hear that," I tell her.

Diana shrugs, her beautiful silky hair pouring over her shoulders. "C'est la vie."

We move from rack to rack, Diana picking out items of interest while simultaneously transforming me into a pack mule. I don't know how much more clothing I can carry. I suppose if I'm being forced to revamp my wardrobe, there are worse places I could be doing it than France.

"Can I ask you a question?" I say. "About what West said."

"I was beginning to wonder when you would."

"Were you there? When he tried to go after Berruci the first time?"

"I was."

"What happened?"

I'm more than aware that I'm pushing my luck. We have a good tit-for-tat thing going, but I risk her closing off again if I come on too strong. Yet my curiosity burns beneath the surface of my skin, leaving me parched for answers.

Diana purses her lips. Tense. Just when I think she's going to clam up, she sighs. "There were six of us on the crew: Michael, West,

Joseph, Henrie, Bannock and me. Berruci has a racket back in Paris and has since moved down to Nice to expand his enterprise."

"West told me he made most of his money through racketeering."

"Yes," she says tightly. "We did the math. On collection days, he'd pull in roughly a hundred million euros in cash."

"A hundred million I'm sure you were eager to take off his hands."

Diana nods, though her expression is grim. "That kind of money ... You can't just dump illicit funds into a bank account, or the authorities start asking the wrong kinds of questions. You have to launder it first. Buy expensive cars and pointless pieces of art, snap up real estate. Until then, you need to keep it all locked away somewhere safe."

"And that's when you decided to strike," I conclude.

"It took us three months to figure out where Berruci kept his stashes. He has several properties scattered throughout Paris. We wanted to hit them simultaneously, but something went wrong." Diana's gaze grows distant. "When I arrived at my location, the police were already waiting for me. Joseph, similarly, walked right into a trap. Cops ganged up on him and arrested him on the spot. Same with Henrie and Bannock. As for Michael and West ..."

A shiver passes through me, the little hairs on the nape of my neck suddenly standing on end. "What?" I urge.

"They disappeared," Diana replies. "I didn't know what happened to them until West called me two weeks ago with a shiny new plan."

The gears in my head kick into overdrive. How odd. I'm clearly missing a part of the story here. How did the rest of West's old crew end up getting caught, but he somehow made it out unscathed?

The mule account I stole from ... I already knew that West was in charge of monitoring it, but I never stopped to consider *why* he was given such a task in the first place. What if West sold them out to save himself? Struck some sort of deal? Clemency in exchange for freedom.

I shove the thought away, already exhausted with all the mental gymnastics. No. That doesn't make any sense. What reason would he have had to do something like that? Plus, being forced to work for Berruci seems like pulling the short stick.

Maybe he was in over his head, I think to myself. *A guy like Berruci is bound to have conditions.*

West doesn't seem like the kind of guy to double-cross his friends. And his story about wanting to protect his niece is admirable. Sympathetic.

Almost by design.

What if I'm being played for a fool? West always seems to know what to say, what to do. He comes across as an unassuming guy, but what if that's his scheme? For all I know, he could be laying it on thick to lower my guard, all for the express purpose of walking me right into a trap.

"You'd better go try these on," Diana says. "The clerk is giving us a dirty look. I'm going to pop out for a bit and see if I can find us something to drink."

"Uh, sure," I mumble, making my way to the cramped changing room in the back of the boutique.

To be perfectly honest, I'm not in the mood to be shopping, but there's little else I can do until West figures out a workaround to this snag in our plans. *If* that's even what he's doing.

I throw shirts on just to take them off again. There's nothing wrong with the items Diana picked out for me, but they're simply not to my taste. I find a simple black tee that I'm partial toward, but after converting the price from euros to Canadian dollars, I decide against it. (The store is *definitely* charging tourists higher prices.)

My real phone, which I've set next to my burner on the narrow changing stall bench, buzzes. A text from Lily.

Lily: Hey! Just wanted to let you know I'm boarding my flight.

Lily: Sending you my itinerary.

Lily: I'm off to Spain!

I take a deep breath. In all the recent mayhem, I'd nearly forgotten about my sister's trip. It looks like we'll both be on the same continent at the same time, though I sincerely doubt our paths will cross. (I can only pray. I *really* don't want to have that conversation.)

I shoot her a quick text wishing her a safe flight before putting everything back neatly on hangers. I leave the changing room to find that Diana is nowhere in sight. Weird. She should be back by now. How hard is it to find a bottle of water?

I leave the boutique and step out onto the street, the heat of the sun quick to warm the top of my head. (Such is the curse of having dark hair.) I have no idea where Diana might have gone. Before I have a chance to reach for my burner and send her a text, I notice something strange. There's a man standing across the street. Normally, I wouldn't think anything of it. The streets are packed full of springtime travelers and locals alike. It isn't a crime to stand around, but . . .

He's staring right at me.

Unnerved, I try calling Diana's number. She doesn't pick up.

It's then that I notice the man isn't alone. Less than a block away, another guy leans against a parked car, watching me with uninvited interest. My skin crawls. Ah, fuck. If this is about to turn into a *Taken* situation, I'm screwed.

As calmly as I'm able, I turn in the opposite direction and start down the street at a brisk pace, resisting the urge to make a run for it. It's only when I dare to glance over my shoulder that I see that they're walking in the same direction. Maybe I'm being paranoid. I take a right, and then another right, and then another right. They're still behind me.

Not paranoid, then.

I'm being *followed*.

My hands shake as I try Diana's number again, and once again, she doesn't answer. Shit. Did something happen to her?

Panic grips my throat. What am I going to do? I'm no runner, and I definitely don't stand a chance if it comes down to a fight. It's only a matter of time before they catch me. For what reason, I have no clue, but I sincerely doubt that their intentions are honorable. There's only one person I can call for help, even if I don't entirely trust him.

I punch in West's number.

He picks up immediately. "Porter's Pizzeria," he jokes, "how may I—"

"I need help," I wheeze. God, I'm out of shape.

"What's going on?" he asks, serious and low.

"Men are following me. I can't get a hold of Diana, and I don't know what to do."

"Where are you? Can you see a street sign anywhere?" I hear shuffling in the background. It sounds like he's on the move.

My hands shake as I look around. "Rue Alexandre Mari. West, what do I do?"

"Stay on the phone with me. I'm coming to get you."

CHAPTER TWENTY

What Better Cardio Than Running for Your Life

West

"CAN'T YOU DRIVE any faster?" I ask Joseph, nearly ready to jump out of the passenger side. Despite being our designated getaway driver, he sure is taking his sweet time. We could have taken a right three blocks ago and avoided all this congestion.

Joseph shrugs, gesturing rudely over the steering wheel at a car that cuts us off. "Will you just tell me what's going on?"

"No time," I say, getting out. The Old Town of Nice isn't much farther. I'll be able to run to Adelina faster than Joseph can drive through these cramped, narrow streets. "Adelina, are you still there?" I ask before slamming the door behind me.

"They're closing in," she says, breathless.

"I want you to walk into the nearest store or café. Someplace packed with people."

"Um, okay. Yeah, there's a restaurant here."

"That'll work. What's it called?"

"La Belle Azure."

"Listen to me carefully, okay? You're going to walk in and ask for a table. You're going to take a seat as close to the kitchen as you can."

"What? I'll be a sitting duck."

"They're not going to do anything with people around. Trust me."

There's a pause. I know she hasn't hung up because of the harsh sound of her labored breathing.

"Okay," she murmurs.

I navigate through the streets, taking tight alleys and sharp turns until I finally pinpoint the restaurant in question. A normal person would enter through the front, but I have to think like an escape artist. Circling around back, I find the door to the kitchen propped open with a plastic milk carton. Either someone forgot to move it after their smoke break was over, or the chefs in the back are hoping to generate a cross breeze to keep cool. Whatever the reason, I use their oversight to my advantage and walk straight in.

Naturally, I don't get very far before one of the chefs spots me.

"Who are you?" he asks gruffly from behind the line.

There isn't any reason to panic. I learned long ago that it's better to go with the flow. I reach into my pocket and flash him my wallet, snapping it closed before he gets too good a look. It helps that I already have my burner phone pressed to my ear. Appearing busy and self-important will help sell the act.

"Health inspector," I answer curtly. "I'm here to investigate a complaint. A customer claims to have seen rats running around."

The chef blanches. "Rats? O-oh, but we . . . This is the first I've heard of it."

"Save me some time and let your manager know I'm here, would you? I need a word with them."

"Of course," he says, scuttling off.

Obviously, I have no intention of sticking around for the meeting. I move through the kitchen toward the swinging double doors, peeking out through the circular viewing window. Adelina is right there, just within reach, an undeniable tremble in her shoulders. There are two men roughly three tables away, staring her down like wolves eyeing a lone lamb. Could they be working for Berruci? And if they *aren't*, why the hell are they coming after her? Maybe they're bad men who just so happen to be targeting Adelina.

My heart stutters. It feels like too much of a coincidence, but there's no way Berruci knows. How could he?

Something isn't adding up, but I'll have to leave my theorizing for later. For now, I need to get Adelina out from under their claws.

"I'm here, but don't turn around yet," I say into the phone.

Adelina takes a deep breath. "What's the plan?"

"Working on it."

I scan our surroundings. Even if we make a break for it, Creep #1 and Creep #2 can easily close the distance and grab Adelina before I can spirit her away to safety. It isn't until I see a busy busboy, a large plastic tray full of dirty dishes and empty glasses piled high in his arms, that I decide to make my move. He's just about to enter the kitchen through the double doors when—

I push through them, grab Adelina's hand and pull her in after me. The men give chase, just as I knew they would, but are slowed down by the busboy. They crash into him, causing the poor kid to drop his tray and scattering bits of porcelain, glass and metal cutlery all over the floor. One of the men slips in someone's leftover salad, smacking his head against the tile floor, but the other guy manages to barge his way after us.

"*Run!*" I shout, dragging Adelina through the kitchen and out through the back.

Creep #2 is gaining on us. We fly past groups of people, many exclaiming in alarm and confusion as we shove on by. I hold on to Adelina's hand tightly, but I can feel her fingers slipping. She can't keep up, her strides too short and her stamina quickly draining. I need to think of something—and fast. Leaving her behind isn't an option.

I had no choice with Michael, but it will be different with her.

"Over here," I say, noticing a guided tour ahead of us. It's a large group of men and women—roughly twenty people, by my count—all of them moving together as a dense herd with their backpacks strapped onto their fronts for additional safety. We aren't going to blend in by any means, but they will certainly protect us with ample cover.

I tear off my baseball cap and slap it on the first tall blond man I come across before shoving our way through the crowd and pulling Adelina around the nearest corner. We're well hidden by the sea of people, but I press her against the brick wall and blanket her with my arms and body anyway to keep her out of sight. Adelina pants against my chest, her cheeks flushed and brow covered in sweat as she grabs fistfuls of my shirt.

"Breathe," I whisper. "It's going to be okay. I've got you."

I watch carefully as her pursuer comes into view, making a beeline for the guy I forced my hat onto. He grabs the blond by the shoulder, spinning him around.

"What the hell's going on?" the tourist snaps.

The thug's confusion is brief, swept aside by a look of irritation. He starts off the wrong way down the street, continuing his search. Adelina and I let out sighs of relief. We're in the clear for now.

"Are you okay?" I ask her.

"I think so." She nods, struggling to catch her breath. "I can't believe you came."

I chuckle. "Why wouldn't I?"

"I thought . . . I thought maybe . . ." Adelina clings to me, shaking as she hugs me tight. "Nothing. Never mind."

I hold her firmly, wishing there was something I could do to soothe her nerves. It was lucky she called me when she did. I can't imagine how terrified she must have been. "Tell me what happened."

"We were shopping. Diana said— Oh my God. *Diana*. I don't know what happened to her, she . . . Do you think they took her?"

"We're going to figure this out."

"But what if—"

I cup her cheeks and look into her eyes. She's on the brink of hyperventilating. "Stay calm, Adelina. I promise you, everything's going to be okay. I'm going to call Joseph and have him pick us up and take us back to the hotel."

She swallows hard. I see the doubt in her eyes, the fear. And the thing is, I can't even blame her. If she tells me that she's out—that she wants to go home—I don't think I have the heart to stop her.

"A-alright," she murmurs.

I pull my phone from the back pocket of my jeans and dial Joseph's number, keeping one arm wrapped securely around her waist. Adelina rests her cheek against my shoulder, and I press a kiss to the top of her forehead.

She makes no effort to move away, and I, for one, don't want to let her go.

CHAPTER TWENTY-ONE
Down, but Not Out

Adelina

THE RIDE BACK to the hotel is . . . *tense*, to say the least.

Both Joseph and West tried to get in contact with Diana, but to no avail. Those men who were after me might have had accomplices. Maybe they planned on nabbing us both but took the opportunity to grab Diana when she left the boutique, figuring it would be easier (and cause less of a scene) if they went after us separately. A divide-and-conquer approach. As we drive, it's hard for me not to imagine the worst possible scenario, though I'm not ready to give up hope. There's a chance Diana got away, just like I did.

West sits with me in the back of the car. He holds my hand the entire time, absentmindedly stroking my thumb with his. Unlike on the airplane, I happily accept his comfort, grateful for his warmth and steadiness.

I don't know what I would have done without him. I keep running the events in my head over and over again, my skin crawling at the realization of how close those men got to me. If West hadn't shown up when he did . . . I can't even imagine the kind of trouble I'd be in.

When we finally arrive at the hotel, the few yards between the parking lot and the main lobby don't feel quite real. My steps are jittery, unstable. Like I'm tiptoeing over eggshells, my body ready to run off at the first sign of danger despite weighing a thousand tons.

"It's the adrenaline crash," West explains, as if reading my mind. "It doesn't last long."

"Really?" I grumble. "I feel like I need a year-long nap."

He chuckles. "We'll get you something to eat and you'll feel right as rain. Carbs should do the trick."

We don't get very far into the lobby before Joseph, who entered first, comes to an abrupt standstill. I nearly knock into him as he points ahead, jaw agape. Sitting in one of the lobby's blue guest chairs is a woman, her long black hair a windswept mess. Her knees are scraped up, as are her palms.

Diana.

"Oh, good," she says upon seeing us. "You're not dead."

Joseph rushes forward, kneeling in front of her to get a good look at her injuries. There's a deep notch between his brows and a tenderness in his eyes when he says, "T'as rien?"

"Ouais, ouais, ne t'inquiète pas," she insists with a nod.

My relief is quickly followed by urgency. "Where were you?" I ask. "We've been trying to call for ages."

"Two guys tried to jump me," she replies. "I must have dropped my phone when I was getting away."

"They hurt you?" West asks, drawing attention to her scraped knees.

"No, I stumbled while on the run." Diana stands, Joseph diligently taking hold of her elbow for support. "I think we need to abandon this job."

West frowns. "That isn't an option."

"Berruci clearly has the upper hand here."

"We don't know those were his men."

"Oh, please," she says with a scoff. "Who else could they be?"

"Diana—"

"We don't have a full crew, we don't have eyes inside, and now we've lost the element of surprise. I say we cut our losses and go home. You were in over your head then, and you're in over your head now. Fifty billion dollars doesn't mean anything if you aren't alive to spend it."

West's jaw tightens. "That isn't an option for me."

Because of Jack, I think. This was never about the money for him, but I can understand where Diana is coming from too. This time was a close call. Next time, we may not be so lucky.

Game theory was one of the first concepts I learned in my introductory courses at MIT. Understanding how to analyze scenarios and make decisions is a fundamental principle when it comes to most programs. Computers have to take in data, weigh the odds and understand what options offer the highest possibilities of success and failure within seconds. Game theory applies here too.

If we go through with the job, we *might* succeed. But there are so many variables to consider, so many things that could go awry.

If we *don't* go through with the job, at least we're guaranteed to keep our heads. Maybe I can help West and Jack go into hiding. Forge brand-new identities and get them to move to a far-off country well out of Berruci's reach. Opening up fresh bank accounts is kind of my forte, after all. I'm sure building a new life for them will be a walk in the park.

And yet, I can't help but wonder what will happen if West decides to abandon his plans. Once he starts running, he won't ever be able to stop. He will spend the rest of his life watching his back, triple-checking the locks. Constantly worrying that Jack might be snatched off the street like I almost was. He knows just as well as I do—that's no way to live.

What we need is some way to even the playing field. Not by a lot, but just enough to give us a fighting chance.

That's when it hits me.

"The guard," I mutter aloud. "The one Berruci beat up. What if we turned him?"

Diana blinks at me. "What guard?"

"The first night we did reconnaissance, West and I saw Berruci wailing on one of his guards. Working for a guy like that can't be easy."

"You mean you want to try for an inside man?"

"It's exactly who we need to round out the crew. Despite all of our prep work, Berruci's a wild card. With a man on the inside, we'll not only learn the full layout of the villa, but we'll have someone who can keep us informed about Berruci's comings and goings. What he's plotting. *And* an inside man can connect me to the security network, which will give us a leg up."

There's a murmur of tentative agreement. It's a crazy idea, but if it works, this could be a huge breakthrough for us.

"Okay," Joseph says. "But who's going to talk to him?"

"I'll do it," West says. "There's too much heat on the ladies. Stay here while I take care of it."

I shake my head almost immediately. "I'm coming with you."

"Ad—Qwerty, please. You need rest."

"I'd feel safer."

The moment I blurt it out is the same moment I want to die of embarrassment. Did I really just say that out loud? I'm perfectly capable of taking care of myself, but the thought of waiting around while West does all the work doesn't sit right with me. Not to mention I don't want to be alone, twirling my thumbs in my room like some easy target. If I'm with West, I won't have to worry as much.

He nods. "Alright," he replies. I count my lucky stars that he doesn't tease me for it.

"Are you sure you can convince this guard of yours?" Diana asks.

"I think so. After what Berruci did to him? If I were in his shoes, I'd be pissed off enough to switch teams. I just need to talk to him."

"And how exactly are you going to do that?"

"After a beating like that, he probably had to check himself into a hospital." West turns to look at me. There's a slight tilt to his head as he softly asks, "Do you think you'd be able to find him for me?"

I crack my knuckles. "Leave it to me."

CHAPTER TWENTY-TWO

Who Doesn't Like a Little Praise?

Adelina

THE GOOD NEWS is that thanks to the picture of his ID (and the one West accidentally snapped of his butt), I was able to determine that the guard's name is Elliot Dupont.

The bad news is that Europe has crazy-impressive privacy protection laws when it comes to personal data, so it unfortunately took me over two hours before I was finally able to pinpoint Elliot's phone.

I'm sure many of us don't think of our phones as anything more than a way to call up friends and family, play mobile games, or scroll through social media. In reality, they make us walking targets. Apps on your phone are constantly transmitting information about you to ad exchanges to give advertisers the best shot at turning a click into a purchase. What's included in that information? General age range, gender, recent browser searches, and—you guessed it—your location.

(I could go into a whole spiel about how we live in a surveillance state, but I don't have time for that. Plus, it makes me sound like a conspiracy theorist. Which I'm not. At least, not about *this*. Our phones are absolutely listening to us.)

By limiting my search to everything within the municipality of Nice around the time of the incident at Berruci's villa a week ago, I was able to find the exact pings off Elliot's phone through publicly accessible code, and traced a route directly from the villa to Hôpital Pasteur a little after West and I fled the scene.

West and I are sitting in the visitor parking lot, our rental car tucked discreetly between two large SUVs. A few people have been in and out through the main entrance, but nobody has paid us any mind.

"How are you going to get past the front desk?" I ask. "It's well past visiting hours."

West tilts his head to the side, no doubt strategizing. "I'll wing it."

"That's very reassuring," I reply dryly.

"Stay in the car, okay? I'll be back in about twenty minutes, give or take. If you hear alarms going off, start the engine immediately. We'll need a quick getaway."

"I don't *want* to stay in the car," I protest.

"What if I crack the window and turn the radio on for you?"

"Fuck off. I want to come with you. If you can distract the receptionist, I can use their system to find out which room Elliot is staying in."

West hums thoughtfully. "That's definitely much easier than what I was planning."

"What were you going to do?"

"Seduce them, probably."

I glare at him. "What if it's a guy behind the desk?"

He pumps his eyebrows. "I hope he's a hunk. I'd love to be swept off my feet." When I groan, West throws his head back and laughs, his rich voice filling the cabin of the car. And I'm almost . . . glad for it. It's nice to see him return to his old self. After the shitshow that was today, it's a welcome sight.

"I'm *joking*," he goes on. "Besides, you know I only have eyes for you."

My stupid, traitorous heart skips a beat. "Do you really want to keep playing this game?"

"Do you want me to stop?" he asks. Slowly, he leans across the center console, leaving only a few inches of space between us. All of the air suddenly rushes from my lungs, but I can't bring myself to look away. "All you need to do is say the word," he continues, his voice huskier than a moment before, "and I promise I won't bother you anymore."

The logical part of my brain tells me to run, but when my treacherous eyes flit down to the curve of his lips without my permission, I find myself suddenly lightheaded. He could kiss me, if he wanted to. A quick lean forward to crash our mouths together. Wasn't I the one who dared him to try to make me see stars?

I know this is foolish. Dangerous, even, to allow for such a terrible distraction. I wouldn't be here in the south of France (about to partake in a massive violation of personal health information, no less) were it not for the man seated beside me. Yet there's something tempting in his smirk, a challenge that I can't bring myself to shy away from. When West pushes, it's a thrill to push back.

"I don't want you to stop," I murmur softly. "I want you to touch me."

West leans forward, stroking my cheek with his hand. I'm enraptured by the warmth of his fingers and the tenderness of his touch. He closes the gap between us, leaving me waiting with bated breath, but our lips never make contact. Instead, he hovers barely a whisper away. He stares deeply into my eyes, slipping his hand back to brush his fingers over the sunflower tattoo tucked behind my ear. Sometimes I genuinely forget that it's even there, so I'm surprised at his sincere caress, and even more surprised that West bothered to notice it in the first place.

His other hand roams of its own volition, tracing a line down my neck toward my shoulders. My pulse comes much too loudly in the quiet stillness of the car, his ravenous gaze setting my blood on fire. He continues his way down over my breast, sliding over my belly, before slipping his hand beneath my shirt with a curious glint in his eyes. My breath hitches at the contact of skin on skin, his fingers slowly sliding back up to push aside the fabric of my bra. He squeezes, lightly pinching my nipple.

"*Fuck,*" I whimper, pressing my knees together in an attempt to ignore the heat flooding between my legs.

"Do you like this?" he asks, voice low and rough with something I don't dare name.

I nod, too dizzy for words.

"And this?" His hand slides down, the motion slow and controlled, shamelessly stroking along my inner thigh. Pleasure pulses in my core, building pressure with every passing second.

"West—"

"Look at you. An absolute mess."

"Kiss me," I rasp, barely keeping it together.

He glances down at my lips and grins. Just when I think he might finally indulge me—

"I'll think about it," he says, pulling away to open the driver's-side door.

I can't help but sputter, my whole face burning like I've tripped headfirst into lava. "Are you kidding me?"

"Let's go, mon tournesol. We've got work to do."

"What does that mean?" I call after him, flustered and pent-up as hell.

West laughs like the menace to society that he is. I swear to God I'm going to kill him.

But for now, we infiltrate.

I'm beginning to realize that a lot of what we do comes down to luck. We're lucky that it's a relatively quiet evening at the hospital, only a handful of patients with their family and friends milling about. We're lucky that there's only one young woman (dressed in scrubs patterned with yellow ducks) working the front desk. We're also very lucky that the moment West steps in through the automatic sliding doors, Miss Ducky Scrubs takes such immediate and keen (and not at all subtle) interest in him that I'm effectively rendered invisible as he saunters up to her.

"Salut," he greets, casually leaning against the edge of the counter. I'm not exactly sure what they say after that, since I'm too concerned with slipping away unnoticed. I don't venture very far, choosing a spot on the wall to lean against and deliberately turning my back to her as I pull out my phone and pretend to be enthralled with whatever's on screen. I have to wait for an opening.

A text from Lily sits waiting for me. She's attached a picture of herself at some restaurant, new travel companions gathered alongside her. She's snuggled up to a very handsome man. I can't help but smile. I'm glad *one* of us is having a fun time in Europe. Hopefully her new *friend* isn't as much of a relentless tease as West.

Lily: Just landed in Barcelona! Thinking of you!

Miss Ducky Scrubs giggles loudly, the sound drawing my attention over my shoulder. West has convinced her to leave her station, probably inviting her for a coffee or maybe to show him the way to the gift shop. Whatever his play is, it's working. I notice West's nimble hands move toward her hip, expertly swiping the ID card clipped to her shirt. He plucks it off her in one swift motion, holding it out to me between his middle and forefinger. West throws me a subtle glance, his way of saying *here you go.*

I glide past them quickly, but not *so* quickly that I capture her attention, grabbing her ID card on the way past. My heart is in my throat. How on Earth does he make sleight of hand look so easy? He could pluck the tail off a rat and it likely wouldn't even notice.

The computer at the front desk is nothing fancy, but it does require a card swipe to log in. Credit where credit is due: it's far more secure than a written password. After I run her ID through the reader, the computer beeps lightly, allowing me access to the hospital's admittance records. Unfortunately, everything's in French, but it's nothing a quick *CTRL + F* shortcut can't solve. When the search bar slides down in the upper right-hand corner of the screen, I waste no time typing Elliot's name.

Elliot Dupont—Chambre 412C

Bingo.

I log out of the computer and ensure I've left everything how it was, but I keep the receptionist's ID on hand. Never know when it might come in handy. West has managed to usher the nurse toward the vending machines on the other side of the waiting room. He leans casually against the side, her attention square on his dazzling smile. I leave the way I came, giving West a nod of confirmation as I traipse past and start toward the elevators with purpose. It's all about looking like I belong. The second I appear confused or lost is the second someone inevitably asks me what I'm doing here.

West joins me a minute later, just as I knew he would, his hands tucked nonchalantly in his pockets as we wait for the elevator car to arrive.

"Any trouble?" he asks.

"He's on the fourth floor," I reply dutifully.

West smiles. It's not his usual blinding mask, meant to throw me off-kilter. This smile is quiet and earnest, comfortable in a way I've never seen it before. "Attagirl," he says, so impossibly gentle, before the elevator doors slide open and he steps inside.

A delightful shiver passes through me, my heart suddenly aflutter. *Attagirl.* It's only a word. Three short syllables, and yet it has me craving more praise. Does that make me pathetic? I shouldn't be fazed by a simple compliment, but I guess that's what happens when you grow up the way I did.

Mom wouldn't just point out what she perceived as flaws; she'd fixate on them. Lily and I hit our growth spurts earlier than the rest of our class, and when we started putting on a bit of weight (a perfectly natural thing to happen to pubescent girls, mind you), Mom put us on a diet. She'd passive-aggressively poke at my arms, pinch at the skin on my back. Nothing was ever good enough. *I* was never good enough.

The ride up to the fourth floor is quick. We make our way through the labyrinthine halls. My sneakers squeak against the polished gray tiles, the buzz of the fluorescent light panels above our heads filling my ears.

We're just about to round the corner when West stops abruptly, holding up an arm like a barrier. I nearly knock into him.

"What are you doing?" I ask under my breath.

"Someone's guarding the door."

I peek around the corner. Sure enough, a man is seated to the left of the hospital room door in a blue plastic chair. He looks bored out of his mind, head tilted back against the wall for support. Is he a concerned colleague of Elliot's come to visit?

"He might nod off if we give him a minute," I muse.

West shakes his head. "We don't have that kind of time. If a doctor or a nurse spots us and asks us why we're here, the jig is up."

"And you were giving *me* a hard time about 1940s lingo."

"Can you blame me? It's catchy."

I huff. "How do we get past him, then?"

West looks around, his attention falling upon a heavy door. There's a sign stuck to the front, and although my French is rusty, I know what it says. Personnel autorisé seulement—*authorized staff only*.

"Still have that ID card?" he asks.

I produce it from my pocket and hand it to him. West swiftly taps the plastic to the electronic reader beside the door and—with a quick *beep, click*—the door unlocks. We hastily make our way in. It's a staff changing room, small blue lockers lined up along the walls. The coast is clear for now, so we search through any lockers that haven't been properly shut.

West finds a pair of aquamarine scrubs and holds them out to me. "Change into these."

"Right here?"

"Are you shy?"

Oh, this man really knows how to push my buttons.

I strip out of my clothes right in front of him, unabashedly accepting his unspoken challenge. He doesn't look away, his stare burning as I unzip the front of my jeans and let them fall to the floor. West traces the length of my legs with nothing but his gaze. I pull my shirt off next, not once breaking eye contact. It's a thrill like no other when his throat bobs, his jaw ticking and his pupils blown wide.

West manages a single step forward before I click my tongue, shaking my head in disapproval. "You know what? I *am* shy. Be a dear and turn around, would you?"

"What if I want to kiss you now?" he asks, his words hoarse.

I smile unsympathetically. "You had your chance in the car."

"Damn." West sighs dramatically as he places a hand over his eyes. He turns around too, for good measure. (*Such* a gentleman.) I throw on my pilfered scrubs and find that the shirt is a little tight around the chest, and I worry the starchy fabric will make it difficult to run should we need to, but the pants fit well enough.

"Alright," I say. "I'm done."

He's still faced away, as promised, but he must have found himself his own scrubs because he's already thrown off his clothes to put them on. West stands there in a pair of navy-blue scrub pants, working his shirt over his head. For some strange, confounding reason, my mouth waters at the sight of his broad back. I can make out the movement of muscles beneath smooth skin. Some small part of me hopes that he'll turn around again so that I can admire his tattoos and—

God, what is this man doing to me?

"Okay," he says, reaching into two separate lockers to produce a white doctor's coat for each of us. "Final touches."

"Is this really necessary?"

West winks at me, that annoyingly handsome twinkle behind his green eyes. "The trick is in the details. A good disguise and an air of confidence is all you need to convince others you belong."

A smile stretches across my lips. "Glad we agree."

He helps me into my coat like a gentleman trying to impress a lady on their first date. His hands briefly brush over my shoulders, and while I try not to think anything of it, there's no stopping the delightful little shiver that runs down my spine.

"After you, doctor," he says coyly.

By the time we make it back to room 412C, the man we saw sitting outside is no longer there. Annoyance licks at the back of my neck. We'd been playing dress-up, and for what?

West enters first. Probably a good decision, since I don't know the first thing to say. The man from before sits at Elliot's bedside, wearing a look of obvious concern. Elliot himself looks worse for wear. Currently unconscious, he's hooked up to a handful of different monitoring machines. Purple blooms around his right eye. His lip is split and swollen. Bandages are wrapped around his forehead, neck and both arms. I shudder, realizing now how grateful I should be that West covered my eyes. Berruci must have done a number on him to put him in a coma.

"Bonsoir," West greets with a breezy tone, picking up the medical chart hanging at the foot of the patient's bed. He's a natural, I notice. So comfortable in his own skin, in this room, moving as if being a doctor really *is* what he does for a living. "Faites pas attention à nous. On vérifie juste ses signes vitaux."

"Quand est-ce qu'on pourra enfin rentrer chez nous, docteur?" the man asks.

My head spins. I took French classes in middle school and enjoyed my lessons enough that I studied it all the way into high school, but I hardly remember anything now. West and the man speak too fast and with a regional meridional accent that makes it difficult to follow along, though I am able to pick up "rentrer" and "chez nous" and fill in the context.

When can we go home?

My heart thuds against my rib cage. How does this man know Elliot? West arches a brow and asks, "Êtes-vous . . ."

"Je suis son frère," the man responds.

My ears perk up. They're brothers. An idea pops into my head. Maybe we can use this to our advantage.

"What's your name?" I ask.

"Allistair." He frowns at me with justified suspicion. "Qu'est-ce qui se passe?"

"Do you speak English?" West asks him, tilting his chin in my direction. "For her sake."

"A little," he replies. His accent is incredibly thick. "Who are you? Did Berruci send you? Please don't hurt him. Je vous le promets—"

West holds up a hand. "Easy, friend. We're not going to hurt you. In fact, we're going to help."

"What do you mean?"

"You want out, don't you?" West asks. "Most do, once they realize the shit Berruci likes to pull."

"There is no way out." Allistair shakes his head. "I was such a fool. I thought it was just another security job. Long hours, but very good pay. By the time I realized who we were working for, it was too late for us to leave. I've . . . I've seen things. Terrible things."

West's expression hardens and I wonder if this is how he felt all those years ago. Trapped with nowhere to run and no one to turn to.

"My little brother . . ." Allistair's shoulders deflate, weighed down by his obvious worry and fear. "Elliot is a good man. He did not deserve this. That stupid gate . . . It wasn't his fault it malfunctioned."

"Work with us," West says gently. "We can make things right."

"You still haven't told me who you are. This could be some sort of trap. Un test de fidélité."

I take a step forward. "This isn't a—"

West takes my hand then, giving my fingers the lightest of squeezes. He doesn't say anything, but his meaning isn't lost on me. *Let me handle this*, his eyes say.

"Don't be afraid," he says, reminding me very much of when we first met back in Vancouver. "My associate and I have a plan."

Allistair stands straighter. "Quoi?"

"If you help us, we'll cut you in," West clarifies. "All you have to do is be our eyes and ears."

CHAPTER TWENTY-THREE

An Offer He Can't Refuse

West

"HOW DID IT go?" Joseph asks when we return.

Diana is seated next to him. I pretend not to notice the way they stop holding hands the moment Adelina and I walk through the doors, peeling apart from whatever intense conversation they were having. They looked close enough to kiss. Or fight. It's really hard to tell with those two.

"We found his brother," I say. "He also works for Berruci. I made him an offer and—"

"He didn't bite," Adelina informs, disgruntled.

"Actually, I believe what he said was that he'd think about it."

Joseph grumbles incoherently under his breath, anxiously combing his fingers through his brown curls. I can read the room well enough to know that the crew is starting to warp beneath the pressure.

"Everyone, relax," I say. "It's a good sign."

Diana frowns, her elegantly shaped eyebrows and sharp cheekbones adding to her already severe air. "How is this a good sign? What if he tells Berruci that you approached him?"

"He won't."

"How can you be so sure?" Adelina asks.

Why do I feel like I'm being interrogated? Diana and Adelina would make an excellent bad cop/badder cop duo. "You saw the look in his eyes," I tell her. "There's no love lost between them. Allistair and Elliot are in over their heads and are in desperate need of a way out. He'll see that we're his only option."

"And if he doesn't?"

"If we don't hear back from him within twenty-four hours, we'll figure something out."

Beside me, Adelina's phone rings in her pocket. Not a phone call, but the alarm she's set. She hastily cancels it and, with a few quick swipes of her thumb, reschedules her insurance text. I won't lie—it kind of stings that she doesn't trust me yet, though I can't exactly fault her either.

Adelina yawns. "If you don't mind, I'm going to stress about this in the privacy of my room. Goodnight, everyone."

I watch her go, amused by the way she trudges off. My gaze must linger for a little too long, because Diana clocks it and rolls her eyes.

"Close your mouth," she says, "you look stupid."

The first thing I do when I get upstairs is indulge in a hot shower. The hotel's old pipes creak and groan when I step under the spray, the buildup of steam fogging the mirrors and clinging to the tile walls of the small bathroom. It's easy to let my mind wander, a hundred different thoughts racing through my head.

I wonder how Jack is doing. This is the longest I've been away from her since we moved to California. Her babysitter has been dutifully sending me daily messages along with brief clips of Jack at dinnertime, but it's not the same. I'm eager to return, which is all the more reason to wrap this job up as soon as possible.

The rest of the crew is right to be concerned about Allistair, but I'm confident. As the mastermind behind this entire operation, I took a calculated risk. Having a man on the inside will give us access to

Berruci in more ways than one. Why put ourselves in harm's way just to get a glimpse of what he's got downstairs when we've got a pissed-off employee and a key to the palace? Ten billion dollars and the chance to avenge his brother should be more than enough incentive.

If Michael were still around and someone offered me this kind of deal, I wouldn't even hesitate.

After toweling off and slipping into a pair of joggers and a heavily wrinkled shirt from the bottom of my suitcase, I contemplate ordering some takeout. I haven't had the chance to eat tonight, and for a moment, I wonder if Adelina hasn't either. I've just opened my side of the joint doorway when—

Her side swings open too.

Adelina blinks up at me. "You *do* know that the room comes with an ironing board, right?"

"Go easy on me. I've been living out of my suitcase for weeks." I lean casually against the doorframe. "To what do I owe the pleasure?"

"My shower isn't working," she says with a huff. "I tried calling the front desk, but nobody's answering."

"Want me to try giving them a call?"

"No, it's fine. Can I just borrow yours instead?"

"Sure, help yourself."

Adelina squints at me skeptically. "Really? No lewd comments about wanting to join me? I practically lined that one up for you."

I chuckle. "I'm a flirt, not a creep. I know where to draw the line."

"Much appreciated," she says with a sweet smile. It will never cease to amaze me just how much her face brightens when she lets it. "Let me grab my towel."

She doubles back and disappears around the corner, offering me a glimpse into the mayhem that is her room. There are papers scattered everywhere, scribbled with what I can only assume are draft lines of code. Scraps pepper her bedside table, the floor and the corner writing desk. I can't even begin to scratch the surface of what her process must be like, but one thing is clear—she's been working overtime.

"How's your program been coming along?" I ask.

"Not bad."

"Will it be ready in time?"

"Definitely. All you'll have to do is plug it in, and the program will take care of the rest."

"So what's all this, then?" I ask, gesturing to the trail the tornado left behind when Adelina finally reappears.

"I've been working through different versions trying to get out all the bugs," she says sheepishly. "The program has to identify, copy and upload all relevant information while forcing a server connection, and only has seconds to do it . . . not to mention I'm trying to get its upload speed under a minute."

"Upload speed?"

"Even with a direct injection into the domain controller, the virus needs time to take hold. If I can get it under thirty seconds, it'll be perfect."

"I'm sure you can do it."

"Are you always so optimistic?"

"I've seen what you can do, Adelina. Why wouldn't I be?"

I find myself leaning toward her, unable—or perhaps unwilling—to escape her orbit. She doesn't seem to be in a hurry to leave either, judging by the way her heated gaze flits from my eyes to settle on my lips.

"Have you thought about it?" she whispers. She's referring to when she asked me to kiss her in the car.

"I have," I reply. "Do you still want me to?"

"I do."

My heart hammers against the inside of my chest. "Me too."

"Then why haven't you done it yet?"

"Because I'm worried," I murmur.

Adelina laughs softly. "What? That it'll ruin our friendship?"

"Ah, so you admit we *are* friends."

She pushes against my chest, though without any real force. "You're impossible."

I'm not sure if it's her proximity or the heat of her palm through my shirt or the light floral scent I catch from her hair that sends my mind into a tailspin. My body reacts of its own accord, an arm lassoing her waist to pull her tight against me. I grasp her chin in my free hand and tilt her head up for the perfect angle—but I don't dare make my move.

"You don't understand," I mutter, dangerously close to losing all sense of control. "I'm worried that I won't be able to have *enough*."

CHAPTER TWENTY-FOUR
Touchy Feely

Adelina

I GRAB HARSH fistfuls of his shirt, though I can't tell if I'm clinging to him for balance or control. It's hard to think straight with the solid press of his chest beneath my palms and the heat of his strong arms wrapped around me. West looks like he wants to take a bite out of me, and at the rate things are escalating, I just might let him.

"All this teasing—and for what?" I ask him, proud when my voice doesn't come across as shaky as I feel. "I don't like being toyed with, West. Either put up or shut up—"

Our lips collide with dizzying force, sending a spike of adrenaline through my body. West corrals me up against the nearest wall, swiftly lifting my arms to pin my wrists above my head. He presses the full weight of his body against me as he deepens the kiss, greedy and ravenous and desperate. I'm overwhelmed by the way his free hand slides down to hook my thigh, hiking my leg up over his hip.

His tongue sweeps past my own, commanding and firm in a way I didn't think he was capable of. West leaves me no time to breathe, each kiss followed up with another and then another. Little white dots begin to speckle my vision. When he rolls his hips against me, an embarrassingly squeaky moan escapes from my lungs. He chuckles when he hears me, the low vibration of his voice resonating in my very bones.

"Mon tournesol, je vais te faire chanter toute la nuit."

"What does that mean?" I rasp, too lightheaded to do anything other than trust him to hold me steady.

"Want me to teach you?" he asks with an all-too-pleased grin. His chest rises and falls quickly, his cheeks a light dusting of pink. It's nice to know that although he sounds calm, he is just as affected as I am.

I manage a nod. The surrounding room is little more than a pleasant haze. He releases my wrist, bringing his hand down to stroke the pad of his thumb along the line of my jaw, stopping to caress the tattoo behind my ear. He dips down to press a long, almost reverent kiss to the decade-old ink. "Mon tournesol," he whispers against my ear. "*My sunflower*." West then releases his grip on my wrists and takes one of my hands to press firmly against his chest. "Je vais," he continues the lesson. "*I am going to*."

My breath hitches. "You're going to what?"

He breaks into a devilish grin, tracing a line up the front of my throat. "Te faire chanter," he finishes. "*Make you sing*."

I am suddenly putty in his hands. Nobody has ever spoken to me this way before. Between his heated gaze and the low rumble of his voice, West has me thoroughly hypnotized, ready to fall apart the moment he so much as snaps his fingers. I've forgotten myself, unable to move or speak or focus on anything other than the solid weight of his body blanketing mine.

"Toute la nuit," he says. I've never heard his voice so dark and gruff. "*All night long*."

"Go on, then," I urge. "What are you waiting for?"

In one fell swoop, West kisses me again—just as hungry and deliciously rough—while lifting me up off the floor. With my arms wrapped around his neck and my legs securely around his hips, West carries me toward his bed. He sets me down on the mattress with ease, kissing me like it's the only thing he knows how to do. My fingers crave to explore, slipping beneath the fabric of his shirt to begin their expeditious climb up toward his hard chest. When he gently bites on my bottom lip, a low laugh escapes me.

"What?" he asks.

"I *knew* you were a biter."

He spoils me with his brilliant, blinding smile. "How far can I take this?" he asks after a particularly spellbinding kiss, his hot breath tickling my skin. "I don't have any protection, but I can make you feel good in other ways."

A delightful shiver courses through me. "Whatever you want," I murmur.

"No," he says, gently sliding a hand over my belly, past my hip and down to dig his fingers into the meat of my thigh. "Whatever *you* want, Adelina. Let me please you."

For a moment, I forget how to form a proper thought. West is a lot of things. Frustrating to no end, irritatingly handsome, and a generous lover to top it all off? There's no way a guy like this is real. Maybe I was riding up the elevator to my apartment and the cables snapped, and this whole escapade in the south of France has been little more than a hyperrealistic coma dream.

"Adelina?" West murmurs against my cheek. "Are you alright?"

"Y-yes, I just . . ."

He pulls away slightly, the faintest trace of a notch between his brows. "We don't have to do anything if you're not comfortable."

"No, that's . . . It's been a really long time for me, that's all."

His shoulders relax. "How long?"

"You'll laugh."

"I wouldn't dare." There's a mischievous glint in his eye, but I tell him anyway.

"About nine years."

West's jaw drops. "No way. What, uh . . . What happened there?"

I take a deep breath, hating the way my face feels like a stove burner set to high. "It was my second year of college. I'd been seeing this guy on and off. He was nice, I guess. We eventually got to a point where we wanted to take things to the next level. When I told him I was a virgin, he said he'd take good care of me. That he was going to 'rock my world.' Let's just say it was over *really* quickly."

I laugh. "But I guess it was my fault. I built it up too much in my head, you know? I expected some mind-boggling experience, only to end up with *that*. He pretty much ghosted me after. Saw him with someone else a week later. I figured, why put up with it? Why trust someone to take care of me when I can just take care of myself? Next thing I know, I'm twenty-eight and so wrapped up in my work that even if I *did* want to get back out there, I wouldn't know how."

West sits up, and I honestly can't blame him. I'm more than aware that I've ruined the mood. Leave it to me to take us from hot and heavy to pathetic and sad.

"Sorry," I mumble. "I shouldn't have said anything. I'll just go back to my room—"

Before I have the chance to stand, West pulls me onto his lap so that I straddle him between my thighs. He wraps me up in a tight hug.

"He was a boy, not a man," he says against my ear. "A real man would have taken care of you in every sense of the word."

"Like you?" I tease, trying to ignore the butterflies in my stomach.

"Yes," he answers firmly. West drags his hand down the front of my shirt, curving around my breast before moving down to my navel. His fingers hover just above the band of my jeans, waiting. "Will you let me prove it?" he whispers into my hair.

I'm just about to tell him yes. Yes, I want him to show me all the ways I can lose my mind. Let me forget how we ended up here, thousands of miles away from home, about to take on one of the most dangerous marks I've ever had the misfortune of crossing.

But then his phone rings. Someone is video calling. We both glance over to his bedside table and peer at the screen.

"It's Jack," I read aloud for him.

West's posture shifts, suddenly tense as a springboard. I stand up, mildly amused at the way he reaches for the nearest pillow and places it to cover his lap. "I'm sorry," he says, his voice hoarse. "I need to get this."

"Don't apologize, it's totally fine." I hover awkwardly, my gaze meandering over to the bathroom. "Is it still okay if I borrow your shower?"

"Of course, feel free."

After hastily recovering my towel and change of clothes (which I'd apparently abandoned on the floor at some point), I retreat into the bathroom and seal the door shut behind me, setting my phone down on the small counter. I'm frankly thankful for the privacy, because I can feel myself teetering on the edge of a major freak-out session. Am I hurtling toward a terrible mistake if West and I take this any further? Why can't I stop thinking about his searing touch and that ravenous look in his eyes? Is it a good idea to involve myself with someone who I know next to nothing about?

And why, despite my better judgment, do I want to crawl back onto his lap all over again?

My skin is pruney by the time I'm finished, having stayed under the spray for twice my usual length of time. I'm not sure if I'm trying to be considerate and give West enough time to talk to his niece, or if I'm trying to avoid any possible awkwardness that might arise from having literally confessed to suffering from the world's longest dry spell.

As I run a towel over my head, I approach the bathroom door to hear the low murmur of West's voice, followed by a little girl's high-pitched giggle.

"Marley made me flapjacks with blueberry smiley faces on them," she says.

"Flapjacks for my Flapjack. Were they any good?"

"The blueberries got too squishy."

"That's supposed to happen, sweetie."

"Why?"

"When blueberries get hot, their sugars break down. That's what causes them to get squishy."

"Why?"

West chuckles. "You know what? I'm not too sure. We'll have to find a scientist to help us. Maybe they can answer your question."

I feel a little bad interrupting their conversation, but I don't know how much longer I can stand here, breathing in the steam of the bathroom. I jostle the doorknob a little, creating something of a commotion to give West a heads-up. Maybe it's a courtesy thing. I'm sure West doesn't want to entertain questions from his niece about who I am. I crack the door open, but I don't step out completely, clinging tightly to the doorframe.

"My patch is itchy," Jack says.

"Don't scratch at it, honey. Ask Marley to help you change it, okay?"

"When are you coming home?"

West pauses. "Soon, sweetie."

"How soon?" She pouts.

"Once I'm done with work, I'll be on the first plane back."

"But I miss you."

"I miss you too," West says softly.

"Can't you come back *now*?"

My heart twists just listening to her. The poor girl sounds like she's about to cry.

"I'm going to be home before you know it, Flapjack," West replies. "And when I am, we'll spend the whole day at the park. How does that sound?"

"Fine," she mumbles, even though she doesn't sound enthused about the idea at all. "I love you, Uncle West."

"I love you too."

Only when I hear the call end do I leave the confines of the bathroom. West is seated where I left him on the bed, running a hand through his hair as he exhales deeply. There's a heavy sag to his shoulders, an exhaustion that seems bone-deep. It occurs to me then that *I* did this to him. If I'd chosen some other account to steal from, he might never have been forced into this position. Guilt stabs me in the gut. This plan to go after Berruci may be his idea, but I'm the one who inadvertently set off this chain of dominos.

"Flapjack's a cute nickname," I say gently, sitting down beside him on the edge of the bed.

"I know." West grins, but it's not as sunny as it usually is. He must *really* be tired. He's good at pretending otherwise, but I'm getting better at reading him. "Should we pick up where we left off?"

I shake my head. As much as the thought of fooling around excites me, I can tell he has a lot on his mind. "It's been a long day. Maybe another time. Although . . . is that movie-marathon offer still on the table?"

A thrill rushes through me when his smile returns in full, dazzling force. "Always," he says. "Want to make a pillow fort too?"

"Don't push your luck."

"If we end up cuddling, I'll let you be the big spoon. You give off that energy."

I roll my eyes and toss him the TV remote. "Fucking right I do. Now pick a movie and make sure it has subtitles."

West laughs. "Yes, ma'am."

CHAPTER TWENTY-FIVE

Shady Meetings Are Always Held in Public Spaces

West

BY THE TIME I wake up, the digital clock on the bedside table reads 10:14 a.m. It's not a habit of mine to sleep in. My years spent child-wrangling have forced my body and mind to adapt to an early-bird mindset. Between Jack's boundless energy, her asking me to make breakfast, and trying to figure out where the hell she flung her left shoe before we head out for the day, there's rarely an excuse to stay curled up in bed. But for the first time in six years, I finally have a reason to indulge—and it starts with a big capital *A*.

Adelina, as it turns out, is not a big spoon. For accuracy's sake, I think it's better to classify her as a murderous koala. She has her arms around me, which I normally wouldn't take issue with—because who doesn't like being held in the soft embrace of a woman?

The only problem is that she has me in a literal *chokehold*. I can't draw a proper breath. My heart is pounding in my ears. I wouldn't be surprised if I'm blue in the face.

I tap her elbow roughly. "*Can't. Breathe.*"

"Hm?" Adelina yawns.

"*Umbrella.*"

Thankfully, she comes to her senses just in time. With a gasp, Adelina releases her death grip on my throat and pulls away. "Oh my God, are you okay?"

I give her a thumbs-up. "There are probably worse ways to go."

Only then do I realize that the pounding I thought I heard in my head is actually coming from the front door. Someone is out in the hall, banging their fists, eagerly trying to get our attention. My mind turns to the worst-case scenario. Could it be Berruci? Maybe he's discovered the truth and learned that I'm here in France instead of searching for his thief. My fears are assuaged when I hear—

"I swear to God," Joseph hisses. "If you're dead in there, I am going to kill you. Open up already!"

Adelina is the first to jump out of bed, giving me a hesitant look before retreating to her room and shutting the suite doors firmly behind her.

Well. I guess she isn't too keen on being seen together. Not that anything really happened last night to be embarrassed about. We fell asleep halfway through a midnight run of *Amélie*.

When she told me about her dry spell, I almost felt relieved. Glad, even, to know that I wasn't the only one severely out of practice. Ever since I became Jack's guardian, I haven't had much time for dating. I didn't realize just how pent-up I was until I kissed Adelina last night. No wonder we keep pushing each other, daring the other to make a move. We're both subconsciously searching for an outlet, waiting on deck and ready for our turn to play ball.

I pad across the rough carpet and open the door to a very irritated Joseph. His arms are crossed over his chest, foot tapping away like he's trying to send me a message in Morse code. It's strange seeing him so distressed.

"About time," he huffs.

"Good morning to you too," I say dryly. "To what do I owe the pleasure?"

"Diana and I have been waiting for an update. Has the inside man called?"

I run a hand over my face. My stubble is rough against my palm. I'm going to have to shave soon. "Come on in. I'll check right now."

Rifling through my things, I eventually locate my burner tucked beneath my pillow. There's a brief voicemail waiting for me, Allistair's words clipped and quiet, as if worried he might be overheard.

"He wants to meet," I say in partial relief. "He didn't get into specifics. Only gave an address where to meet him."

"Okay. I'll come with you, and we can—"

"He wants to meet alone."

Joseph frowns deeply at this, and I understand why. This could be a trap. I could be walking directly into an ambush, for all I know, but I see no other option. We need a man on the inside, or our entire plan may as well have been brainstormed by an improv group. But maybe this is the paranoia talking. Allistair likely wants to be cautious too. Adelina and I had him outnumbered at the hospital at a particularly vulnerable time. If I were in his shoes, I would do what I could to ensure my own safety. He wants to meet at a café, which is fine by me. Alone together in a crowd of possible witnesses is as safe as it gets.

"I'll meet him in an hour," I say as reassuringly as possible. "You can circle the rental around in case I need to make a quick getaway."

"Are you sure this is a good idea?"

"Don't worry. I'm a slippery son of a bitch. If anything goes wrong, I'll get out of there."

"No," Joseph says. "I mean you and our hacker."

"I have no idea what you're talking about," I reply casually.

"Oh, please. Since when do you smell like flowers?"

"Nothing gets by you, huh?"

"I hope you know what you're doing. If you end up getting distracted because of some woman and this all blows up in our faces, I will never let you hear the end of it. Understand?"

"What about you and Diana?"

Joseph pauses. "We're just friends."

"And I assume that little hickey on your neck there is just a mark of friendship?" I ask coyly. "Getting more than friendly with our investor, are we?"

He brings a hand up to cover the light bruise on the side of his neck, fighting a grin. "That's, uh . . . She promised me it wasn't noticeable."

I laugh. "Hypocrite."

"I guess I am." Joseph laughs too. "Just hurry up and get dressed. I'm getting anxious. Do you really want to be the reason I go gray before forty?"

"Alright. I'll be down in a bit."

When he leaves, I hear the suite doors creak open behind me. Adelina pokes her head around the frame, looking at me intently.

"I have to go," I explain.

"I heard. Give me a second to get dressed."

"I'm going alone."

"Like hell you are. You need backup."

"We can't risk spooking him."

"And given how vital you are to our plan," she says, "we can't risk you going by yourself."

"No, Adelina."

"You let me come with you yesterday."

"That's because we had the element of surprise," I reply firmly. "He asked for a meeting alone, so we need to uphold our end. We can't act in bad faith."

"Why? Because of that stupid honor among thieves schtick?"

"Precisely."

She shakes her head in obvious disapproval. "This is so stupid."

Unable to help myself, I reach up to smooth out the notch between her brows. "I wouldn't have you come with me anyway."

"Why not?"

"Given how vital *you* are to our plan," I say, "I need you to stay here and work on that virus, and when I get back, we'll finally be able to move on to phase three."

I stroke her cheek with my fingers, marveling at the way Adelina relaxes against my touch. "Fine," she mumbles.

"Can I get a kiss for good luck?"

"Are you sure? I wouldn't want to be a *distraction*," she says dryly.

"Don't listen to him—"

Adelina hops up on her toes and plants a sensuous kiss on my lips, catching me by surprise. My hands find her hips, pulling her close as she teases me with the tip of her tongue. She tastes minty, like toothpaste, with a delightful note of underlying sweetness. I think I could get lost in the sound of her soft, contented sigh, be perfectly happy to spend the rest of the day learning all the ways I can hold her tight.

When she pulls away, I give chase, determined to savor her for a few more seconds, only for her to press her fingers to my lips.

"There will be more," Adelina whispers, "when you come back safely."

I nod, kissing her fingertips instead. "I will."

"Good boy," she says before stepping into her room and shutting the door.

The address Allistair provides leads me to a small café by the beachfront. I have a clear view of the promenade, as well as the calm ocean waves sweeping up onto the sand. It's surprisingly chilly out thanks to the wind sweeping in off the water, but there are plenty of people out enjoying the sunshine. Sometimes the safest place for a congregation of thieves isn't in the shadows but beneath the protection of day.

I spot Joseph driving the rental car around the block every now and then, discreetly checking in on me from behind the wheel. He comes around every ten minutes or so, giving me plenty of opportunity to bail without making things so obvious that it will raise Allistair's suspicions.

I agreed to come alone, and technically I have. Seated by myself at the table in the far corner with my back against the wall, I'm in the perfect position to see Allistair coming in through the front door. I already scoped out the exit—just like Michael taught me to do—and I've chosen this spot because the back exit is only a few yards away. Michael made sure I knew how to cover my bases.

Allistair arrives on the hour. I'm grateful for his punctuality. There's nothing quite like the anxiety of sitting alone waiting for shit that may or may not hit the fan. We greet each other with a sturdy handshake. To an outsider, this looks like a perfectly friendly interaction. They would never be able to tell that my muscles are clenched and my heart is pounding a mile a minute. Years ago, a meeting like this wouldn't have fazed me. I've been out of the game way too long, and I hope it doesn't show. I need Allistair to put his faith in me, to chance it with us rather than cave to his fear of Berruci, and he's never going to agree to work with me if he thinks I'll snap under the slightest pressure.

We both take a seat, ordering two espressos if only to keep the waitress from hovering over us while we discuss business. He looks like he had a rough night—tired and restless and emotionally drained. There are dark circles under his eyes, and I'm fairly certain he's wearing the same clothes we saw him in at the hospital.

"How is he?" I ask politely. "Your brother."

"The doctors say his recovery will be slow, but he will be alright."

"I'm glad to hear it."

Allistair reaches into his pocket. My muscles tense. While I'm confident he isn't about to draw a weapon, it's better to err on the side of caution. There are no guarantees in this line of work.

Thankfully, it's nothing nefarious. Allistair produces a small black thumb drive. I reach for it, but he closes his fist around the drive and pulls his hand back. Figures. This wouldn't be a proper meeting without a little tug-of-war.

"I have conditions."

"I assumed you would."

He sets the thumb drive between us in the middle of the table, a bargaining chip as much as it is a bomb. "Everything you asked for is on that drive," Allistair informs. "Personnel files, our daily rotations and Berruci's personal schedule."

I do my best to swallow my excitement. This is better than I could have hoped—a stockpile of ammunition for the taking. If we can keep track of Berruci's comings and goings down to the nearest second, we'll be able to move forward with our plan without so much as a hitch.

"How much would I have to pay you to deliver a package for us in my place?" I ask. "If I were to have you insert a USB directly into Berruci's server, for instance."

"I don't have that kind of clearance," Allistair explains. "I work the gate and patrol the perimeter; only Berruci's top lieutenants have access downstairs. Even if I tried, I wouldn't be able to get past the lock."

"What kind of lock?"

"Key card. The internal code is updated every use. Even if I stole you a key, there's no guarantee it would work."

I hold my breath. Damn. I could have saved myself so much time, but I get it. He's already sticking his neck out for us. "What is this information worth to you, friend?" I ask.

"When all of this is over, I want to take my little brother away from here. A different country where we can start fresh. That takes money."

"Everything does."

"Whatever your cut is," Allistair says, "I want double."

I do the mental math. Fifty billion six ways is . . . Well, let's just say it's not as neat and tidy as it could be. "I'll have to talk it over with my crew," I reply.

Allistair shakes his head. "No. I'm risking everything just being here. You either agree now, or I walk."

Ah. I guess we're playing hardball.

I personally have no qualms about taking a smaller cut. I'll still come away with enough to set Jack up for life and ensure Berruci can never get his mitts on her. And I'm sure Adelina won't mind too much either. She doesn't strike me as the greedy type. She can still help all the causes she's passionate about with that kind of money. Diana probably doesn't care, so long as Berruci gets what's coming to him. Joseph is the only one on our crew who might make a bit of a stink, but I can always take from my cut to make up the difference if it comes down to it.

In the grand scheme of things, it's a small price to pay for the treasure trove of information an inside man can provide. I can't even fault Allistair for wanting more. He's just being a good businessman. A good brother.

I stick my hand out to shake. "Welcome to the team."

"Actually, I have one more condition."

"What is it?"

"I want Berruci for myself," he says darkly. His fists are clenched, the vein at his temples pulsing with anger. "I want revenge for Elliot."

I'd be lying if I said I didn't want the honor. After Jack and I managed to escape to the States, there was a time when all I could think about were ways to take Berruci down. But I can see how badly Allistair wants this. There's a fire in his eyes—a fire we can *use*.

I nod slowly. "He's all yours, my friend."

CHAPTER TWENTY-SIX
Time to Dig Deep

Adelina

"HE KEEPS TOUCHING the camera," I grumble, staring at the live feed on my laptop. "Is there a way you can tell him to stop?"

"We didn't want to risk an earpiece giving him away, remember?" West pulls up a chair to sit beside me, resting his elbows on my desk. The airplane hangar is particularly cold today. "So how does it work? This little program of yours."

I type while I talk, determined not to waste any time. "This *little program* is analyzing the footage captured by the camera pen in Allistair's front pocket. As he completes his rounds, the computer digitally measures and reconstructs the layout of Berruci's villa, correcting the blueprints we already have to give us an up-to-date map so we can plan your route more accurately."

"Did you write it yourself?"

"No," I confess. "It's a repurposed construction tool. Mostly for interior decoration, mind you. There are some companies out there who will conduct walking tours of empty houses or apartments, and then they upload what they've captured into their computers to show off potential designs to clients."

"Interesting," West muses. I can't tell whether he's being genuine or if he's mocking me.

"What is?"

"I figured a genius like you might have whipped something like this up from scratch."

I can't help but laugh. "I'm no genius. There are entire forums dedicated to open-source coding. There's no point in doing it myself when someone's already done it before me."

When West doesn't respond, I turn and find him staring. The corners of his lips are turned up in a smile. Not the one he normally wears, though—the one he uses as a mask. This time, his smile is sweet and warm, the green of his eyes reminding me of springtime fields after a heavy storm.

"Tu as le plus beau des rires," he says, the words rolling off his tongue with a mesmerizing musicality. "J'aimerais que tu le fasses plus souvent."

I frown. "What does that mean?"

West shrugs. "Learn some French. They say learning languages is good for your brain."

"Or you can just speak in English, you weirdo."

He chuckles and reaches out, his fingertip just barely grazing the side of my neck. "I was asking about your tattoo," he says.

I bring a hand up and rub my neck self-consciously. I'm fairly certain he's lying, because he used *way* too many words to ask such a simple question. Then again, what do I know? My French is just as bad as my Cantonese. "Sometimes I forget it's even there," I mumble.

"Are sunflowers your favorite?"

I set my jaw, hesitant to share my thoughts. I guess not letting things get personal between us is officially out the window. It's been out the window for a while, actually. I was so adamant about keeping him at arm's length that I didn't notice how easy it would be for him to duck under. When did I start to let things slip? Was it when he told me about his niece? When he came to my rescue? When I let him kiss me?

West has shared a lot of himself with me, but I haven't done him the courtesy of the same. Surely it isn't the end of the world if I share a story or two.

"My sister," I tell him slowly, keeping my eyes on the laptop screen. Allistair has made his way through roughly half the villa now, taking his time—as I'd instructed—to give the camera a chance to drink in every detail of what we're up against.

"Yes, I recall."

"I think it was at our tenth birthday party. Someone gifted her with a whole bouquet of lilies. I remember crying because I wanted to be named after a flower too. My dad snuck out from the party to run to the florist, and he picked up a big bouquet of sunflowers to gift to me. Supposedly, he thought they were the most beautiful flowers in the world. Then Lily started crying because she took that to mean *she* wasn't the most beautiful flower in the world. And then *I* started crying because I hate seeing my sister upset, and Dad tried to backtrack and . . ." I grin, feeling ridiculous now that I've said it out loud. "Dad always liked to say that whenever I was feeling down, I should think of myself as a sunflower."

"Why is that?"

"Because they face toward the sun so that all their shadows fall behind them."

"He sounds like a wise man," West says.

My chest tightens. "Yeah, he was."

He tilts his head to the side, reminding me very much of a curious golden retriever. "Was?"

I swallow hard, unable to bring myself to explain. I know it's been nearly six years. I should be over it by now. But the memory of how I left things, our last conversation . . . it's settled sediment deep within my core, heavy and ugly and cold. If I could go back in time and take back what I said, I would do it in a heartbeat—though the *what-if* game is a dangerous one to play. It has no winners, no conclusion.

Thankfully, something on the screen grabs our attention, sparing me from the painful answer.

Through the camera pen's feed, we can see Allistair standing at the top of a set of incredibly steep stairs. The walls on either side of him are gray, made entirely of hastily poured concrete. Before he's able to take a single step, however, he stops abruptly. There's no audio connection, but the way he turns suggests that someone's talking to him. Two armed guards come into view—guards I recognize from the personnel files Allistair provided us.

West is already scrolling through on my iPad, matching their faces to their profiles. The one standing to the right has distinctively large ears, while the other sports a buzz cut and a scar bisecting the left side of his upper lip.

I watch the feed carefully as Allistair backtracks, gesturing with his hands like he's trying to appease two rabid raccoons. Much to my disappointment, he doesn't make it down those stairs. They're sending him away.

"That's going to be a problem," I mutter. "If we don't get a sense of the space—"

"It'll work out," West assures. "He'll try again on his next round."

"How can you sound so sure?"

"We're thieves, mon tournesol. We have to roll with the punches."

"Wait," I mumble, taking a closer look at the personnel files. "Those were the guys who came after me. So Berruci *does* know."

"Shit," he grumbles. "But how? We were so careful."

My mouth goes dry. I think I might be sick. There's really only one possibility, but I don't entirely trust it. "Do you think . . ."

"What is it?" he urges.

"Do you think we have a mole?"

West frowns at this. "That's absurd."

"Think about it. The day Diana decides to make nice and take me shopping also happens to be the same day Berruci sends his men after me? What if she did that because she wanted to give them a window of opportunity?"

"Stop it, Adelina. Diana and I go way back. She wouldn't do something like that. Plus, she was chased too."

"We don't know that," I say sternly. "She claims she was followed and managed to get away, but all we have is her word."

"She got hurt."

"Cuts and scrapes are easy to fake."

"What are you doing?" West asks, an edge to his tone.

"I'm trying to be logical." I grit my teeth hard enough that my molars squeak inside my skull, sending a terrible vibration shooting down my spine. "Stop making excuses and think for a second. Diana told me about how the Paris heist went wrong. That the police were tipped off before you could make a move."

West's expression grows dark. "She told you about that?"

"You were the only one who managed to get away."

"What are you implying?"

I hold his gaze, the words sitting on the tip of my tongue. What I'm about to say might be a mistake, but I've been wrestling with my suspicion for long enough. "Tell me the truth. Did you sell them out? Is that how you came to run the mule accounts for Berruci? You thought you could get away clean, but he had conditions?"

West rises, the air around us suddenly turning cold. "Sell them out?" he murmurs, crestfallen. "No, Adelina. I didn't sell out my friends. And I didn't expose you to Berruci either, since that's clearly what's on your mind."

"West—"

"I could have. The moment I found you, in fact. But I didn't because you are my *best shot* at protecting the one person in my life who I hold dear." The muscles in his jaw jump. "I told you before that Berruci is well-connected. He has informants crawling everywhere.

He basically owns this city. Maybe we were sloppy and someone reported us, but I guarantee you that no one here is a mole."

I swallow hard, his unwavering conviction leaving me breathless. "Okay," I murmur. "I'm sorry."

West paces in a circle, seething in quiet fury. He won't look at me. "The moment we start fighting among ourselves is the moment Berruci wins. I can't let that happen again."

"Will you tell me?" I ask quietly. "About that day. Why did you agree to put yourself under his thumb?"

He stands there, hands on his hips and as still as a statue, taking his time to consider. "I didn't agree to anything," he says slowly. "My brother made the decision for me."

"Your brother?"

"Michael. Jack's father."

"He betrayed you?" I ask, alarmed.

"No," West mutters, looking me in the eye. "He *saved* me."

CHAPTER TWENTY-SEVEN

Brother Mine

West

Six Years Ago
Paris, France

IT SHOULD HAVE been a momentous occasion, what with Michael's new bundle of joy. I never could have imagined my big brother with a kid. Yet there he sat at the very front of the funeral hall, five-day-old baby fast asleep in his arms, newly widowed and somehow keeping it together. I admired that about him. If the world was ever on the brink of collapse, he was the only man I knew who could hold down the fort.

But it broke my heart too. I was all too familiar with what it looked like to don a mask.

I hadn't known his wife, Jacqueline, very well. Being five years older, Michael left home well before I did. Who knew what sorts of misadventures he got up to while I was stuck inside, counting the days until I could finally rejoin him. He would visit often, sent lots of gifts and letters. And when I finally turned eighteen, he was there to pick me up—alongside his gorgeous blonde girlfriend. I never knew my brother had that kind of game.

Jacqueline was nice, though. Sweet. Had dreams of being a dancer, but ultimately made the pivot to teaching art. I always thought she and Michael made an odd match, but that was the kind of shitty opinion you were supposed to keep to yourself. So long as they were both happy, who was I to judge? I was there when they eloped. I was there when they found out they were expecting. They should have had a fairy-tale ending, not . . . *this*.

All I knew was that there had been complications. Michael refused to tell me the details, and I didn't dare push. He may not have shed a tear, but I knew his was a silent pain. The funeral had finished over an hour ago, and the other guests had already given their condolences and left, but Michael hadn't moved from his spot. I had no intention of leaving without him. If he needed time, I wouldn't be the one to rush him. As if sensing her father's grief, Jack—named in honor of her mother—had been nothing but an angel these past few days, rarely crying and sleeping easy.

"I can hold her, if you want," I offered. "Get some fresh air. You look like you could use it."

Michael glanced at me, arching a skeptical brow. "You? Hold a baby?"

"What's the big deal? It's just like holding a ball."

"It isn't."

"I'm sure I'll be fine for ten minutes."

"Mathieu, I would not trust you to hold my daughter even if the floor were padded and you were dressed in a suit of pillows."

"Your lack of faith in me is hurtful and you *will* buy me dinner to make up for it."

Michael huffed. It wasn't quite a laugh, but I still counted it as a win. Cracking jokes, making a fool of myself for his sake . . . it was the card I liked to play most if it meant I could make him feel even the slightest bit better. Ease some of his stress. Poor bastard was only twenty-seven and already graying at the temples, though I would attest to being partially responsible. It was no small test of patience, having me as a little brother.

"We can postpone the job tomorrow," I said quietly, though in the still silence of the funeral home, it felt like the equivalent of a scream. "We'll try again next month."

"No," he replied. "We've worked too hard and too long to get everything in place. This time tomorrow, we'll be rich enough for as many fresh starts as we want."

My skin tingled with excitement. Oh, how I had been dreaming of this day. For us, it was never about buying up mansions and showing off fast cars. Ever since we were kids, all we'd wanted was stability. Some peace of mind.

I remembered those long, terrible nights when Mother and Father would argue over the bills. Which ones could they afford to pay next month? Would they choose the rent over this week's groceries? They both worked two jobs to try to make ends meet, labeled by the more fortunate as "lazy" when they were, in fact, the hardest-working people I knew. They worked themselves to the bone week after week, their paychecks going out as fast as they'd come in.

I understood the value of a dollar early, dreamed of the doors it could unlock. I personally never agreed with the old adage that money couldn't buy happiness. Like hell it couldn't. Happiness meant food in your belly, a roof over your head and the clothes on your back; all purchased with—surprise, surprise—money. It was the whole reason why I started pickpocketing tourists to try to ease some of my parents' burden. Where was the harm? These people could clearly afford to travel, to spend freely along the Champs-Élysées. A fenced watch here and there wouldn't harm anyone. I didn't steal for the thrill or because I thought it was cool.

Strict parents made excellent liars, and necessity made excellent thieves.

But we were older now, with far larger aspirations than merely scraping by. Or just surviving in a world that didn't care if we slipped through the cracks. With this score, we would be set for *life*. And who better to take from than someone with more than enough to spare?

Michael eventually stood, baby Jack shielded in his arms, as though determined to protect her from all the terrible things in the world. "Let's go home," he said.

I followed without hesitation.

Michael assigned me not to one of the luxury suites Berruci owned but to a smaller stash house a few blocks from the Seine. I moved in on the hour, hidden under the cover of night. It was raining heavily, but that worked in my favor. People weren't keen to go for late night strolls when it was pouring, so the chances of running into any witnesses were as good as zero.

It took me all of thirty seconds to jimmy the lock on the door, and another thirty to climb the stairs two at a time to get to the upper floor. The money sat there on the table in the center of the room, wads of multicolored euros bundled together with paper bands. This was easy.

Maybe a little *too* easy.

Despite the tantalizing prize before me, I refused to move an inch. Michael's reports said I should expect to sneak around at least three guards, but they were nowhere in sight. Between the flimsy lock, the cash laid out like a comical gallery display and the creeping sensation crawling up my neck, I knew something was wrong. But what?

An alarm blared, high and shrill, cutting through the frigid air. The flash of red-and-blue lights flooded in from outside on the street.

A setup.

Downstairs, the heavy thud of boots rapidly making their way up. There was no escape—or was there?

I dashed across the room, ignoring the table of money. It was probably booby-trapped with ink packets or marked bills. Making for the window, I shoved it open and dared to peek outside. It was only the second floor, but it was a terrifying drop all the same. I had no choice. I slipped through the opening, clinging to the ledge, my legs dangling beneath me.

I let go, landing awkwardly on my heels only to fall onto my back. My shirt was soaked against the wet pavement, but at least I managed to keep from hitting my head. With a groan, I rolled over and pulled myself to my feet. I couldn't feel anything other than the frantic beat of my heart. Without thought and without hesitation, I ran as fast as my legs could carry me, my thoughts in utter disarray.

Were the others okay? How did Berruci know we were coming?

My phone buzzed in my pocket. A call from my brother.

"Are you okay?" I asked the moment I picked up. "The cops showed up. I don't know what happened. I had to abandon the take and—"

"Cops showed up at my location too," Michael replied in a rush. "Diana's been arrested. I can't get a hold of the others."

"What the hell just happened?"

"I don't know. I think we've been made."

"Fuck—"

"Meet me at the rendezvous point. I'm going to get Jack."

"What? Why?"

"If Berruci knows, he'll be on us within the hour. We need to *leave*."

It was a hastily slapped-together plan, and it showed.

We had a suitcase each. Passports were in our pockets. Michael had an extra duffel bag crammed full of diapers and baby clothes for Jack. There wasn't any need for a visa to the United States from France, so it was just a matter of buying the tickets and getting the hell out of town.

I held my breath the entire time we were lined up for security. Once we were past the metal scanners, there was no way Berruci would be able to get his hands on us. We would be in the clear. All we had to do was make it through.

I could practically taste freedom, my skin buzzing with electricity. We were getting a fresh start, a new life. Granted, we didn't have much money to our name, but better to be poor and free than dead and rich. The path before us was full of endless opportunities.

"Step out of line, please," the security guard said to us just as we were about to slip out of our shoes and put them in the waiting plastic bins.

I tried my most relaxed smile. "Is there a problem?"

"You've both been selected for a random search."

Michael and I exchanged a wary glance. No way. This was just a coincidence, that was all. A really poorly timed coincidence. Everything would go smoothly so long as we cooperated. Making a scene was only going to cause more trouble.

We were led to a sparse room adjacent to the security check with white walls and awful fluorescent panel lights. The security officer confiscated our passports.

"These will be returned to you," he explained. "It's our policy."

"Can you tell us what this is about?" Michael asked. The security officer said nothing and left the room.

"It's fine," I said, trying to remain calm. "We're fine."

They kept us waiting there. Five minutes. Ten. Thirty. As we encroached on the hour, my skin started to crawl. My knee bounced, my fingers tapping against the metal table that was bolted to the floor. Beside me, Michael was perfectly still, other than patting Jack on the back rhythmically in a soothing pattern. He could sense, just as I could, that things were most certainly *not* fine.

Cold, harsh dread washed over me the second Berruci stepped in through the door.

"How?" I asked in disbelief. "How the hell did you—"

"Everyone can be bought for the right price," he said, taking a seat across from us like he owned the place. For all I knew, maybe he did. Berruci strummed his fingers against the table, letting us stew in our own uncomfortable silence. "You thought you could take from me, did you?"

I swallowed. "We're—"

"Sorry?" he interjected. "Don't make me laugh."

"What do you want?" Michael asked.

Berruci leaned back in his seat. "What else are you supposed to do with rats? You exterminate them."

The room spun. I was going to be sick. How did this all go so terribly wrong?

"Please," I murmured. "There has to be something we can do."

Berruci stroked his chin, his eyes closed as though in thought. "Alright," he said eventually. "Here's what's going to happen, gentlemen. I'm going to let one of you leave."

I blinked at him stupidly, barely able to understand past the rush of blood in my ears. "One of us?"

"I can't let you both go without a slap on the wrist. That wouldn't send a very good message." Berruci leaned back in his chair. "I'm going to see this as a business opportunity. My enterprises have been raking in more money than we can spend, and I need a handful of offshore accounts to spread things around. Create a messy paper trail. You know the drill. Since you're headed to—America, was it?—you may as well do me a favor since you're so determined to leave."

"We can open accounts," Michael said hastily. "Not a problem."

Berruci shook his head. "It's more of a one-man kind of a job."

I knew for a fact it wasn't; it never hurt to have several mule accounts at once. Berruci was being obtuse on purpose. Nobody crossed him without facing consequences.

Baby Jack stirred in Michael's arms, her uncomfortable whimpers breaking into an all-out cry. My brother did his best to soothe her, rocking her back and forth, shushing her gently, but nothing seemed to work.

My heart raced. I wasn't sure what Berruci had planned for the person who stayed behind, but I sure as hell wasn't going to let Michael take the fall. Jack needed him. They could start a new life together in the States. I wasn't going to separate a father from his daughter. I would rather face Berruci's wrath than let it come to that.

"I'll stay," Michael said before I had a chance.

No, I wanted to scream, but my voice died in my throat. "Michael—"

"Perfect," Berruci said. "I can appreciate a man of action."

I gripped my brother's shoulder. "Don't be an idiot. She needs you."

Michael hugged Jack closer to his chest. "You two are the most important people left in my life. I'm not going to let anything happen to either of you."

"Can't we at least talk about this?"

"There's nothing to talk about." Michael moved to place Jack in my arms. "Take the baby."

I shook my head. "No."

"Mathieu." There was a terrible tremble of finality in his tone, as he transferred the baby to me in a rush. "Take care of her. Please."

I was wrong before: holding a child was nothing like holding a ball. I was terrified, not of her, but that I would accidentally be too rough. She was so small and delicate and *precious*. How could Michael be sure I wouldn't fuck this all up?

"There's a car waiting for us outside," Berruci said to Michael. "I hope you're smart enough to come quietly."

Michael set his jaw. "Yes, sir." He stood up from the table, bending over to press a kiss to the top of Jack's head before pressing his forehead to mine. "Stay out of trouble. I love you, little brother."

"Wait—" I pleaded.

Berruci and Michael left the room together, a metaphorical gun to my brother's head.

Jack continued to cry hard enough for the both of us.

CHAPTER TWENTY-EIGHT
Apologies Shouldn't Be a Struggle

Adelina

Present Day
Nice, France

WE HAVEN'T REALLY spoken much, not that I can blame him.

It's been four days since I heavily implied West might be a traitor. He doesn't seem angry, but that makes me more nervous than it probably should. If I were in his shoes, I'd be livid. If only he'd snap at me. Yell. Then the anxious bubble in my chest might finally burst and give me some sense of relief. I'm more comfortable navigating through a person's anger than I am their indifference. I can tell I've hurt him, and that doesn't sit well with me. The right thing to do would be to apologize . . . I just don't know how.

West and Joseph continue to build up the course based off the new dimensions Allistair has provided us. He texted to say he'll try to get footage of downstairs today. I hope he pulls it off. Berruci's bunker is the most vital location with regards to our plans, and it's the only blind spot we haven't managed to cover.

Eager for something to do, I pull up my code editor and go through my virus line by line. She's almost complete, and I'm 99.9 percent sure that it will work exactly as intended on the day.

It's that last 0.1 percent that worries me.

There's always a chance I've missed something. A dropped value, a duplicated bracket, an errant decimal. Or maybe some redundant line of junk that ultimately causes the whole thing to crash. I'm a weaver, diligently trying to find and correct missed warps and knotted wefts. It *has* to be perfect. And that isn't just my A-type personality talking. If I can't do my part, this whole thing will have been for nothing.

"Hungry?"

I jump in my seat, whipping around to find West standing there with two takeout containers. I was so engrossed in my work that I didn't hear him approach. Is it stupid how much I missed his face? And his voice. And the way my stupid heart skips when he looks my way.

"Where'd this come from?" I ask.

"Diana ordered something for us to eat."

I frown. "And had it delivered *here*?"

West chuckles. "Of course not. Joseph went with her to pick it up. They just got back."

I check the time on the computer. An hour flew by and I barely even noticed.

"Thank you," I say, taking the food from him.

He sits down beside me as I pull open the container's lid and am greeted by the rich garlic aroma of the dish's red sauce. It's a pasta, topped with seared scallops and juicy pink prawns. My stomach growls with a vengeance.

"Diana's spoiling us," I murmur.

"A well-fed crew is an efficient crew," West replies, digging into his meal.

We eat in silence.

And it gets to me almost immediately.

"West, look . . . I'm really—"

"All's forgiven."

I don't know if I want to laugh or frown. "You didn't let me finish."

"No need."

"So you're not angry with me?"

"I was . . . upset, but for only a little bit." He offers me a gentle smile. "I understand, Adelina. Really, I do."

"Then why have you been so quiet?"

"Didn't think you'd notice."

"You're the most talkative guy on the planet. How could I not?"

"You seemed agitated. I wanted to give you space."

"I don't want space from you," I blurt out. My face turns red, my eyes widening in horrified realization that I just said that out loud.

West leans against my workstation, wearing that stupid smug smile of his. "Is that so?"

"That's not—I didn't mean it like that."

"Like *what*?" he teases. "Goodness, Ms. Choi. Could it be that you're fond of me?"

Warmth blooms in my chest, sending an electric thrill crackling up my spine. "You're . . . not so bad."

"Coming from you, that's the highest of compliments."

"Shut up and eat."

He laughs and I feel . . . better. *Good.* Certainly lighter than I was a second ago. West is so wonderfully (and frustratingly) easy to talk to. I'm so used to people lording my missteps over my head that his easy acceptance, his quickness to forgive, is a welcome breath of fresh air.

My computer screen flashes, an incoming video feed beaming in.

On screen, we're treated to a first-person POV as Allistair makes his usual rounds. It takes him twenty minutes to complete a full loop before finally arriving at the stairs. There are guards everywhere, potential land mines scattered throughout the villa. My palms are sweaty. It's like watching someone trapped in a fish tank full of piranhas. If he does anything to draw their attention, it'll be an absolute feeding frenzy. It looks like the coast might be clear. He descends the stairs and makes it down into the bunker, providing a new vantage point I can use to feed the reconstruction software.

Stretching from the base of the stairs is a long, narrow hall with white walls and polished tile floors. The ceiling is lined with fluorescent panels, lending to the sterile atmosphere. At the very end of the hall is a thick door, sealed shut on heavy hinges. Drilled into the adjacent doorframe is some sort of electronic panel.

I hold my breath when someone opens the door from the other side, fearing Allistair might be caught. He books it back up the stairs, but not before my program is able to capture several key frames of the interior, the algorithm estimating the dimensions of the room. It's the finer, slightly blurry details in the image that make my stomach roll.

"Holy shit," I mutter under my breath.

It's an armory, a storage unit and a server command center all rolled into one. I can see the main computer in question hooked up to a grid of large screens running everything from stock market analysis to bank statements.

"This place looks like it could withstand a raid," West grumbles. "Maybe he built it because he was starting to feel the heat from the feds."

"You're going to go in *there*?" I ask, incredulous. "If anything goes wrong, you'll be pinned down."

"It's the only way. Can you zoom in?" West asks. "You know, enhance the image or something like they do on *NCIS*."

"I hate that show. That's not how any of that works."

"It isn't?"

"You can't enhance pixels that aren't there."

"Well, damn." He sighs, running a hand through his hair. "Allistair says that the lock relies on a key card, but the codes change after every use."

"Not a problem. I know how to spoof it."

"Really?"

"Don't sound so surprised." I lean back in my seat and sigh. "At least we know it's a straight shot to the servers. And it doesn't look like there are pressured floor panels or lasers that could set off an alarm."

He leans forward, staring at the screen. "From what Allistair's shown us, the guards are incredibly punctual, but there's a five-minute gap in their rotation."

I nod. "That matches up with our notes."

"Then that's our window."

"You really think you can do this?"

"I can do anything I set my mind to, sugar." West pumps his eyebrows suggestively at me, and I offer him an unimpressed look.

"Call me that again and I'm going home," I say, rising from my seat.

"Alright, alright." He throws his head back and laughs. "I know exactly what we can do."

"Tell me."

"Mon tournesol, no heist is carried out without practice."

CHAPTER TWENTY-NINE Put Your Phones on Silent, People

West

"AND . . . YOU'RE DEAD, mon ami," Joseph announces, his eyes glued to his watch. "Run the formula again, Qwerty. This one's no good."

While I return to the beginning of the maze we've created, Adelina quickly types into her computer, the fans inside whirring to the max as it generates an alternative route for me to take. It's nothing short of impressive. The program she's using is a modified version of the ones Micromouse maze solvers use to get from point A to point B in the shortest possible distance and time. Naturally, I don't have four wheels or sensors to tell me which way to go, nor the capability to make split-second decisions, but by adjusting the algorithm Adelina's been able to shave my time down from five minutes to three minutes and fifty-seven seconds.

Still not fast enough, though.

I hate to say it, but I think the problem might be *me*.

We've been at it all morning. I've worked up a sweat, and my lungs burn with a vengeance. I'm not out of shape, per se, but this is definitely the most intensive workout I've had in years. No matter how fast I run, no matter how hard I push myself, I can't get my time below three minutes.

"Maybe we should take a break," Diana suggests. "No sense in killing yourself before the big day. Wouldn't want you blowing an ankle, now would we?"

"You can go," I wheeze. Good God, am I about to keel over? This wouldn't have been an issue in my early twenties, but now my joints ache when the weather gets a little too cold and my back hurts just getting out of bed. "I'm not ready to quit yet," I say once I've caught my breath.

"Suit yourself," Diana says pointedly. I can tell she has doubts. It's not very encouraging.

By the time I pick myself up off the floor, I find Joseph hovering near Adelina's computer station. He leans casually against her desk, a hand on his hip. I can't quite make out what they're saying to one another, so I have to will my legs to carry me over to get a better listen.

"A buddy of mine says the casino's security system is super lax," Joseph tells her. "If you work your magic, we could pull a fast one on them and make away with upward of—"

"Sorry," Adelina interjects. "I'm just not interested."

"Promise me you'll at least think about it?"

She false-starts, eventually shrugging a shoulder. "Sure."

"Wonderful," Joseph says, rubbing Adelina on the upper arm. I'm sure it's a friendly gesture, but something in my gut clenches at the sight. I thought I told him to leave her out of whatever half-baked scheme he's cooking up.

I make my way over and clear my throat. "All good?"

Joseph nods, chuckling as he leaves, giving me a wide-eyed look that is too innocent to be convincing. Jack pulled the same move when I caught her trying to sneak ice cream bars after breakfast. He makes his way over to Diana, speaking in low murmurs before reaching out to tuck a loose strand of hair behind her ear. Diana rolls her eyes, but she doesn't look too put off by the gesture. They leave through the hangar's main exit, and I can't help but wonder what they could possibly have to talk about.

"He isn't bothering you, is he?" I ask Adelina.

"Nothing I can't handle," she replies. On her computer screen, her program is recalculating in the background, tracing a new route through the virtual model of the villa, which I will have to duplicate to the best of my ability in real life.

"The problem I think you're running into is the stairs leading into the bunker," she says, analyzing the code. "Do you think you could jump the distance? It's only twenty steps."

"*Only* twenty?" I grimace. "I'd rather not blow out my knees, thank you."

"I think you need a little motivation."

"You think taking down Berruci isn't motivation enough?"

Adelina gives me a mischievous grin. "Let's race," she says. "Loser buys dinner." She stands up from behind her desk, shrugging off her jacket. Adelina doesn't look particularly fast. I could easily outpace her in a pinch, and yet she doesn't seem the least bit deterred.

"I don't think this is a very fair matchup," I say.

"Scared you'll lose?"

A smile stretches across my face. "I'm warning you now that I'm a very sore winner."

"I guess we have that in common. First one to the door and back?"

"Fine by me," I say. "Are we going to count down from three, or—"

Before I have a chance to finish my sentence, Adelina reaches up and grabs hold of my shirt, pulling me down to catch me in a bruising kiss. Startled, I instinctively grip her by the hips, enjoying the way she hums contentedly against me. Thoughts stumble out of my head, leaving nothing but a blank slate. What was it we were doing again?

I get my answer when she suddenly peels away and runs. Adelina cackles wildly as she makes her way toward the makeshift villa, weaving in, out and around the metal trusses we've used in lieu of proper walls. I laugh and give chase. She has a head start, but I'm gaining quickly.

While she sees it as a race, I treat it very much as a game of tag. Adelina may have caught me off guard, but I've been maneuvering through these faux halls all day. The moment I have her within my grasp, I circle her waist with my arms and hold her close. I swing her around, lifting her off her feet as she giggles breathlessly. We stumble together, ending up on the cold concrete floor of the hangar in a tangle of arms and legs.

She ends up on top of me—not that I mind in the slightest—her hands pressed against my chest for stability. I adore the flush of her cheeks and the way the corners of her eyes crinkle when she smiles.

Has she always been this beautiful? Adelina is very much like the night sky. Dark and cold and something to be wary of. But when she smiles like this, it's like gazing at the dawn, when the first golden rays peek out from behind the horizon to show you that there was never anything to fear. That the night sky can bring with it its own quiet splendor.

I wonder if I should put a stop to this before I'm too far gone. Once we've dealt with Berruci, Adelina will return home to Vancouver, and I'll need to go home and take care of Jack. Adelina has her life, and I have mine. She said it herself—this is one and done. I'll likely never see her again, and allowing myself to indulge is only setting myself up for disappointment.

Yet I can't seem to help myself. I bring a hand up to trace my fingers over the shape of her grin, sweeping them over her cheeks to admire the softness of her skin. I comb my hand through her short hair before pulling her down to capture her lips with mine. Her skin is delightfully hot to the touch. What once was a race has now evolved into a wrestling match. It's clear she enjoys being on top, pinning me on my back while she straddles my hips.

And while I would normally indulge her, she isn't the only one who wants to play this game.

Locking my arms around her, I throw my weight up and over, rolling her onto her back so I can be the one on top. Her soft *oh* gives way to a light giggle as I deepen our kiss. I'm tempted to spend the rest of the day like this—maybe even the next week, if I'm able—exploring all the different ways I can earn her gasps of pleasure.

"Touch me," she pleads.

Who am I to deny her?

Propping myself on my elbow beside her, I unzip the front of her jeans and slide my hand beneath the band of her underwear, relishing the way she grinds against my touch. Nothing delights me more than the way her mouth falls open and her pupils blow wide as I draw tight circles against her.

I take my time to tease, to explore, applying pressure one moment only to ease up the next. Adelina's hips buck against my hand, searching—begging for more of that sweet friction. I lay claim to her mouth, take command of it, savoring the rush that comes when she whimpers against my lips.

"West . . ." she moans languidly, trembling with pleasure beneath my hand. A light sweat coats her forehead, her cheeks a lovely pink. Adelina looks at me from beneath heavy eyelids, her lips parting as she pants, hot breath ricocheting off my cheeks.

"God, the *sounds* you make," I groan.

"Please don't stop," she whines. Breathless. Desperate. Filthy.

"You're soaked, Adelina. Does this feel good?"

"Yes," she rasps. "West, I think I'm going to—"

"Not yet," I tell her firmly. "I'm not done playing with you. Understand?"

Although her eyes widen in brief surprise, Adelina quickly nods. "Yes."

"That's my girl."

I easily slip a finger inside her, her sensitive walls clenching around my knuckles. Adelina whimpers, ferociously gripping onto my shirt as I search for that one spot I know will make her see stars. "Look at you," I murmur, crooking my finger again and again. I add another finger and enjoy the way her eyes roll back. "T'es trop bonne." *You're so damn hot.*

Our kisses are bruising, our skin feverish. It's a pleasure like no other to see her unravel, to have her cling to me like the world's about to fall apart. I think Adelina's on track to becoming a problematic obsession of mine.

"You're getting so tight," I say against her lips. "You fucking *need* this, don't you?"

Adelina moans my name. At least, I think she does. Her ragged breathing makes it difficult to get a word out.

"What a pretty little mess you are," I muse. "Do you like my fingers that much?"

"West—West, I can't take it anymore."

"I can tell. Go on, mon tournesol. Let me see you come."

She writhes against me, coming undone around my fingers with an impassioned cry. Adelina is a sight to behold, the air around us crackling. I wrap her up in my arms as she kisses me sweetly, leisurely dragging her hands through my hair.

"Oh my God," she sighs.

"You sounded like you enjoyed yourself."

Adelina laughs lightly. I swear just the sound is enough to get me high. "Your turn," she insists.

"Let me take you back to the hotel," I say, nipping at her earlobe. "We can have more fun there."

"You're so forward, Mr. Porter," she says with a wry grin, throwing my words back at me.

A phone rings, the sound piercing through the tension in the air. Adelina and I both ignore it . . . only for it to go off again. Either it's an incredibly persistent telemarketer, or someone is having an emergency that desperately requires our attention. I really hope it's just a wrong number.

"I think it's mine," she says apologetically.

"Ignore it?" I suggest hopefully.

Adelina laughs, rising to her feet. "It might be my sister. It could be important."

I remain seated there on the concrete floor, perfectly happy to catch my breath. I'm a gentleman, after all. It wouldn't be comfortable to walk around with my very obvious *problem* on full display.

I suppose I should be grateful that someone felt the need to interrupt, because at the rate things are going . . . Well, after what Adelina told me about her letdown of a first experience, she deserves better than a romp in some repurposed airplane hangar. I want to give her a bed of fluffy pillows and warm blankets. Maybe a hot soak and a nice dinner. I want to make her feel like a queen, not some quick fuck in the heat of the moment. She deserves better than that.

And I could give it all to her if she asked.

It occurs to me then that her phone hasn't actually stopped ringing. It continues to blare, an unwelcome sound echoing off the high walls of our safe house. I turn to see Adelina with her phone in hand, but she doesn't pick up. Instead, she stares at the screen, paler than I've ever seen her.

I stand, a creeping sensation crawls its way up my spine. "Adelina?"

She swallows. Is she about to be sick?

"Adelina, what's wrong?"

She manages a shaky inhale. "It's my mother."

CHAPTER THIRTY

I Think I Might Be in Trouble

Adelina

HE GIVES ME a confused look. Why wouldn't he? West doesn't know that just the sight of Mom's caller ID is enough to send me into a downward spiral. I haven't even answered yet, and I can already imagine all the terrible things she'll have to say. Or worse—how she'll give me the silent treatment until I'm the one to break first.

Mom loves to do that. Whenever we're having an argument, she ices me out, letting me suffocate in my own silence until I can't stand it anymore. It never used to occur to me just how messed up it was that I would prefer to have her yell at me than say nothing at all. At least if she yelled at me, she could get it off her chest, and we could put whatever heinous crime I'd committed behind us and move on. But when she bottled it up, I was left to walk on eggshells, terrified that she would explode at any moment. I'd rather get it over with and risk minor cuts rather than major burns.

I consider ignoring my phone, but she's video calling and that *never* happens. It could be a pocket dial. It's highly likely that Mom was trying to get in contact with Lily and accidentally mixed up our numbers. Apart from our awful encounter at Lily's celebration dinner, we haven't exchanged so much as a text message in six years. This has to be some sort of mistake. It's far more likely that someone has stolen Mom's phone and accidentally gave me a ring.

But it isn't long before the doubts creep in. What if it's important? Someone could be dying. Mom must have something urgent to say if she's the one reaching out. What if I miss her call the way I missed Dad's and I live to regret it?

I can't do that to myself again.

With a trembling hand, I accept the call.

Mom's face fills the screen. She didn't always look like she was carved from stone. I remember her smiling a lot when I was a little girl. Always when I did something she approved of, of course, but I craved her warmth and praise more than anything. Whenever I did something exemplary (earned an academic award, won first place at a school track and field meet, became captain of my robotics team), I shared in her pride. I *loved* it when she boasted to her friends and family, adored that sparkle in Mom's eyes when she showed me off. To me, her love and approval were one and the same.

I wish I could go back in time and slap some sense into me. Or maybe give myself a hug. Because that line of thinking is a double-edged sword. At some point, her disapproval was ever-present, and therefore her love was always out of reach. Conditional. Weaponized.

"Yes?" I say dryly. My guts are in knots. She's going to yell at me any second now.

"Are you proud of yourself?"

"What?"

"You talked her into it." Her words are sharp. Bitter.

"Talked who into what?"

"Lily. She's not talking to me."

I set my jaw. "I'm sure she's just busy. She's traveling, after all."

"Not one phone call or text message since the family dinner!"

"Can you blame her? You embarrassed her."

"*You* embarrassed her," Mom snaps. "Ga sai la."

I don't know what that particular phrase means, but her tone is aggressive. Probably nothing nice.

"I didn't do anything," I insist, heat creeping up the back of my neck. "You were the one making a scene."

"Always making excuses. You were the one who left."

My eyes prickle with the sting of salt. It's true I left, but . . . shit, am I remembering wrong? It's been a while since the dinner, and I've frankly had a lot on my plate since then. I recall being prepared to be combative, but I'm always like that where Mom's concerned.

"That's not what happened," I reply, my voice wavering. "And even if I did—"

"So you admit it."

"That's not what I'm saying—"

"And now you've convinced your sister not to talk to me either! You two are so ungrateful. How can you do this to your own mother?"

My mind spins as she continues berating me. Her admonishments flow over me, wave after terrible wave. Mom lists all the ways I've wronged her. How she put a roof over my head, provided three square meals a day, made sure I did well in school—all to be treated like this. And as she tells me I have no respect, no sense of honor—I retreat into myself. Her words float into my ear, but they lose all meaning. We've done this song and dance before. It's better if I close my heart to it, just blank my mind and let the storm pass.

They're just words, I tell myself. *They can't hurt me*.

"What are you even going to do with your life?" Mom asks. "Stupid girl—dropping out of school. You couldn't put up with one more semester? All that time and money wasted. Who will hire you now? How are you going to make money and take care of yourself?"

"It's *my* life, Mom," I hiss, snapping back to reality.

"A life *I* gave *you*, you selfish—"

"Adelina," West says clearly. "Hang up the phone."

Mom frowns. "Who is that?"

My heart stutters. I don't know what to do. I'd completely forgotten West is even here. Embarrassment and shame flood through me.

Did he hear all of that? He must think I'm so pathetic, being scolded like a child. *I* think I'm pathetic.

West looks me in the eye, bringing a hand up to gently brace my wrist. "Will you please give me your phone?"

I nod. At least, I think I do. Every inch of my body is numb, my mind devoid of all thought. It's easier to deal with her that way. To become transparent and allow everything to pass through rather than face it directly. I just want to disappear.

West takes my phone and glares at the screen. "I don't know who you are, but you don't get to talk to Adelina that way."

"I'm her *mother—*"

"*Don't. Talk. To. Her. That. Way.*"

Mom launches into a full tirade in Cantonese. I can only catch bits and pieces of it. (Something *none of your business, gweilo* something something.) Even with a language barrier, her meaning is loud and clear. Instead of trying to listen, to pause and reflect, she doubles down. Mom grows louder and angrier because she thinks that makes her right. She's been caught out, but she would rather scream at the top of her lungs than lose face. It might kill her to admit that maybe, just maybe, she is in the wrong.

West ends the call and sets the phone on my desk without so much as a *goodbye*. I'm both impressed and horrified at how easily he does it. I wish I had that kind of willpower.

"Are you okay?" he asks me, so soft and sweet it gives me whiplash.

I'm not sure how to respond after that shitshow, so I do the only thing I can think of. Forcing a smile onto my face, I say, "I'm fine." West frowns, and I suddenly want to light myself on fire. He's disappointed with my response. Disappointed with *me*. "I'm *fine*," I try again, more insistent. More desperate. If I say it over and over again, at some point it will be true. "I'm totally, totally fine."

I am a grown woman. I should act like it. Sticks and stones, or however that stupid saying goes. I'm used to Mom's mistreatment. I've endured worse.

West takes a step forward and brushes the pad of his thumb over my cheek, wiping away tears. I can't bring myself to look him in the eyes because we both know I'm a liar. But he doesn't push. Doesn't even remotely attempt to pry an answer out of me because he knows, just as I know, how brittle I am right now.

"I . . . I want to go back to the hotel," I mumble.

"Okay," he says. "I'll drive you."

"I just need a nap. A reset." I laugh quietly. It's fake and uncomfortable. "I'm sorry you had to see that. My mother, uh . . . You know what? Never mind. Family drama, right? We've all got it."

"Adelina—"

"Yeah, a nap sounds good."

"Adelina," he whispers. I finally manage to look up at him and he . . . he looks heartbroken. "You're the most brilliant woman I've ever met."

I'm the first to look away. "Stop it."

"No," he says, pulling me into a tight hug. I melt against his touch, happy to no longer be adrift. There's a pleasantness to be found against his solid frame, a comfort in knowing that he wants me close. "I mean it. The work that you do . . . it's nothing short of amazing. You've helped countless thousands without an ounce of the recognition you deserve. What that woman said—"

"My mother."

"I don't give a fuck. She could be the Queen of England—it doesn't make a difference. Nobody has the right to speak to you that way." West presses a kiss to my hair, holding me with such surety I fear I'll grow spoiled. What a tragedy it will be once I've learned to crave his touch, only to never see him again when the job is done.

My shoulders tremble, stifled sobs soaking into his shirt. I bury my face against his chest, eager to hide from him, the world, from everyone. West holds me that much tighter. If he notices that I cry even harder, he makes no mention of it. I can't remember the last time I felt this . . . adored. Appreciated. *Safe*.

Which is precisely why I know it's going to hurt like hell when we finally part ways.

"Will you talk to me?" he asks in whispers. "Tell me your story, Adelina. I promise you'll feel better if you do."

I swipe at my eyes, struggling to regain control of my breathing. "Okay."

Adelina

Six Years Ago
Cambridge, Massachusetts

I WAS IN the thick of it, surrounded by mountains of textbooks and stacks of loose papers. Midnight was approaching, but the library always extended their hours when the end of the semester rolled around. For many students, it was both a safe haven and a place of astronomical stress. I had just polished off my third (or maybe my fourth?) energy drink of the evening, but I didn't care that it was bad for my health. Heart failure be damned. Nothing was more important than killing it this week.

If my calculations were correct, I was sitting pretty at the top of my class. So long as I cleared this exam in the ninetieth percentile, I would once again secure my position on the Dean's List. Sure, I was running on fumes, but I had to prove that I was the best. It's like Mom always used to tell me: Success only comes to those who work hard.

By the time I finished my fifth practice module, I was starting to go cross-eyed from having stared at my laptop screen too long. A terrible pressure pounded against the inside of my skull. A normal person might have taken it as a sign to pack up and get some well-deserved sleep, but the cloying sensation deep within my gut told me that it wasn't an option. I needed to do more work, study harder, be better than all the rest.

This was my last year at MIT. Several of my classmates already had internships lined up (courtesy of parents or other relatives), and while I had been tapped by a couple of recruiters for some decently big names, I knew I could do better. The only way I was going to secure my future was by outperforming everyone else. Nobody ever remembers or notices a slacker, which was why I had to be the one on top. A shining example. I needed to turn myself into someone companies would *fight* each other for.

I was either perfect, or nothing.

My phone buzzed on the table, the vibrations rattling me awake. A text message? At this time of night? With a yawn, I checked the screen to find a message from Dad.

Dad: Make sure you're eating well.

Dad: Take a break every now and then!

Adelina: I will, thx.

My phone started to buzz in earnest. He was calling me now. I leaned back in my chair with a sigh. Seriously? I had so much work to do.

"Hi," I answered.

"What are you doing up so late?" Dad asked with a chuckle. "You need your beauty rest."

I dragged a hand over my face. "I know."

"Are you at the library by yourself?"

"Yeah. My roommate has some friends over. I couldn't concentrate."

"That's not safe, Adelina. You should have someone walk with you."

"I'm fine, Dad."

"Isn't there a campus program where you can have security escort you back?"

The pressure behind my eyes was getting worse. "I'm *fine*, Dad. How are things at the food bank?"

Dad worked full-time at the Vancouver Food Drive Society as its main coordinator. If there was one thing he really knew how to do, it was stretch a dollar. Donations were always in flux, with people's generosity surging around the holiday season, but the rest of the year was when the food drive struggled. Dad was the one to reach out to the local municipality about additional funding, or to strike up deals with local farmers to buy fresh produce at a reduced rate. It wasn't a flashy job by any means, but it was honest work that he genuinely seemed to love. To him, there was nothing more fulfilling than helping those in need.

"Not too bad," he said. "Spent the morning tossing expired cans someone brought in."

"I can't believe they treat the drive like a dumping ground."

"Maybe they didn't know."

I huffed. "You're too forgiving, Dad. Of course they knew. They probably just wanted to clean out their pantries."

He laughed. "That's what your mother said."

"Look, my first exam is tomorrow. I'm going home right now, okay?"

"Okay, okay. Please text me when you get home."

"I will. Love you."

"I love you, too."

I hung up with a tired laugh, slowly gathering all of my work to shovel into my backpack. I lived off campus, so it was a brisk fifteen-minute walk before I got home. Toeing off my shoes at the door, I texted Dad just as promised.

We had three hours allotted to complete the exam, but I finished in two. I pretended not to notice all the dirty looks I got from a few of my male classmates as I vacated my desk, traipsed down the aisle and handed my stapled booklet to my professor at the front of the gym. I was riding high. There wasn't a single question I didn't know how to answer. Number forty-three stumped me for a bit, but I eventually worked it out.

One exam done, five more to go.

A part of me wanted to go straight home and take the rest of the day off, but there was no rest for the wicked. I was on a hot streak, my brain already attuned for learning, so I headed straight to the library and parked myself at a table where I fully intended to camp out for the night.

Once I put on my noise-canceling headphones, I was lost to the world. Computational cognitive science was probably my weakest subject. I pored over my notes, flipped through every possible page in my textbook. At some point, my stomach grumbled, begging for a dinner break. I chewed on a small bag of almonds I'd packed instead. I was going to eat everything in sight once I was back home to enjoy Mom's cooking. Until then, I could soldier through.

My phone buzzed. Another text message from Dad.

Dad: How did it go today?

Dad: Wishing you lots of luck!

When I didn't respond right away, too caught up in trying to finish reading a paragraph, I was met with a flurry of new texts.

Dad: Mom says good luck too.

Dad: Did you remember to book your flight?

Dad: Try to get a connection through Montreal, it's cheaper than direct.

Dad: Have you eaten today?

I set my jaw. I knew Dad cared, but between the irritating buzz of my phone and all the work I still had ahead of me, my muscles were starting to tense. My headache from the night before was back in full force now, and grinding my molars certainly didn't help.

When he texted me again, I called him directly.

"A-Ba," I said, exasperated. I was so, *so* tired. "I'm at the library."

"Oh, sorry. I didn't mean to disturb." Dad sounded genuinely apologetic. He probably forgot about the time difference again. Even though this was my fourth and final year at MIT, he still sometimes forgot.

I took a deep breath and exhaled slowly. It was just the stress getting to me. There was no reason to get mad at him. "It's fine," I said. "I booked my flight already, don't worry. I haven't eaten dinner yet, but I will soon. I can't concentrate when you text me every five minutes."

I felt like absolute crap the moment I said it, but I didn't have the mental capacity to put it in a nicer way. Juggling being an overachieving student and an attentive, dutiful daughter was too hard in that moment.

"I understand," he said gently. He didn't sound upset, which I was grateful for. "This old man worries about you. Work hard, Addy."

"I always do," I said irritably and ended the call.

Modeling with machine learning—done.

Dynamical system modeling and control design—done.

Robotic manipulation—thank God, that one's done.

I was restless to get the hell out of there. My flight was scheduled first thing tomorrow morning, and I was practically chomping at the bit to get to the airport. There was a wonderful buzz in the air, an excitement at the thought of nearly finishing the semester. All I had were two more exams, these ones unfortunately back-to-back. I was in for a tense six hours, but the silver lining was that once they were done, I'd finally get to go home.

A whole group of students was gathered outside the classroom in the hall, a few still shuffling through their notes in a last-minute cramming session. The professor opened the door at five minutes to the hour, and we started to shuffle in. I was just about to take my seat when my phone buzzed.

Dad was calling.

The exam was about to start. I had no choice but to ignore the call and turn my phone off. He probably wanted to confirm what time he needed to pick me up from YVR, but he would just have to wait until I was done.

There was something about computer science that made it easy to slip into a flow state. I tuned everything else out, enjoying the challenge and the satisfaction that came whenever I got a question right. All those late nights spent studying had paid off. I could do this. There wasn't a doubt in my mind that I'd end up with the highest marks in my year. Everything I had learned over the last few years poured out of me and onto the page, showcasing not only everything I had absorbed, but everything I understood.

I finish one exam, and then another. I took great pride in walking out of the room first both times. Sure, I looked like a hotshot, but I'd *earned* the right to walk out with my head held high.

My first deep breath of winter air was exhilarating. I was finally free for the holidays. I couldn't wait to catch up with my family, to recount all the things I'd gotten up to. I fished my phone out of my pocket and turned it on. Dad would want to know my itinerary for tomorrow.

My phone blew up with alerts. Twenty missed calls from Mom. At least fifty unread messages from Lily.

Lily: ADDY.

Lily: ADDY ANSWER YOUR FUCKING PHONE.

Lily: IT'S DAD.

I dialed my sister's number. She answered immediately.

"Adelina, oh my God!" she sobbed into the receiver.

"What's going on?" I asked, chest painfully tight.

"Dad is . . . Dad had a heart attack at work. He was in the warehouse alone. When they finally found him—"

My heart sank into the pit of my stomach. A heart attack? No. No, that can't be. He called me a few hours ago. I swore I was going to get right back to him.

"Mom and I are at the hospital now," Lily said, breathless. Listening to her was surreal—my own voice delivering the terrible news. "Addy . . . he didn't make it."

"This is the last of his stuff," Bernice, one of the only full-time staff at the food drive, said as she helped pack up the box. Dad's office was empty, stripped of every trace of him. It had to happen at some point. It had been two weeks since the funeral, and the newly appointed drive coordinator was going to need the office space come the turn of the month.

"We're so sorry for your loss," Bernice said for the tenth time since Lily and I arrived. For what it was worth, Bernice seemed to be taking Dad's passing pretty hard too, but I was getting sick of people telling me they were sorry. Sorry for what? It wasn't *their* father they'd ignored. "Edwin was so loved by the community," she went on. "We're really going to miss him."

"Thank you," Lily said again.

I tuned out after that, their chatter nothing but a muffled sound in my ear. I combed through the box of Dad's things. Mostly desk accessories. Little things that brought this otherwise gray box of a room some much-needed color. Some succulents in small pots, a few crayon drawings that Lily and I drew for him when we were barely out of diapers . . . and a framed photo.

I picked it up and stared at it. It was of Mom, Dad, Lily and me on graduation day. Lily and I were dressed in our blue gowns, caps adorning our heads. We were all smiling at the camera in what I now realized was the last picture we all took together as a family.

A terrible sob punched its way up my throat, leaving my lungs empty and chest burning. I hadn't been able to cry at the funeral, but apparently *now* was when my tears decided to betray me. Guilt shredded me to the bone. What would have happened if I'd answered when he called? Why hadn't I spent more time with him while I had the chance?

"Adelina," Lily called to me softly. "Adelina, it's okay."

"I'm fine," I said shakily, swallowing my shame and anger and sorrow. I didn't want to feel like this, seconds away from drowning on dry land. It was too terrifying. Better to ignore it. Bury it deep. "I just need some fresh air," I said, pushing past my sister to leave.

It was one of those rare days where it was as sunny as could be, not a single gray cloud to be seen. What a cruel joke, to have such pleasant weather on such an awful day. Even the luxury of the crisp breeze did little to settle my nerves. I sat down on the curb just outside the building, too weary to do much else.

The sound of laughter caught my attention. There was nothing delightful about it. Grating and nasally and obnoxious. I looked up to find a group of teenage boys gathered around an expensive-looking car that sat askew in its parking lot stall. A couple of them sat on the hood, the others drinking out of soda cans. I didn't take issue with them being here. It was a free country. They were just hanging out.

(Though I would argue that there were better places than outside a food drive.) It's what they did next that pissed me off to no end.

They took their half-empty cans of soda, walked over to the donation bin that fed straight into the building's warehouse—

And poured the contents of their drinks inside. When they were done, they tossed the cans in too.

They all laughed, cackling like hyenas. Red-hot fury engulfed me. How could they do such a terrible thing? How could they treat this place—a place that Dad loved and tried so hard to do right by—with such disrespect?

"What the fuck are you guys doing?" I snapped, rushing toward them. "You can't do that."

"Oh, sorry," said one of the boys. Except he didn't *sound* sorry. He had a mess of dark-brown hair styled with too much product. The leader of this little gang, I had to assume. "I thought it was the trash."

"You have to clean this up," I demanded. "People need the food in there! Either clean it up or pay to have the food replaced."

He shrugged, unapologetic. "Not my problem." They started to turn away, laughing at me as they got into the brown-haired kid's car.

I was incensed. Did I need to call the cops? No, they probably wouldn't arrive in time. These brats were getting away scot-free.

But not if I could help it.

I memorized their license plate number before they managed to drive away. They messed with the wrong woman. I was hurting. Pissed. And, unlucky for them, I happened to have a can-do attitude.

CHAPTER THIRTY-TWO Full Steam Ahead

Adelina

Present Day
Nice, France

SUNRISE SNEAKS UP on us, the golden morning rays peeking in through the crack in the curtains. I'm not entirely sure how we wound up curled up together in my bed, surrounded by soft pillows, but I'm certainly not going to complain. I guess we got to make that pillow fort after all.

West and I lie facing each other, our hands clasped as the hum of the room's AC system covers our conspiratorial whispers. My eyes are puffy and scratchy. I normally would be embarrassed about last night, but I'm all cried out. Everything is finally off my chest.

I like that West is so easy to talk to.

"You know it wasn't your fault, right?" he murmurs, tracing the tips of my fingers with his own. "Whether you picked up the phone or not . . ."

"Yeah," I reply quietly. My head sinks against my pillow, too heavy to move an inch. "The month after the funeral was rough. I remember thinking, *What's the point*? I was miles from home trying to make my family proud, but now Dad was gone and . . . I don't know. Maybe I could have chosen a school closer to home. Spent more time with him. Concentrated on stuff that actually mattered.

I couldn't focus on any of my classes and wound up dropping out in my last semester."

"And by the sound of it, your mother must have been *thrilled*."

I huff a laugh. "I had to go to therapy to deal with the way she treated me. There's tough love, and there's whatever she's trying to do. All she seemed to care about was how embarrassing it was to have a dropout for a daughter. It was exhausting, dealing with her negativity. Cutting her off was the only thing I could do to protect myself."

West gives my hand a squeeze. "I'm glad you did."

I peer deeply into his eyes, bracing for some sort of punchline. It never comes. "You are?"

"Why do you sound so surprised?"

"Everyone in my life told me I was making a mistake. My aunts and uncles and cousins all sided with her. They asked me how I could treat my own mother that way, but . . ."

"But?" he prompts.

"None of them ever stopped to ask *why* I would treat her that way. They judged me. Called me selfish. Never once stopping to think maybe there was a reason I'd resort to something so drastic. And . . . I don't know. Sometimes I thought maybe they were right. They had my head so warped that *I* was the one who felt guilty."

"If someone slaps you every day and then blames you for leaving, *they're* the problem. Verbal and emotional abuse aren't any different."

"I know that now. It took me a really long time to come to terms with it. Still am, I think, but I'm getting better."

West shifts beside me, moving to hug me tight against his chest. His weight is comforting, tethering me to our little slice of reality. He presses a chaste kiss to my forehead. "I'm glad to hear it."

I melt against him, failing to remember the last time anyone held me so tenderly.

"What did you do about that kid? The one who was tossing garbage," West asks.

"Believe it or not, I almost didn't do anything. I was fuming for *days*. A quick Facebook search and I found him—Charlie Bower. Turns out, he was the kid of some hotshot tech CEO muscling his way into Vancouver. They lawyered up as soon as we tried to sue for damages. He was going to get away with it.

"Then the idea hit me while I was in the shower. People like that have more money than heart, so what if I . . . *relieved* some of their funds? Little enough that they won't miss it, but more than enough that it could help the drive. Everyone likes to preach kindness and taking care of their neighbors, but they never actually do anything. This way, I *was* doing something. Imagine my surprise when it not only worked, but I got away with it."

"And a new thief was born," he says, amused.

"It's not the most interesting villain origin story out there, but it's mine."

"Trust me, Adelina, you're no villain." West combs his fingers through my short hair. "The furthest thing from it."

I laugh softly. "I'll take your word for it."

"Thank you for telling me."

"Thank *you* for listening."

West cranes his head to glance at the clock on the bedside table. "We need to get to the hangar soon. How about I head downstairs and scrounge up some breakfast?"

"Are you sure that's a good idea?"

"Their continental spread not to your liking?"

I roll my eyes. "No, I mean going to the hangar to train. I kept you up all night."

West pumps his brows. "Yes, you did."

"You know what I mean." I push against his chest with a groan. "You're tired. You can't practice the route while sleep-deprived."

"I raised a six-year-old all by myself. I haven't known a full night's sleep in ages." West sits up, selfishly taking all of his warmth along with him. "Don't worry. Once you get a couple cups of coffee in me, I'll be wound up the whole day."

"Wonderful," I reply dryly. "Can't wait for your inevitable caffeine crash."

Only once he rolls out of bed do I finally turn over to find my phone crammed beneath my pillow. It's low on battery, but that's not what bothers me. I can see the scheduled text I have programmed sitting there, waiting to send. A cloying sensation simmers in my guts.

He watches me intently as I delete it right in front of him, along with the picture I took of his passport. "I don't need it anymore," I murmur.

West smiles, a mix of joy and gratitude, as he dips down to cup my face. "Thank you, mon ange," he says before giving me a deep, tender kiss. It's so sweet and appreciative and beholden that I could cry. I adore the way he holds me, looks at me, *talks* to me, like I'm something revered. "I'll be right back, okay?" he says, giving me a smile before leaving out the door.

I giggle to myself, curling up in his side of the sheets and surrounding myself in the scent of pine and fresh laundry. The bed's getting cold without him. Hopefully West comes back soon.

As I put my phone aside, I think back to what Mom said about Lily not returning her calls. Strange. I'm sure she's just busy. Or, short of that, maybe my sister is finally tired of putting up with Mom's behavior, too.

My familial problems can wait, though. Right now, I have more pressing matters to attend to.

"How long has he been at it?" Diana asks as she leans against my desk.

"All afternoon," I reply.

"Any progress?"

"He's managed to shave ten whole seconds."

"Not bad."

"But not great," I mumble. "Joseph's working on his distraction plan as we speak. We might be able to give West a wider window of opportunity."

It's at this exact moment that Joseph walks in with a large crate stuffed full of fireworks. Diana and I exchange weary glances. At this rate, we'll take whatever zany plot he can come up with.

My attention doesn't linger for very long, returning to West as he dashes through the obstacle course. He's getting impressively fast, each round offering some new insight on how he can improve his time. Practice makes perfect, though I'm beginning to fear it won't be enough.

"Time!" he exclaims as he comes flying over the finish line.

I hit the space bar on my computer, halting the program. I gawk at the results. "Holy shit."

"What is it?" he asks, panting.

"Two minutes and fifty-eight seconds!"

"Are you serious?"

"Yes!"

West laughs as he rushes over and picks me up out of my seat, spinning us around in utter delight. "I did it! I told you I could!"

I can't help but laugh too, his joy downright infectious. This means we have a chance.

Joseph groans. "Am I still going to be able to use all of these?" he asks, referring to his crate of explosives.

"We'll keep them on hand," Diana says. "You never know. West may end up with a leg cramp."

"I'll make sure to do my stretches," West says dryly.

Someone's phone rings, the sound interrupting our celebration. All four of us reach for our burners.

"It's mine," West says before answering. "Hello?"

I shiver when his smile fades, slowly twisting into a stern frown. West doesn't say anything, quiet the entire time until he finally nods and says, "Okay. Thank you."

"Who was that?" I ask.

"Allistair."

"Is everything okay?"

"Berruci has made unexpected plans to leave for Monaco tomorrow. Some sort of business trip. He'll be taking many of his personal guards with him, which means—"

"Which means this is our chance to strike," I conclude, my heart skipping.

I glance at Diana and Joseph. It's not the plan we've laid out, but having Berruci out of the picture greatly minimizes the risks West will have to face. There will no doubt still be guards to attend to, though the security will be more lax. There's no guarantee that nothing will go wrong, though.

"Is your virus ready?" he asks me.

"Yes. All you have to do is insert the USB."

West nods slowly. "Then there isn't any point in putting things off. We make our move tomorrow."

Joseph beams. "It's time to make some money."

CHAPTER THIRTY-THREE Like Thieves in the Night

Adelina

I'M NO STRANGER to high-pressure situations, but this really takes the proverbial cake. I knew this day would come, but now that it's at our doorstep, I find myself rethinking absolutely everything.

My virus is perfect. I've tested it over and over again, ironing out every little bug, optimizing every function. I've done everything that I can, my role for this reverse heist (as West once called it) officially fulfilled, yet I can't help but feel like there's more to do.

My laptop dings, the notification informing me that everything has been successfully uploaded to the USB. It's nothing out of the ordinary. Just your run-of-the-mill USB purchased from a local office supply store. After removing it (always be sure to safe-eject, people), I turn it about in my hand. It's wild to me how our entire plan hinges on something so incredibly small.

Taking a deep breath, I open the door to West's room, only to find him video calling someone. How inconsiderate of me. I really should have knocked.

"Sorry," I say in a rush. "I'll come back."

West waves me over, shaking his head as if to say *Don't worry about it*. "You got to play soccer at lunch?" he asks. "How was it?"

"It was fun!" Jack replies, bright and bubbly. "One of the boys scored on his own goal."

West laughs. "Oh, well. Mistakes happen."

"Who's that, Uncle West?"

I hold my breath. I'd been trying to stand out of frame, unwilling to disturb.

West grins up at me. "Would you like to say hi, Adelina?"

My heart skips. Being introduced to his kid feels like a huge deal. "If you're sure that's alright."

"Yeah. I want you to meet her."

My cheeks heat. In a strange way, I feel almost honored. Being introduced to his niece is no small thing.

I take a seat next to him on the edge of his bed. West tilts the phone and I suddenly come face-to-face with an adorable girl with bright-blonde hair and chubby cheeks. I know they're niece and uncle, but their resemblance to one another is uncanny. If West is the sun, then Jack is a dazzling smaller star.

"Hello," I say. "Your uncle has told me so much about you."

"How do you know Uncle West?"

"We, uh . . . work together."

Jack gasps. "You're a superspy, too?"

I give West a questioning look, to which he replies with an almost pleading expression. "That's right," I say slowly. "But you have to keep it a secret for us, okay? No one can know."

"Okay," Jack replies with a giggle. "When are you done with your mission?"

"Very soon, sweetie," West says. "Day after tomorrow, in fact."

Jack's face lights up. "Really?"

"Really, really. We'll be on the plane headed straight home afterward."

"Then we can all spend the day at the park together. Just like you promised?"

West nods. "That's right, kiddo. Now, make sure to eat your vegetables and brush your teeth really well. I'll be checking with Marley when we get back."

Jack sighs like she's just been assigned the most impossible task in the world. "Okay."

"I love you, Flapjack. I'll be home soon."

"I love you too."

When the call ends, I shake my head. "A superspy? Really?"

"What?" West says with a shrug. "It's a brilliant cover and I won't be told otherwise. If people ask her, they'll chalk it up to an overactive imagination. I can't have her telling everyone I'm a thief, now can I?"

"I guess you have a point." I laugh softly, handing him the USB. "Thirty seconds. It needs thirty seconds to upload. If you replicate your time from earlier, it won't be a problem. Plug it in and ditch it if you have to. The virus will take care of the rest."

"Thank you," West says warmly, pocketing the USB before taking my hand. "I have a favor to ask of you."

"I'm kind of in the middle of the last thing you wanted me to do."

West grins, but it quickly fades into something far more serious. I almost hate to see it. "If anything goes wrong tomorrow—"

I shake my head. "Stop it."

"Adelina." He stands and gives my hand a light squeeze. "If anything should happen to me tomorrow, I've opened an account under Jack's name. I've managed to squirrel away enough for her to live comfortably. Will you make sure she gets it?"

"West—"

"Please. You're the only one I trust to do this."

My throat closes up. The fact that he's telling me all this . . . I'm sure he's only being cautious, making the necessary preparations, but I don't like that he has to make them at all.

"It won't come to that," I say.

"If it does—"

"*If* it does, then yes. I'll handle it. But it won't come to that, right?"

He nods, bringing his free hand up to caress my cheek. "Right," he replies before leaning forward to kiss me.

But I pull back before he can. My guts are in knots and the world around us feels like it's about to fall apart. I crave the heat of his hands, eager to distract myself with his touch and smell and attention, but before I allow myself the chance to indulge, I need so much more.

"Promise me everything will be okay," I say.

"Adelina—"

"*Promise* me."

His brows furrow in thought. "I wouldn't want to lie to you."

My stomach flips. "That's not what I want to hear at all."

"I'm confident," he says quickly, like it's a consolation, "we've prepared the best we can."

I struggle to stand on bones made of jelly, making my way over to peek through the crack in the window curtains. The night is peaceful. Maybe a little too peaceful. In twenty-four hours' time, we'll be in the thick of it. I know West is right. We've done everything we can to give ourselves the best possible chance at success. We've planned, practiced . . . and now all that's left is the execution.

The bedsprings creak as West rises too, stepping forward to close the distance I've created. He wraps his strong arms around me from behind, dipping down slightly to press a tender kiss to the crook of my neck. "We've always been aware of the risks," he says.

"I know," I murmur, turning to face him. I rub my palms over his broad chest in slow circles, almost as though the gesture will somehow soothe my own anxiety. "It just *feels* real now, you know?"

"There's no point in worrying yourself sick over what may or may not happen. Focus instead on trusting me to see our plan through."

"I *do* trust you."

West nods slowly. He takes his thumb and lightly strokes my bottom lip, the warmth of his skin as comforting as it is tantalizing. "Will you let me take your mind off things? Don't think about tomorrow. Concentrate on me. On us."

My heart stutters for an entirely new reason. Caught beneath his heated gaze, I can't help but nod, the coil in the pit of my stomach growing tight. "Okay. Okay, I can do that."

He pushes his thumb forward and parts my lips. I obediently open my mouth, allowing him to press his thumb against the flat of my tongue. West smiles, something ravenous in his green eyes.

"Don't think," he commands, voice deliciously low. "Just get on your knees."

There's nothing forceful about his hold. Far from it. I'm free to move as I wish, but I won't. It's the implication of control that sends heat to pool between my legs. All I have to do is turn off my brain, finally allow myself to relinquish all my worries and stress. I trust West to take care of everything else.

I kneel before him, looking up expectantly. I dare to suck on his thumb, relishing the obvious strain against the front of his jeans.

"Undo my belt."

It's so easy to follow his instructions. Especially when he looks at me like that—like I could never do anything wrong. With slow, careful movements, I make quick work of his belt buckle and unzip the front of his pants. West is already hard, his want seeping through the cotton of his boxer briefs.

"Take my cock out, Adelina."

I squeeze my knees together and ignore the hot, throbbing sensation between my legs. Dear God, his voice is downright sinful.

And I fucking *love* it.

Hooking my thumbs over the band of his underwear, I do as I'm told. His cock springs free, long, swollen and weeping at the tip. An electric giddiness washes through me. On top of being kind, funny and frustratingly clever, *of course* he'd also be well-endowed. Whatever higher power there may be, they clearly have a favorite among mortals—and that would be Westley fucking Porter.

I lean forward, but West shakes his head and applies the faintest bit of pressure against my tongue with his thumb. I frown deeply, my confusion clear.

"I don't think you want it bad enough," he says with a chuckle, finally removing his hand so that I'm able to speak.

"You're a relentless tease," I grumble, wrapping my fingers around the base of his shaft. I give him a slow, deliberate stroke, enjoying the way West tilts his head back and moans.

"You like it."

"Maybe I do."

He combs his fingers through my short hair. "Go on then. I want to see you wrap those pretty lips around me."

Electricity crackles through my veins. I want that too. I want it so much that there isn't an inch of my body that doesn't ache.

I take him into my mouth slowly, losing myself in the heat of his skin and the weight of him in my hand and the low, satisfying rumble of his languid moan. Hollowing my cheeks, I suck in earnest, working my way down his length until I can't bear it anymore.

"Fuck," he hisses. He grips onto my hair at the roots, guiding my head until there's no question—he's fucking my mouth and undeniably enjoying it. "Adelina, you're a fucking *dream*."

His praise only serves to spur me on. I look up and find his eyes screwed shut, his muscles tense. So this is what it looks like when a man is clinging to the last remnants of his sanity. It never occurred to me just how powerful I could feel while on my knees, but now that I know, it's an addictive sensation. In this exact moment, I've forgotten all about what's to come tomorrow. What I need more than anything in the world is for West—this charming, handsome, wonderful man—to need me just as much.

My jaw aches. I can feel him swell against my tongue. Before I get the chance to drive him over the edge, West grasps my chin and takes a step back, leaving my mouth unbearably empty.

"Up," he demands. My God, could he sound more ruined?

West offers me his hands. No sooner am I on my feet than he brands me with a searing kiss. It's so intense that it knocks the air from my lungs and leaves my head spinning.

"Don't let go," I murmur against his lips. "Don't stop."

West deepens the kiss, his hands trailing down to grip either side of my waist. "Je n'en rêverais pas," he says. "I wouldn't dream of it."

I finally manage to gather the coordination needed to pull his shirt up and over his head, then drag my hands down the front of his chest, appreciatively stroking his beautiful tattoos. West uses my fleeting distraction to corral me up against the nearest wall, his deft hands making quick work of stripping me out of my clothes.

The cool air brushes my skin, sending a delightful shiver down my spine.

"Magnifique," he says, voice low against my ear. "Do you need me to translate that one for you too?"

I laugh, breathless, circling my arms around his neck. "I understand that one. Though you should probably keep it simple for me."

West lifts me up off the ground, and I instinctively wrap my legs around his hips. I've never felt closer to another person before, bare chest to bare chest. "Mon ange, ma chérie, mon amour. Me laisseras-tu te faire plaisir ce soir?"

I groan. "That's not simple at all."

West chuckles as he carries me to the bed, laying me down on the mattress with the utmost care. He kisses a line down my neck, trailing over my collarbone and the peaks of my breasts, teasing his way down my belly to then kneel by the bedside to press his lips to my inner thighs.

"Je veux te connaître."

"What does that mean?" I ask, already writhing beneath his touch.

"I want to know you."

"You already do."

"No, Adelina." West peers up at me from between my legs. The hunger in his eyes sends my heart skipping. "I want to know you in *every* sense of the word. Will you let me?"

My cheeks warm. It should be illegal, the way he talks. "Yes, please," I reply.

I can feel his smile against my skin, his greedy fingers holding my hips in place as he proceeds to tease with the tip of his tongue. Pleasure surges through my veins, crackling arcs of lightning hopping up my spine. He is relentless in the best of ways, applying pressure one second only to ease off the next, experimenting to find what my body appreciates best but my mind has never truly understood. My unfortunate first experience was *nothing* compared to this. I think I'm well within my rights to consider this a mulligan.

Tension builds in my belly. My pleasure is a pressure cooker, building with such startling intensity that it isn't long before everything comes to a sudden release. My back arches as I grip the sheets for some illusion of stability, my cry of ecstasy loud enough to rattle the walls. A euphoric haze washes over my mind, bringing with it a gratifying buzz through the tips of my fingers and toes.

West rises to his feet, leaving me for an instant to retrieve something from his suitcase in the corner of the room. It's almost embarrassing how badly I miss him despite the fact that he's only a few feet away. I crave his touch, need his smile, yearn for his soft whispers against my skin.

"What are you looking for?" I ask.

He holds up a pack of condoms and throws me a cheeky, nearly smug wink. "Did a little shopping after the last time we fooled around. Hope I wasn't being too presumptuous."

I don't bother fighting my smile. "Not at all."

When West finally returns, I happily comb my fingers through his hair, stroking my thumbs over his jawline. His face is a bit rough with stubble, but I find that I enjoy the friction.

"Will you go slowly?" I ask sheepishly. "Only at first. It's been—well, you know—forever."

The next kiss he gives me is so achingly gentle that it's almost enough to break my heart. Who gave this man the right to be so sweet, so kind? It's a kiss that tells me everything I need to know, yet he tells me anyway.

"Je prendrai soin de toi." West smiles and, not for the first time, I find myself staring in awe up at the sun. "I will take care of you," he translates.

And take care of me he does.

Settling between my thighs, he aligns himself, pressing the tip of his cock against my entrance. There's a bit of pressure, a pinch, but he spoils me with a flurry of light, apologetic kisses.

"Bear with me, love. You're doing great."

I circle his neck with my arms, holding him as close as I'm able. *Vulnerable* doesn't even begin to capture what I feel right now. But I trust West. I trust him so much.

His movements are slow, every touch soft. If I were a painting, I would be a watercolor, all of his strokes careful and executed with undeniable lightness. Even his words of praise, secrets whispered to me in both French and English, are a tea steeped with honey.

"Tu es si belle."

"West—"

"C'est bon, ça?"

I moan, a high and breathless sound.

He nibbles on my bottom lip. "Chante pour moi."

All of a sudden and all at once, pleasure erupts from deep within my core. I am drunk and high and on another plane of existence, briefly forgetting all earthly worries. I tremble in his arms, drowning in wave after wave of ecstasy. He kisses me through the crest and then the descent, nothing but light giggles and lazy smiles between us. Just when I think we might be done—

He flips me onto my stomach.

CHAPTER THIRTY-FOUR
Language Lessons

West

"WE'RE NOT FINISHED," I say before I grab Adelina roughly by the hips and bury myself deep inside, pinning her against the mattress with my weight. "That was just a warm-up."

She moans, gripping the sheets as I set a slow pace. *Infuriatingly* slow, because after weeks of stifling tension, I fully intend to make the most of tonight. I'll stretch every second into an hour if I have to. There's no telling what tomorrow will bring, but there's one thing I'm certain of: I have a beautiful woman in my bed, and I'm going to savor every moment she's willing to give me.

"Fuck, Adelina. You feel so good."

"West, I—"

"Yes, angel?"

She wiggles her ass against me, whining with need. "I need *more*."

Using my knee to spread her legs farther out, I help myself to a new, deeper angle. I dip low and murmur against her ear, "Anything for you."

I drive myself deeper, intoxicated by the softness of her body and the way my fingers leave an impression on her skin. Her walls clench around my cock, every thrust met with the slap of skin and the creak of the bed beneath us.

"Faster," Adelina pleads. "West—*faster*."

"I don't know. Do you deserve it?"

Adelina whines against the sheets but doesn't reply. It upsets me that her answer isn't immediate. It should be more than obvious. I can tell she's thinking again, caught up in that brain of hers.

I roll my hips against her. "Then answer is *yes*, Adelina. Say it."

"I . . ."

"Say '*I deserve it.*'"

"I deserve it," she echoes, breathless.

"'*I deserve to feel good.*'"

"I deserve to"—I thrust into her hard, her voice coming out as a squeak—"to feel good."

"'*I'm beautiful.*'"

She huffs a laugh. "A little full of yourself, huh?"

"Adelina."

"I'm beautiful," she whispers.

"And '*I'm perfect.*'"

Adelina grows quiet at this, leaving me no choice but to reach around and grasp her by the chin, turning her head so I can look at her. Her eyes are glassy with brewing tears, her brows stitched together in doubt.

"I don't—"

"Would I lie to you?"

"No."

"Then *say it.*"

She takes a deep breath. "I'm perfect."

I nod, rewarding her with a kiss. "Yes, you fucking are."

My pace increases, a growing crescendo that brings with it an untamable wildfire. I chase her pleasure, feeling the way her body trembles and her breathing grows tight as I push her over the edge, her euphoric cry music to my ears. She's unlocked something inside of me. A hunger, a desire—something so intense and feral it almost scares me. I knew this was going to be a problem. I *knew* that if I had a taste, I would never be able to get enough.

"Two," I rasp before I stand and drag her to the edge of the bed.

"West, what—"

I give her no time to rest, roughly turning her onto her side and lifting her right leg over my shoulder. She could be a work of art, what with her mussed hair, skin glistening with sweat, and her face twisted up in sweet agony. My beautiful girl is painfully close, so I drop a hand down to draw tight circles against her clit. Her mouth falls open and her eyes roll back. This time, she comes with a silent scream.

"Three," I announce proudly.

Her chest rises and falls rapidly. "What are you counting?"

I smile. I'm sure she'll figure it out.

Gathering her up in my arms, I lift her off the bed. Adelina wraps her legs around me, making it easier for me to carry her to the nearest wall and fuck her up against it. Rough. Unrelenting. She kisses me hard enough to leave my lips bruised. I'm sure we're going to piss off the neighbors, but to hell with it. If all goes according to plan, we won't be here tomorrow to receive their complaints.

"West, I don't think I can—"

"Yes, you can. Can you give me one more, love?"

She makes a noise that sounds a lot like *okay*, but it's hard to tell when I'm too busy exploring her mouth with my tongue. I take her back to bed, surrounding her in soft pillows and warm sheets because she deserves nothing less. I return to taking things slow, our bodies so entwined it's difficult to tell where I stop and she begins.

She takes me so well. Every time I thrust into her, I hope she understands what it means. No matter where, no matter when—she is mine, mine, *mine*.

This time when she reaches the peak, I'm right there with her. We fall over the edge, wrapped up so tightly in each other's arms that the rest of the world may as well not exist. Nothing else matters except our heavy breaths and racing hearts.

"West," she says my name, combing her fingers through my hair. It's all she can say. Again and again, better than any song or sweet prayer.

"Hold on to me, baby. I've got you."

I gingerly carry her to the bathroom and set her down on the edge of the tub, quick to fill it with warm water. I hold on to her hand the entire time as steam fills the small room, the calm that settles over us the closest my heart has felt to peace in years. When the bath is ready, we slip into the water together, her back flush against my chest.

"How do you feel?" I ask as I reach for the shampoo. I take great pleasure in washing and rinsing her hair, loving the smile that spreads across her lips.

"Good. A little sore, but really good. *Tired.*"

"Shame to think we could have been doing this the whole time."

Adelina laughs softly. "Yeah."

I dip down to press my lips to her shoulder. If only this night wouldn't end. Maybe I could hide her away here, keep her to myself forever. Make love to her, fuck her, savor every inch of her skin for as long as I live and breathe.

"How do you say '*don't worry*' in Chinese?" I ask after a long while.

"Oh, my Cantonese is terrible, I don't think—"

"I want to learn. Can you teach me?"

She pauses, searching for the words. "I think it's . . . *mm sai daam sam.* How do you say it in French?"

"Ne t'inquiète pas."

She turns to face me, water sloshing with her movements, and brings her fingers up to smooth the small furrow between my brows. I can't help but smile. Does she have any idea how far gone for her I am? "Ne t'inquiète pas," she repeats.

I press a kiss to her forehead. "Mm sai daam sam."

At no point during the rest of the night do we dare bring up what's to come tomorrow. For now, we have this. That's more than enough.

CHAPTER THIRTY-FIVE
This Is What I Would Call a Pickle

West

"WATCHES SYNCED?" I ask Joseph, triple-checking the one wrapped around my wrist. "I'll enter the villa on the hour after the patrol passes. I'll need you at the pickup point in—"

"I know, old friend," Joseph says with a chuckle. "You can count on me."

"The ladies are all set up?"

"They're in the other rental five clicks that way," he informs, pointing. "Allistair is working on getting her hooked up to the external cameras, but from that point on, you're on your own."

I rub a hand over my chest, hoping to dry my palms. There's no point in being nervous. This is what everything has been building up to, and I'm as prepared as I'll ever be.

"Let's get rich," I say.

Joseph grins, conspiratorial. "Let's get rich."

With one final breath and a moment to steel myself, I turn and start toward the outer perimeter of the villa. It's so much more ostentatious than the model we set up at the hangar. Although it's the middle of the night, Berruci's property is illuminated by exterior lights bordering all the stone paths. To make matters worse, his team of guard dogs have been set loose to run amok in the backyard, blocking me from drawing any closer to my planned point of entry.

No matter. I came prepared courtesy of Allistair's intel.

I climb over the high garden hedge and land on the manicured lawn with a soft thud. The dogs notice me almost immediately, their hackles raised as they flash their sharp teeth, low growls coming to a crescendo in the backs of their throats. With my hands already flying to my pockets, I pull out the bits of dried steak Allistair recommended I pack and toss them their way, praying it will be enough to ingratiate them to my presence. Short of that, it will buy me a few precious seconds before they maul me to death.

Thankfully, the treats do the trick. I'm able to sidle past toward the west-facing window on the ground floor without a hitch. Allistair has already left it unlocked—all according to plan. I lift the window open and squeeze through. The moment my feet hit the ground, muscle memory locks in.

I sprint down the hall at top speed, the surrounding air screaming past my ears as I take a hairpin turn to the right. I'm through the west wing in under thirty seconds, dashing through the main foyer like a sudden breeze, no trace of me left behind. Somewhere up above, I hear voices and heavy footsteps. No doubt the guards on their rounds on the second floor. They'll be sweeping through the main floor soon. All the more reason to haul ass.

Three minutes left. Almost there. I'm cutting it close, but we all knew that would be the case.

I get to the staircase leading down into the bunker, ignoring the cold sweat dripping down my back. The flight has fifteen steps. During practice, I was able to jump the final five. With the clock counting down, I decide to try my luck with six.

Rolling to spread out my momentum, I land with the tiniest twinge in my lower back and crack in my knees. Not bad for a retiree like me. I might have shaved two seconds, though this is hardly the time to celebrate. I make a break for the door at the very end of the hall, pulling my phone out to confuse the lock's RFID—using the very same program Adelina used to break into my hotel room in Vancouver. Extra points for recycling.

The lock beeps, the little indicator light blinking green. I breathe a tight sigh of relief. Oh, Adelina, you beautiful genius.

Ninety seconds remaining.

I push the door open and step into the dark bunker, the thick concrete walls making the air around me both cold and thick. There is nothing save for the sound of my labored breathing and the electronic whine of a single LCD desktop screen across the room, a computer and its giant server connected to it.

This is it. Every ounce of dirt on Berruci is on that computer. Without a moment's hesitation, I dash forward and jam the USB into the server's closest available port.

Thirty seconds. It needs thirty seconds to upload.

The lights snap on, leaving me blind. I stumble forward, feeling around aimlessly as my vision struggles to adjust to the burning brightness. Someone grabs me from behind, locking their arm around my throat. I surge back, driving my elbow into their gut, but they don't budge. I've been caught.

Shit. Fuck.

How the hell did this go downhill so fast? Our whole plan hinged on a seamless infiltration and extraction to avoid the possibility of a confrontation. I was supposed to be a ghost, not a fighter. Brute force was never an option. There's no way the patrol managed to catch up to me that quickly, and I'd have seen them come through the door. Whoever this is was lying in wait. They *knew* I was coming—but how?

A flood of memories threatens to drown me. This is just like last time. But how is that possible? It's hard to think now that my windpipe is being crushed, and I have no choice but to throw plan A out the window and set it on fire.

It's time to improvise.

I drive my elbow back again, this time as high as I'm able, in order to catch my assailant in the nose. He staggers back, releasing me from his chokehold. I twist around, getting a good look at him as I throw the meanest left hook I can manage. It's one of Berruci's personal guards.

No. No, if he's here, that means—

I take a hit to the face. Stars splash across my vision. I suddenly realize that we're not the only ones in the room. I count four—maybe even five—of Berruci's strongest men. It's a dogpile. No matter how hard I struggle, I can't win the upper hand. My arms are wrenched behind my back and I'm forced to my knees, pinned in place by their weight. Someone grabs me by the hair and forces me to look up.

My eyes land on Berruci as he yanks the USB out of the computer, glaring at the little device with a sneer. Dammit. Has it been thirty seconds? I wasn't counting. I have no way of knowing if Adelina's code injected itself.

He clicks his tongue and moves to stand across the room, behind someone tied to an office chair. Berruci turns it, the wheels squeaking with the movement. Sitting before me is a woman. It takes me a moment to register her face. I think I might be sick.

"Adelina?" I croak.

Except it isn't her. The woman looks exactly like her, but her sleek black hair is long and flowing. Not Adelina—but her *twin*. Lily looks unharmed. A little rattled and teary-eyed, but alright on the whole.

"What the hell is going on?" Lily asks, trembling. "Who are you? How do you know my sister?"

"A commendable effort, dear boy," Berruci says with an air of calm. "And here I thought you would have learned your lesson after your first spectacular failure."

All I can do is stare at him in disbelief. Why is he here? How does he know about Lily? A cold dread filters through my heart. Someone betrayed us, told Berruci about our plans. It had to have been Allistair. He must have chickened out at the last possible moment and played a triple-cross, setting me up to believe that Berruci was out of the country only to catch me by surprise.

"I know what you're thinking," he says smugly. "You're trying to figure out who ratted you out. I'm a little disappointed you didn't realize sooner."

This is bad. This is really, *really* bad. I don't think there's anything I can say or do in this moment that will get me out of this situation alive, but I try anyway.

"Let the girl go," I say. "She's got nothing to do with this."

"I know," he replies. "But her sister does, and I'm very much looking forward to meeting her."

A terrible pressure pulsates behind my eyes. Berruci knows about Adelina. But how can that be? Allistair was never formally introduced to her, and she never once mentioned her name to Diana or Joseph. My theory crumbles before my very eyes.

Behind me, the security door beeps. Shoes clack against the polished tile, one foot heavier than the other. I crane my neck to see none other than Joseph, wearing a smile so smug I want to knock it straight off his face. Following hot on his tail are two patrol guards, Allistair in their custody. They have his hands handcuffed behind his back, his purpling eye a testament to the fight he put up before his capture.

"How?" I demand, sick to my stomach. "*Why?*"

"Joseph informed me there was a mole hiding under my roof," Berruci explained. "But he didn't have a name. So I devised a plan to snuff them out. I told my guards that I'd be making a last-minute trip out of the country, giving a different location to each. I had no doubt that the snitch would share this window of opportunity with you. Allistair called you, didn't he? Told you I'd be flying out to Monaco. Joseph reported back to me immediately, and that's how I sniffed him out."

I grit my teeth. Damn, that's . . . actually really clever. I genuinely didn't think Berruci was capable of an intelligent thought, let alone such a devilish trick.

"Sorry, old friend," Joseph says, though he doesn't sound particularly sorry at all. "Don't worry. Adelina will be joining us shortly."

I glare at him. "How did you . . ."

"You weren't as careful as you thought. You let her name slip right in front of me and didn't even notice. All I had to do was use my network—"

"Fuck your network," I hiss.

"—and see what came up. Since I knew Adelina went to MIT, it was a simple thing to pull up the enrollment lists. Even found an article online with her posing with some robotics team. And then Diana let me know she had a sister. After that, all I had to do was search her up on Instagram. Imagine my delight when I discovered her feed was full of geotagged images a skip away in Barcelona."

I grit my teeth. Goddamn *geotagging*—the stalker's favorite tool.

"Why?" I bite out viciously. "Why did you do it?"

He shrugs casually. "When someone offers you a better deal, you take it."

"It's always about the money for you."

"I was always up-front about that."

"Six years ago . . . were you the one who sold us out? You've been on Berruci's payroll the whole time?"

"Not the *whole* time," Joseph says. "When it became clear I wouldn't be getting any more jobs out of you, I thought . . . what the hell? Let's go with the guy who's willing to offer me a better payday."

I want to scream, rage simmering beneath the surface of my skin. "You could have turned us in at any point. Revealed our hotel or ambushed us at the hangar. Why didn't you?"

Joseph scratched his jaw, contemplative. "Why go through the trouble? Our failed attempt to nab Adelina already had you both spooked. Didn't want to risk having you two bail altogether. You were going to deliver yourself to Berruci anyway, so I figured I'd save myself the trouble."

"Where's your honor?" I snarl through gritted teeth.

"Grow up, Mathieu. That's not a thing."

Berruci chuckles. "Desperation is a good look on you." He steps out from around Lily's chair and makes his way over, daring to crouch in front of me. "I gave you one simple task: find me the hacker who stole my money. But you couldn't even do that. No, you had to get smart. Try to turn this into a scheme. Once a thief, always a thief, hm?" He reaches into his pocket and pulls out his phone, opening it up to show me a handful of pictures he has saved on his camera roll. He holds it up in a twisted version of show-and-tell.

The first picture is of me and Adelina working together in the hangar. The second is of us at a distance, speaking together on the train from Paris to Nice. The last one is of us together in the hotel suite in Paris, Adelina helping tend to my bloody nose. All the air rushes out of the room. I thought we had been alone then. Joseph had yet to arrive, which means . . .

"Diana took those?" I ask, though a part of me already knows. "She's in on it too."

"It was her idea, actually," Joseph replies. "When she called me to tell me about the job you were putting together, I thought she was joking. You didn't just leave me behind, Mathieu. You left *her* to rot in jail. I likely wouldn't have agreed to work with you again, but she insisted. I'd never seen that woman more determined to screw you over. Hell hath no fury, am I right?"

"But *you* betrayed her."

"Yeah. But she doesn't know that."

"I thought you cared about her."

Joseph's expression softens, but only slightly. "I *do* care. Once you're in the ground, Diana will never have to know that I was the one who sold her out."

My heart thuds loudly against my rib cage, and I'm unable to concentrate on anything other than the fact that Adelina is with Diana right now. She's in danger.

"Leave them out of this," I plead. "Punish me however you see fit but let Adelina and her sister go."

Berruci clicks his tongue. "You're in no position to be making deals."

"Please. I'll do anything."

He chuckles. "That's exactly what your brother said."

My stomach twists. I'm drowning in cold sweat. Things weren't supposed to end like this. What will happen to Adelina? To Jack?

"Are you going to do to me what you did to him?" I ask, my voice hoarse. "Dump my body in the ocean? Throw me in a ditch somewhere?"

Berruci *laughs*. It's a low, menacing cackle that makes my skin crawl. "You think that's what happened to Michael? No, dear boy. I plan on making good use of you the same way I did your brother."

I frown. "What?"

He gestures to the bunker at large. "Who do you think I got this idea from? I know you believe me to be some unhinged maniac, but I'm clever—"

"Not to mention boastful."

Berruci grabs me roughly by the chin, digging his fingers into my cheeks. "I learn from my mistakes. After you tried to steal from me the first time, I thought to myself . . . how do I protect my assets from conniving rats like you? By *thinking* like a thief. Or, more accurately, hiring one on as a consultant."

My jaw drops. Several thoughts race through my mind: Was that really the deal Michael struck with Berruci to ensure clemency for Jack and me? Was he really the one responsible for the construction of Berruci's underground bunker? And most importantly . . .

"Is he still alive?" I ask breathlessly. "Tell me."

"Shall I bring him in?" Berruci asks with a cruel smile. Responding to a quick wave of his hand, a few of his guards leave only to return moments later, roughly shoving a man into the room.

I recognize his eyes first. They're green, just like mine, though where they once had a fiery spark, they now hold a heavy dimness. His blond hair has turned completely gray at the temples, the fine lines at the corners of his eyes and upon his brow physical proof of how much time has passed. He's lost a great deal of his bulk, appearing much smaller than I remember. Standing before me is a ghost of a man, a shell, but there's no denying what my eyes struggle to comprehend.

My big brother, Michael, alive and in the flesh.

I can't believe it. I don't know whether to laugh or cry or some strange combination of both. It almost seems like a cruel tragedy for Berruci to reveal him to me now that all hope is so clearly lost. Knowing him, that's probably *why* he does it.

"I thought I told you to stay out of trouble," Michael grumbles. He doesn't sound angry, but he isn't over the moon with joy to see me either.

"And I thought you were dead," I mutter back.

"Tie them up," Berruci orders his men. "When Diana finally brings Ms. Choi, it'll be a family reunion."

I grit my teeth. "If you so much as lay a finger on her I'll—"

"You'll what?" he challenges. "There's nothing you can do. Face it, West. You've *lost*."

CHAPTER THIRTY-SIX

An Object in Motion Will Stay in Motion

Adelina

CONFESSION: I THINK I'm going to barf.

There's a reason why I've never been super into sports (either participating in or observing). The anxiety of not knowing how things will pan out, mixed with the incessant little voice in the back of my head telling me my team has to win at all costs, inevitably leaves my nerves feeling like chewed-up bubble gum.

I check the clock on the electric car's dashboard, trying to remember what it was like to breathe without this crushing weight on my chest. Diana sits behind the wheel, looking ahead and appearing as intense as ever. It's only been three minutes. West still has time.

"God, I can't stand this," I grumble.

Diana says nothing. I'm sure she's just as stressed as I am. And she probably doesn't want to talk about it any more than I do.

Mm sai dam saam.

I count my lucky stars that it's all quiet. Quiet means we're still in the clear. No sirens, no alarms. Maybe West and Joseph are already making their miraculous getaway. I just have to put my faith in West to see this job through.

Click.

"Put your hands where I can see them."

I turn, straining against my seat belt, swallowing hard when I find myself staring down the barrel of a gun. Diana has a pistol in my face, the hammer pulled back and her finger curled around the trigger.

I fucking *knew* it. Vindication would feel so good right now were I not about to eat lead.

"That's terrible trigger discipline," I say dryly.

"Shut up."

"I know we never really got along, but this is low, even for you."

"It's nothing personal."

"But what about West?"

"West and his harebrained schemes are the reason why I was locked away in prison while my father lay dying in a hospital bed." Diana's nostrils flare, a fire burning behind her dark eyes. "I could have been there for him, but because West screwed up—because he *abandoned* us and let us take the fall—I couldn't even attend my own father's funeral. Do you have any idea how that feels?"

My mouth goes dry. I *do* know how that feels, to not be there for family in a time of great need. And while I'm not unsympathetic, there are risks to this kind of work. Diana should have known that going in. I'm positive that West never intended for anyone to take the fall, but I have a feeling that telling her this may be the fastest way to end up with a bullet in my brain.

"Let's just stay calm," I say evenly. "West didn't do anything, Diana. He told me what happened that night. He had nothing to do with it."

"Of course you'd believe him. You're too emotionally involved."

"It's the *truth*."

"Quiet—"

"Just put the gun away, alright? This night doesn't have to end in murder."

"Stop. Talking." Her grip around the gun is so tight, I can hear the metal rattling. "I'm not going to kill you. Berruci wants to talk to you first."

"Why?"

She shrugs. "None of my business. He only told me to bring you in unscathed."

"You've been working for him this whole time?" I set my jaw, unable to think over the roar of blood past my ears. Slowly but surely, I put the pieces together. "You were the one who sent those men after me. And those outdated blueprints . . . Joseph gave us those on purpose. You're working together."

"You're too damn smart for your own good," she says.

I shake my head, silently fuming. As disappointed as I am with Diana, I'm mostly upset with myself for not seeing it sooner. The signs were all there; I just hadn't bothered to look close enough.

"There are zip ties in the glove compartment," Diana says. "Open it slowly and put them around your wrists."

"And then what happens?"

"I'm going to take you straight to Berruci."

"What about West?"

"Joseph has already taken care of him."

That could mean anything. West could be captured. Hurt. *Dead.*

A shudder passes through me. No. No, I won't even consider the possibility. What I need to do right now is *think*. If I let Diana take me to Berruci, I'm as good as done for. If I try to fight Diana, I risk being shot. There aren't very many options, but I would rather take my chances here than in Berruci's clutches.

Diana doesn't look like much of a fighter. To be fair, neither am I, but a cornered animal is by far the most dangerous kind. The fact that we're trapped in the same car together is both an advantage and a disadvantage. She's at point-blank range but has limited mobility, her arm tucked up close to her body to keep her aim true. How does she plan on driving us to the villa when she's so preoccupied with keeping an eye on me?

The car.

It's practically full to bursting with circuits that make up its onboard computer—a computer I can *hack*. My laptop is literally in my backpack on the floor by my foot. This is going to be dicey, but I'm not going to lie down and let Diana walk all over me.

Slowly, I move as though I'm going to open the glove compartment. Diana's like a hungry hawk watching skittish prey, her gaze hot enough to brand my skin. I find the thick black zip ties in question, but instead of putting them on . . .

I swing my arm up and knock the gun away with all the force I can muster. It goes off, a terrible ringing screaming in my ear. Or maybe I'm the one who screams. It's hard to tell with the adrenaline overriding my system. The bullet hits the passenger-side window, shards of glass shattering everywhere, but the gun blessedly falls from Diana's hand somewhere into the back seat.

She's too stunned to move. Good. Her shock is my advantage. I snatch her wrist and pull her forward, cramming her arm through the steering wheel. I pull back hard on her hand and hug it to my chest, forcing her elbow to lock painfully.

"Let go of me!" she shrieks.

I apply more pressure. "Move and I'll break your arm!"

She doesn't listen. Diana claws at my face and my hair with her free hand. She struggles against my hold, but I don't let go.

"What are you going to do now?" Diana demands. "We're stuck like this, idiot. The moment you let go, I'm going to shoot you."

Using the tip of my foot, I lift my backpack up by the strap and all but shove my hand inside, pulling out my laptop to roughly set it down on the dashboard. It's a trial and a half just to get it open with the way she's fighting me. I mis-click twice, nearly exiting out of the program. I can't be sure if I'm typing the code in correctly, or if it's a jumbled mess.

I slam my fist down on Enter.

The engine rumbles to life all on its own.

Diana freezes, gawking at me.

"Here's another demonstration for you, bitch."

"Adelina, wait—"

With a quick press of the space bar, I run the next command. The car puts itself in drive and begins to accelerate down the street. It picks up speed, the air around us rushing over the hood. Diana screams bloody murder as we go careening, hopping the curb to crash head-on into a tree, the motion throwing my laptop off the dash and sending it tumbling to the floor. The edge of its hard case nails me in the shins hard enough that something cracks. I release Diana's arm at the last possible moment, allowing her to bring her arms up to protect her head, just in time for the airbags to go off with a loud *bang*.

In the same way I understand the physics behind flight, I also understand the fundamental forces at work when it comes to a car crash. It's not the impact but the abrupt stop in your momentum that hurts like hell. I only managed to get us up to twenty-five miles per hour, but the resulting inertia is still enough to do some serious damage. Praise be to the inventor of the seat belt, because while I do end up hitting my head against the airbag, I know it could have been *so* much worse.

I also know it was reckless, but I'm of the mind that if it works, it *works*.

It takes me a moment to collect myself, and to bring my hands up to check for any substantial injuries. I'm numb, for the most part, definitely in shock. I'm sure I'll be in a whole world of pain later.

Beside me, Diana groans. Still alive, thank goodness, but out for the count.

Kicking the passenger-side door open, I stumble out and fall onto my hands and knees, mildly disoriented and *very* rattled. I check my laptop over hastily. Apart from a small crack in the upper right corner of the screen, it still works.

In the distance, I hear sirens. Someone's called the police. I need to get out of here before someone spots me. For a moment, I consider grabbing Diana's gun, but it's a mess in the car and I can't risk leaving fingerprints all over a weapon. Besides, my laptop is far more dangerous than any gun.

Still buzzing with adrenaline and roaring for a fight, I start in the direction of the villa.

This heist has just turned into a rescue mission.

CHAPTER THIRTY-SEVEN

I'm a Damsel and I'm in Distress

West

"I CAN'T BELIEVE you're alive," I mumble for the umpteenth time. Now that we're all bound to chairs, Berruci and his men pay us little mind, huddled together as they no doubt discuss their nefarious plans for us. We pose no threat tied up like this and are therefore not worth their attention.

Michael sighs heavily, the dark circles under his eyes betraying how rough the years have been on him. "You shouldn't have come here. The only reason I took Berruci's deal was to keep you two safe."

"By *working* for him?"

"It could have been worse."

"What does he have you do?"

"Construction, mostly. I draw up plans to make his homes throughout Europe secure enough to withstand police raids. He has me consult too."

"Consult?"

"He's got a big empire, little brother. Berruci is always hungry for the next scheme. Every power grab he's orchestrated in the last six years was heavily influenced by me." A terrible, cold look of guilt fills his eyes when he catches me staring, aghast. "Don't look at me like that. I either lent my expertise, or he'd kill me."

I sit there, crushed by the heavy silence that follows. I think I understand. Michael didn't have a choice. For him, it was a matter of survival. Of getting through to the next day in one piece. It was smart of Berruci, in a way, to use Michael's mind and unique background to do all the hard work.

"Do you know a way to get us out of here?" I ask.

My brother shakes his head. "There's an exit through a small corridor that leads out to the waterfront, but we're outnumbered and they're blocking the way."

What a travesty, to be offered a glimpse of hope only to have it dashed mere moments later.

I look to Allistair, who has been roughly yanking at the bindings around his wrists. All to no avail. "Why wasn't Michael's information included in the personnel files you gave me? It would have been useful to know he was here."

Allistair frowns. "Don't blame me. I gave you everything I could get my hands on."

"Berruci keeps me in the guest house," Michael explains. "Never lets me leave. I don't ever interact with the guards. One of the house chefs brings me food, and that's about it."

I huff bitterly. To think we were in the same place at the same time, but I never knew . . .

"Did you ever try to reach out?"

"Once," he says. "Nearly got caught. Realized it was probably better this way."

"How can you say that? I thought . . . God, Michael. I thought you were *dead*."

"I couldn't risk your safety. My *daughter's* safety."

Guilt festers in the pit of my stomach. I get it. At least, I think I do. If our positions were switched, I'd probably think the same.

"How is she?" Michael asks quietly, almost tentatively. "Jacqueline."

"She's good," I reply. "An absolute angel. She just started first grade."

There's a warm glimmer in my brother's eyes. Unmistakable pride with a trace of longing. "I see."

"We're going to get out of this. You'll get to see each other really soon. I promise."

"Um," a woman's soft voice interjects. Lily's gaze shifts warily between Michael, Allistair and me. "Not to butt in or anything, but what the fuck is going on? Who are you people? Why on earth am I here and how the hell do you know Addy?"

"Addy?" I echo, as amused as I can be considering the circumstances. "Oh, that's cute."

Lily furrows her brows, and it's astounding just how much she looks like Adelina. Her features are a bit softer, in a weird way. She's bright-eyed and has nowhere near the same chaotic energy I've come to adore. "Look, I'm really scared. They grabbed me off the street in Barcelona and won't tell me anything. Is my sister okay? What kind of trouble is she in? What's all this crap about being thieves?"

My chest tightens. "It's a lot to explain."

"Then you'd better fucking *try*."

Man, these Choi sisters are really something else. What am I supposed to say? Telling Lily the truth would only leave Adelina exposed. I could always try to spin a tale, but Lily's already heard more than enough. She likely wouldn't believe my lies.

"Adelina is a hacker," I say slowly. "One of the finest out there. The best, in my opinion. I . . . sort of blackmailed her into working with me."

"And they took me because I'm—what? Collateral?"

"Really? No pushback on the whole hacker thing, huh?"

Lily rolls her eyes. "I know my sister better than anyone. Given her highly specialized skill set, it wasn't that far-off a conclusion. Companies contract people to test their security systems all the time. I logically assumed that's how Addy was making ends meet. I wasn't aware she was dabbling in . . . morally questionable freelance work."

"'*Morally questionable freelance work*'? You sound like a lawyer."

"Where is she?" Lily asks, slapping me with another hard question.

"I don't know."

"What do you mean you don't know?"

If what Joseph said was true—that he and Diana have been plotting to turn us in to Berruci—there's a good chance Diana has already made her move. If not, then she'll definitely act soon. I wish there was a way I could warn Adelina, keep her out of harm's way. When we agreed to this whole sordid ordeal, I promised she wouldn't see any of the action. She was meant to be behind the scenes, not thrown into the thick of it.

"I'm sure she's fine," I say. "They would have already brought her in by now if they had her. We need to focus on getting out of here."

"The grounds are crawling with guards," Michael says. "Even if we manage to free ourselves, there's no way we can fight our way through. Berruci has informants all over Nice too. There isn't a corner of this city he won't have eyes on."

I bite down on my tongue, trying to still my racing mind. There has to be a way out of this. There always is. But the longer I dwell on our chances of escape, the more I realize how hopeless it is. Berruci has us right where he wants us. Joseph and Diana played their parts perfectly. Being a thief requires incredible luck, and I'm afraid that mine has finally turned against me. We don't stand a chance in a fight, and I sincerely doubt that Berruci will entertain the idea of striking another deal with me after I so blatantly tried my hand against him.

We're out of options. This is the end of the road.

Berruci was right—I *lost*. I just can't bring myself to accept that.

"What do you mean you can't reach her?" Berruci demands from across the room, grabbing Joseph by his shirt collar.

Joseph holds up his phone. "She isn't answering. I'm sure she's on her way."

Oh?

My ears burn, an electric current thrumming in my veins. It could be nothing. Bad signal. We're underground, after all. Maybe Diana hit a spot of traffic. Or maybe . . .

Maybe it's a sign that the winds are changing course.

Out of the corner of my eye, I spot the subtlest movement of the mouse icon on Berruci's desktop computer. No one else notices as it slowly trails down to the start menu, pulling up the command prompt and causing the entire system to crash. The screen goes blank and then returns in bright, eerie blue.

The lights flicker. The bunker's isolated ventilation system whirs to life. Loud, obnoxious EDM music plays through the computer's speakers, overwhelming the room. Someone types out a message in bright-green font.

I'm in.

~QWERTY xoxo

"What's happening?" Berruci snaps.

I can't help but smile. "It means you're *fucked*."

CHAPTER THIRTY-EIGHT

The Great Escape

Adelina

THE MOMENT THE program goes live, I receive a notification ping on my phone. West *did it.* I'm so happy I could kiss him. Provided I can save him from Berruci, which I very much plan to do. Now that Berruci's computer has been brute-forced to connect to the internet, I reign supreme. It's finally time for me to wreak havoc.

The first thing I do is tap into the security cameras, studying the live feed from every possible corner of the villa. The east wing is empty, as is the main foyer, though there's a notable presence in and around Berruci's bunker. That's to be expected. He thought he could trap West down there, but I bet he didn't expect to be caught up in his own net.

What does concern me, however, is the realization that not only is West bound and strapped to a chair, but he isn't alone. Allistair has been captured too. And just beside him is a man I've never seen before, but who looks strangely familiar.

The real shock comes when I see *her*.

"Lily?" I gasp under my breath.

My heart hammers against the ladder of my ribs, my palms suddenly cold and clammy. No wonder she wasn't answering Mom's calls. (A fucking *Taken* situation!) That asshole Berruci kidnapped my twin, but to what end? Blackmail, no doubt. A bargaining chip. Given what Diana said about needing to bring me in alive, it's the only logical explanation I can come up with. How dare he rope her into this.

I'm going to make him pay. Fifty billion dollars and then some.

Now that I have unfettered access to his entire network, it's a simple task to manipulate every single electronic on the premises. What I need to do is smoke him out. I won't be able to rescue everyone if they're secure underground. It's a game of chess, and right now, I need to force my opponent into making a blunder.

Tucked away in the villa's lush gardens, I set the building's fire alarms off with a few keystrokes. Next is the house alarm, wailing loudly into the night. I make it appear as though I've opened one of the windows on the second floor. It's all a ruse, of course. A diversion to draw away some of Berruci's men.

I press the space bar to unmute the camera microphones, relishing the panic in Berruci's tone. He shoves Joseph and the rest of his men out of the bunker and up the stairs, then gives Joseph a pointed look. "Your woman failed, Demarr. If you don't bring the hacker to me, consider our deal null and void."

Joseph's lip curls. "I'll find her."

"Hurry up, dammit! She has to be nearby."

I'm in your walls, actually.

It's a privilege like no other to see Berruci's face turn beet red as he reads my message off the computer monitor.

"So you can hear me?" he snarls.

Yeah. Me and the whole neighborhood.

"Why don't you come out of hiding, hm? I only want to talk."

Right. And you're keeping everyone
for a tea party.

Berruci approaches the screen, turning his back on West and the others. "You're in no mood for games. Fine. Neither am I. I want to propose a deal."

`Let everyone go first.`

"That's not how I do business, my dear."

On camera, I spot West shifting slightly in his seat. Now that I have Berruci thoroughly distracted, he's making his move. I'm not sure how he plans on getting out of his handcuffs until I see a glint of something silver slip out from under his tongue. A hairpin. I hold my breath, oddly relieved to know that he didn't listen to my warning about it being a choking hazard. If I can buy him enough time, he might be able to free himself and the others, but I must be convincing. I type slowly, one letter at a time.

`What do you want?`

West twists his head around and drops the pin over his shoulder. I'm not sure where it falls, but I can only pray he managed to catch it.

"You've intrigued me," Berruci says. "Ever since our friend West informed me that you stole from my account, I've been curious about you. He was supposed to find you and bring you straight to me, though he clearly had his own plans."

`Let me guess. You want me to work for you?`

"Think of the money we could make. With my resources and your talents, we'd rake in billions for ourselves."

`So you kidnapped my sister to`
`make sure I can't refuse.`

"Don't worry. No harm shall come to her . . . so long as you do as I say."

What about the others?

"I'm afraid they're not a part of this arrangement. I'm not very lenient on those who cross me. In this case, repeatedly."

I take a deep breath. This is it.

And I don't like working for assholes. No deal.

"You do realize I could kill everyone in this room, right?"

Awful hard to do that without a gun.

Berruci sneers. "What?"

He turns—all too late—to discover that West not only has freed himself and successfully lifted Berruci's pistol from his own holster, but has also managed to free Lily, Allistair and the other man in the room. Looks like West has finally managed to pluck the tail right off this rat. In all the chaos, Berruci made the mistake of sending all of his guards on a wild-goose chase, leaving himself sorely outnumbered.

"Watch your back, dickhead," West says bitterly.

Lily hangs back as the three of them jump Berruci and give him a taste of his own medicine. I look away, not only because I'm averse to outright displays of violence, but because I hear something.

Sirens.

I can't tell if it's the cops or fire trucks or both. Regardless, we're in for a lot of heat if we don't leave. In all caps, I write:

WE HAVE TO GO.

"Can you meet us at the garage?" West calls up to the camera. Berruci is little more than a curled-up lump on the ground, unconscious and bruised and hopefully concussed as hell. Serves him right.

I take in my surroundings. I know the layout of the villa like it's the back of my hand thanks to all the time I spent watching West race through the course.

`Take care of Lily. I'll race you there.`

I don't move an inch until I see West graciously help Lily (literally) step over Berruci, guiding her and what remains of our ragtag crew out of the bunker. Shutting my laptop, I make my way toward the west wing, hugging the outer wall of the villa as tight as I'm able to keep out of sight.

A few blocks away, flashing red lights paint the neighboring buildings. The frantic wail of sirens grows ever louder. Berruci's men are scattered without instruction or clear purpose, most of them likely trying to determine if it's a safer bet to stay or to flee. Either way, I don't want to risk capture. We're at the finish line. We can't give up now.

The garage was built as an extension off the main building. West and the others will be able to enter from the inside, but I need a way to sneak in. I try the door, testing my luck, but find it locked. What I wouldn't give for West's lockpicking skills right about now.

"Vérifiez là-bas!" a gruff voice exclaims. Shit. One of the guards. If they catch me here—

A large hand clamps over my mouth, stifling my yelp as I'm suddenly dragged backward into the garage. I'm no fighter, but my first instinct is to kick and bite and scratch.

"It's me," a familiar voice says quickly. "It's *me*, Adelina."

I turn, as dumbfounded as I am relieved. "West?"

He wraps me up in a tight hug, planting a sweet kiss on my lips. "You're not hurt, are you?" he asks. "Did Diana try anything?"

"I'm fine," I say. "I crashed her car, but I'm fine."

"You what?" West laughs.

I cup his face, distraught to see a few bruises blooming along his cheekbone and jaw. "Are you okay? I was so worried."

"I'm alright now, mon ange."

"Um, *hello*?" Lily stands beside us with her arms crossed. All she has to do now is stomp her foot, but holy shit is she a sight for sore eyes. "You have a lot of explaining to do, Addy. What the hell have you gotten yourself into?"

"We can all catch up later," the mystery man says as he checks each of Berruci's ten different vehicles. I'm not sure what he's looking for. Maybe keys? "We're running out of time," he says.

"Who's that?" I ask West.

"That's Michael."

"Your *brother*? I thought he was dead."

"Nice to meet you too," he grunts.

West shakes his head. "We'll do proper introductions later."

Michael yanks on the door of a parked SUV, whistling at us when it pops open. "Get in."

Michael gets into the driver's seat, Allistair in the passenger. Lily, West and I all clamber into the back, barely having enough time to close the door before Allistair remotely opens the garage door and Michael slams on the gas.

Tires scream beneath us as we launch forward, the engine roaring to life as we peel out onto the main drive. The police are closing in. We might be able to make it onto the main road if we floor it, but then someone steps out in front of us, gun in hand.

Diana. Her brow is sweaty, her eyes bloodshot. She lifts the gun and aims. Michael stomps on the brakes.

"Get out!" she shrieks.

"What do we do?" I rasp.

"Let me talk to her," West says, reaching for the door handle.

"Are you crazy? She's going to kill us!"

"*Trust* me."

West opens the door slowly and sticks his head out from behind it, his hands up in a show of peace.

"You need to let us go, Diana," he says.

"After what you did to us?" she seethes. "You're going to get what you deserve."

"He didn't do anything!" I shout out the door. "It was Joseph!"

Her lip twists into a sneer. "Shut up. I don't believe you."

"We all heard him confess!" Lily adds.

"He said he sold you out," Allistair piles on.

"Diana," Michael says, voice booming with gravitas. "Old friend, you have to believe us. Joseph fucked us all over. He turned on us for a bigger cut."

Tears streak Diana's cheeks. "I don't . . . He wouldn't do that to me."

"Diana," West says, his tone pleading. *Begging*. "I have never lied to you."

Her hand trembles, finger curled dangerously around the trigger. I don't know if we've helped or damned our cause, but I take it as a good sign that we aren't dead yet.

The sound of footsteps crunching over the gravel drive alerts me to a new arrival—Joseph himself, his brow sweaty from running. He takes one look at us in the car, and then at Diana.

"Ma chérie," he says. "What are you waiting for? Kill them."

She hesitates. Doubt flashes behind her dark eyes. "Was it you?" she asks, turning the gun on him. "In Paris. Did you sell us out?"

Joseph laughs nervously, taking a step toward her. "Whatever they told you, they're lying. They'll say anything to save their own necks—"

"Answer me," she snaps.

He takes another step forward. "Diana, let's be reasonable."

"Why won't you just answer—"

Joseph lunges, knocking Diana's arm away much like I did when we were trapped in the car together. The gun goes off, the front windshield shattering to bits.

"Get down!" Allistair shouts.

I do so reactively, but the only thought in my mind is West. I scream his name as he rushes toward the chaos, throwing his weight at Joseph before he can lay his hands on Diana. West manages to tackle him to the ground before grabbing Diana's hand and dragging her toward the car. We all cram into the back. It's a tight fit, but we make it work. Joseph, meanwhile, is quick to recover, Diana's gun in hand. He must have wrestled it out of her grip.

"Drive!" I scream at Michael.

Michael floors it.

Joseph gets off four rounds. I squeeze my eyes shut as bullets go flying. Lily screams. Joseph has to jump out of the way, his legs clipped by the SUV as it careens onto the street. Holy shit. I think we just *hit him with our car*.

When I finally find the courage to open my eyes, I'm startled to find West in front of me, arms outstretched to protect me, Lily and Diana. He slumps back, resting his head against my shoulder.

"West?" I rasp. I tug at his shirt, alarmed when my palm comes away red and sticky. Terror claws through me.

He's been shot.

CHAPTER THIRTY-NINE

Ouch

West

I'VE NEVER BEEN shot before, but, 10/10, I would not recommend it.

But if it means keeping Adelina safe, I'd do it again in a heartbeat.

CHAPTER FORTY

A Very Literal Game of Red Light, Green Light

Adelina

"CAN'T YOU DRIVE any faster?" Lily asks, gripping the back of Michael's seat for support as we bank right. The cops are on our tail, chasing us through the crowded streets of Nice with their sirens on full blast.

"If you think you can do a better job, *you're* welcome to try!" Michael shouts over his shoulder.

"We have to lose them," Allistair snaps. "Take a left here!"

Michael does so, cranking the wheel with such force that the back end of the SUV slides out from behind us. He expertly throws the vehicle into second gear, controlling the momentum of our drift so that we don't spin out.

Michael guns it down the narrow street, the buildings on either side of us threatening to scrape the paint off the sides of our car. It's a one-way road. And judging by the small car rounding the corner just up ahead—*we're going the wrong way*.

Michael shifts into fifth. I can't bear to look.

We miss the car by a mere half inch, catching a bit of air as we hop the curb and swerve back onto the main road. The police car that was in hot pursuit comes to a screeching halt, unable to pull off the same miraculous maneuver. In the reflection of the rearview, the officer reaches for his radio, no doubt calling for backup.

I hold West as tight as I dare, pressing my hand against his wound to staunch the bleeding. Joseph got him in the chest, just below his left shoulder. There's no exit wound, so I can't tell if the bullet managed to pierce anything vital. All I know is that he needs medical attention, and soon.

"We have to get him to the hospital!" Michael exclaims over the chaos.

"And give the police the chance to catch up to us?" Allistair asks.

"We'll have to dump and run," Diana says, helping me apply pressure to the wound.

"No!" I snap. "We're not leaving him behind."

"We don't have a choice," his brother says. "Do you want him to bleed out?"

My stomach churns. "No."

"The doctors *have* to treat him. They can't turn him away." Michael whips the car left, driving straight through a red light. The driver of a vehicle we cut off lays on their horn. "We're not going to get very far with the way he is now. We'll come back for him. I promise."

I grind my teeth, exhaling shakily as I take in West's face. He's pale, his features pinched in pain as a thick layer of sweat coats his brow. Maybe Michael is right. West needs medical attention, and the only way he's going to get it is if we drop him off at the hospital. But the thought of abandoning him makes my heart squeeze. If we leave him by himself, there's no telling what might happen.

"It's okay," he murmurs, so soft and tired. He manages to open his eyes a crack, looking up at me with a weary smile. "I'll be okay, mon ange. Trust me."

"Stop saying that. The last time you said that you got shot!"

I don't realize I'm trembling until Lily places her hand on my shoulder. She looks deep into my eyes and nods, a silent conversation passing between us. Nothing needs to be said. Her reassurance is enough that I begin to mimic her nod.

"Okay," I murmur. "Can we evade the police long enough to get him to the emergency room?"

"I think I can give us a minute's head start," Michael says behind the wheel.

I take a deep breath. "Then a minute will have to do."

Hôpital Pasteur. I wish I could say it was a sight for sore eyes. Never in a million years did I think we'd end up coming back here.

As a team, we move with the utmost efficiency. Michael drives the car straight up to the emergency room entryway. Allistair is out the door in a flash, racing toward the inner vestibule to grab something for West to sit on. Lily, Diana and I pull West out of the back seat, setting him down on the complimentary wheelchair that Allistair returns with. A handful of hospital employees gawk at us, already stepping forward to investigate. The sirens aren't that far behind us.

"Plus vite!" Michael yells from inside the car.

By some miracle, West has enough energy to remain upright. "Go," he urges, voice hoarse.

I caress his cheek. "If you die on me, I'll kill you."

West chuckles, only to wince from the effort. "Yes, ma'am."

I plant a kiss on his forehead before peeling away, climbing back into the car in a hurry. We race off just as a few ER nurses rush out, immediately attending to West with looks of great concern. Hopefully none of them get a good look at our faces.

Just like that, we're back on the road, our momentary pit stop barely slowing us down. It feels like all of Nice is after us. Weaving in and out of traffic, we've turned the city into an obstacle course.

"We can't keep this up much longer," Michael says, his grip on the steering wheel knuckle-white. "They're going to catch us sooner or later."

"Or we'll run out of gas," Lily adds.

"Damn this traffic!" Diana grumbles.

An idea suddenly pops into my head. The answer has been staring us in the face the entire time.

"Hang on," I say, grabbing my laptop from the car floor.

"What are you doing?" Lily asks.

"Giving us a straightaway," I reply, hacking into the city's traffic-control system. It's a little startling how easy it is. Someone in their cybersecurity department needs to be fired ASAP. It takes me two attempts to crack through their firewall. The second I'm inside, I change all the lights ahead of us to green.

If a city's roads are its veins and arteries, I officially have control of its pulse.

Lily gawks at me, equal parts horrified and amazed. "Holy shit."

"They're still on our tail," Allistair says, peering out the window.

"Not for long," I reply, making an absolute mess of the signal rotations with just a few lines of injected code.

Drivers turn left, right, and start straight ahead, only to slam on their brakes. Confusion floods the streets. Everyone starts honking at everyone. Our pursuers are trapped behind the congestion, growing smaller in our rearview mirror as we leave the chaos behind.

We're in the clear.

But our business is far from finished.

CHAPTER FORTY-ONE

Even Houdini Needed an Assistant

West

WHEN I FINALLY come to, I find myself handcuffed to a hospital bed. Talk about kinky.

I pretend to sleep, taking in my surroundings through the briefest glimpses. I'm hooked up to all sorts of monitoring equipment, the machine at my bedside beeping every now and then. I'm alright for the most part, though incredibly sore. Whatever painkillers they have me on are doing an excellent job of muting the ache in my back and shoulder.

I'm not the only one in the room. A police officer and a nurse speak in hushed French.

"When will he wake?" the officer asks.

"I'm not sure, sir. Though it shouldn't be too long now."

"And you're sure he had no ID on him?"

"None at all. And the security cameras didn't catch anything about the people who dropped him off because it was so dark."

The officer groans. "This patient is our only lead. Be sure to tell me the moment he wakes. I have a lot of questions to ask him."

"Yes, of course."

I do my best not to react despite my relief. I gather that means Adelina and the others must have gotten away. Now the question remains: How do I get out of here and catch up with them?

My plan is nothing elaborate. I'll wait for the nurse to go about her checks, and I'll slip out the door the moment I'm left unsupervised. The only problem is that I'm in a breezy, paper-thin hospital gown and I have no idea where they've put my clothes. I doubt I'll get very far with my backside exposed. There's also the added challenge of my handcuffs. I can't pick them open if I don't have any of my tools on me.

Not ideal, but not impossible either. I'm going to have to give it some more thought.

Once the nurse finishes scribbling her notes on my chart, I fully expect her to leave, providing me with a window of opportunity. Except . . .

Except she doesn't do that.

"Ah, finally," she says when her wristwatch beeps. "Time for my break."

I'm sure this hospital has a perfectly nice lunchroom, but for some reason, she decides to claim the room's spare chair and park herself beside me. She leans back and turns on the small TV that's mounted to the wall. "You don't mind, do you?" she titters.

I pretend to remain sleeping. *Are you kidding me right now?*

The nurse flips through the channels until she ends up on the news. The much-too-serious anchors deliver the night's breaking headlines.

"—Valentino Berruci is considered one of the most significant arrests by INTERPOL in nearly a decade. Sources say that an anonymous leak provided authorities with damning evidence of Berruci's involvement in racketeering, weapons smuggling, money laundering and bribery. He was arrested alongside Joseph Demarr, who is known to police. Demarr has entered into a plea deal against Berruci in exchange for partial sentencing."

Ha. Why am I not surprised? I guess Joseph's loyalty is only worth as much as a person can pay, and with Berruci cleaned out, there's really no reason to stick his neck out for the bastard.

I lose interest when the anchors move on to lighter topics like international sports news. I lie there impatiently, waiting for the nurse to leave. Doesn't she have other patients to attend to? Doctors to assist?

"Code blue on four," a man's voice announces over the hospital's speaker system. He sounds . . . strangely familiar, though I can't be entirely sure. Maybe it's the painkillers muddling my brain, but I could swear he sounds exactly like Allistair. "Code blue on four," the man repeats.

The nurse who so graciously helped herself to my TV stands and leaves, responding to the code with urgency.

Finally.

As soon as the door to the room clicks shut, I throw off my thin blanket and inspect the handcuff chaining my left hand to the frame of the hospital bed. It's a standard make, nothing too complicated. If only I had a pin or something just as slender to work my magic. I look around the room, searching for a viable tool, but am dismayed to find there's very little in the room to begin with.

I suppose if I'm desperate enough, I could pull a Houdini and resort to temporarily dislocating my thumb so I can slip my whole hand through the cuff, but just the thought is enough to make me grimace. Recovery time can take weeks, and I'd rather not deal with the discomfort, so I file it away as a last resort.

I've been in tighter spots before. There has to be *something* I can do to escape.

"Come on," I grumble to myself. "*Think*."

Before I get the chance, I hear footsteps approach my door. Someone fiddles with the doorknob, the hinges creaking lightly as they push it open, offering me the briefest glimpse of a woman in light-blue scrubs. The nurse again. Quick to maintain my cover, I throw my blanket back on and go still.

I'm vaguely aware of her to my right as she checks on my vitals.

Push comes to shove, I could always try to charm her into letting me go, but I doubt I'll get very far with the police sniffing around.

"How long do you plan on playing possum?"

I crack an eye open, grinning wide when I recognize her voice. Adelina. She's dressed as a nurse, her outfit complete with a fake ID badge clipped to her pocket. "Took a page out of my book, did you?"

She shrugs. "If it works, it works."

"God, I missed you."

Adelina laughs softly. "It's only been a day."

"I said what I said."

She reaches into her pocket and produces a proper lockpick, handing it to me so I can make quick work of my handcuff. The second I'm free, I cup her face and pull her down into a deep kiss, relishing the warmth of her skin and the scent of her floral shampoo.

"How are you feeling?" she asks me in a whisper.

"Not going to lie, I'm in a lot of pain. Joseph's a terrible shot, though. I think most of the bullet's momentum was absorbed by the passenger-side window, so it didn't end up going too deep. I overheard the doctors say I'll be stiff for a while, but I'll make a full recovery."

"Thank goodness," Adelina sighs. "I can't believe you threw yourself in front of me like that."

"Heroic, I know."

"I was going to say fucking stupid, but whatever works."

I press my forehead to hers. "I don't regret it."

"Do you feel well enough to move?"

"Yes. Let's get the hell out of here."

After I carefully unhook myself from all the monitoring equipment and gingerly remove my IV—unlike in the movies, you're not supposed to just rip that shit out—Adelina hands me a pair of scrubs that she snuck in with her. I came in as a patient, but I'll be leaving under the guise of hospital staff.

With a doctor's cap to cover my hair and a mask to conceal my face, I easily slip out of the room beside Adelina, both of us unnoticed as we start our trek down the hall. My injury makes walking uneasy, every step bringing with it a dull, aching stab. But we can't give up now that we're just about to reach the elevators.

Out of the corner of my eye, I happen to spot Allistair and his brother, Elliot, who's up and about with the help of some crutches. Allistair tips his head in acknowledgement, his smile appreciative. I nod back at him. So it *was* him that I heard over the speakers. Looks like I owe him one.

"Who are they, brother?" Elliot asks.

"Good people," Allistair replies.

Adelina and I get on the elevator, and she all but jams the button for the ground floor. We're in the final stretch, and we're both practically vibrating out of our skin to make a run for it. When we get to the ground floor, there's nothing to stand in our way. The two of us walk out, slipping into the waiting car that Michael's parked beside the curb. Lily is in the passenger seat, looking equal parts relieved and understandably concerned. Diana is in the back, already opening the door for us.

"Doctors," she greets as we buckle up.

We drive away without a hitch.

CHAPTER FORTY-TWO
All's Well That Ends Well

Adelina

Two Weeks Later
Sacramento, California

"ARE YOU STILL mad at me?" I ask as I join Lily on the wraparound porch. The summer heat here in California is very different from the heat back in Vancouver. It's dry, toasty. My skin is already a little burnt, and I was only playing with Jack and Michael in the yard for twenty minutes.

My sister sighs. "I'm not mad, Addy. I'm just . . . processing."

I almost laugh. Lily has been *processing* ever since I told her the truth on the plane. We're in the *lying low* phase of West's master plan, and while I'm grateful for the breather, being subjected to Lily's silence is its own kind of torture. I know my sister. She doesn't get upset often, but when she does, her anger is the kind that simmers and stews.

Jack has invited us all to a princess tea party in the backyard. I have to admit there's something incredibly funny and utterly adorable about seeing Michael, big and burly man that he is, seated cross-legged on the grass with a tutu on his lap (because it doesn't fit) and a plastic tiara on his head. I probably wasn't the only one worried about how Jack would take the news that he was her father, but children her age will believe anything, apparently.

("Your Papa is a superspy, too," West explained when we got back. "And he's finally back from his secret mission!")

If only my sister were as accepting. Then we could sweep this whole thing under the rug.

"I wish you'd told me sooner," Lily says.

"I didn't exactly know how to bring it up."

"Is it always this dangerous?"

I shake my head. "Normally I do this from the comfort of home. It's usually very safe."

"How many people have you stolen from?"

"I don't keep track."

"How *much* have you stolen?"

"I don't keep track of that either."

Lily grips the railing, the wood creaking beneath her fingers. "The other people you've taken from . . . are they just as dangerous as Berruci?"

I take a deep breath, watching Jack pour her father a cup of tea. (It's just water, but Michael drinks like it's the most delicious thing he's ever tasted.) "Some of them are," I say quietly. "But like I said, it's usually very safe."

"What if they come after you? Find you the same way West managed to find you."

"That won't happen again." I glance at her, chewing on the inside of my cheek. The moment I had a solid enough internet connection, I scrubbed that damn article off the face of the internet. Although I did download a copy for myself. It *was* a gift from Dad, after all. It will be for me and Lily to treasure, but for us alone. "You don't approve," I say after a moment.

Lily runs her fingers through her hair. "That's not it. I think . . . Well, I think it's really fucking cool what you're doing."

"You do?"

"Of course. Stealing from the rich to give to the poor? That's *awesome,* Addy." Lily sets her jaw. "It's just that I'm studying to be a lawyer. Do you have any idea how conflicting this is for me?"

"I understand." Jack skips in a circle, waving at Lily and me. We wave back. "You're not going to tell anyone, are you?" I ask.

"No," Lily says firmly. "No, I'm not going to tell anyone. Snitches get stitches and all that, but . . ."

"But?" I prompt.

"Is there really nothing else you could do?"

I smile gently. "I don't know what to say. I've found my calling. Whatever consequences may come, they're mine to bear."

Lily takes my hand and gives my fingers a squeeze. "But I don't want anything bad to happen to you."

I squeeze her hand back. "I'll be fine. I promise."

My sister nods slowly, contemplative. "Alright," she whispers. "Not that you need my approval or anything. I'm sure you were going to keep doing this regardless."

"Probably." I pick at a loose thread on my sleeve. "You should call Mom. She worries when you don't check in."

"About that. I think I'm . . . Well, I'm not going no contact, exactly, but I want to limit how much we interact from now on."

I arch a brow. "Is this a solidarity thing? Because you don't have to not talk to her just because I've chosen not to."

"Being around Mom is like putting my hand on a stove element. Sometimes it's on and burns me, other times it's not and I'm okay, but I'd rather not risk it on a coin toss." Lily shakes her head. "I just wasn't brave enough to stand up for myself . . . or you. Don't get me wrong—I love her, but I love you too. I'm tired of seeing what she puts you through. And I think moving to Nova Scotia for law school will be good for me. It'll give us the chance to breathe."

I smile, bumping my twin with my shoulder. There isn't much to say. I'm proud of her, and I respect her decision. Maybe one day, we'll all be able to exist amicably in the same room together. But until then, the only way to protect ourselves is to take some space.

"Lily! Addy!" Jack calls, racing over to us with something balanced on her palm. She climbs the low steps of the porch and takes Lily's hand. "Papa and I just made a fresh batch of cookies. Do you want some?"

The cookies in question have been crafted out of Play-Doh, topped with an obscene amount of neon-pink glitter. Lily breaks out into a big smile anyway, graciously accepting Jack's offering.

"That sounds *delicious*. I'll be right over."

"Is Uncle West feeling better?" she asks, looking specifically at me. "I want him to come play too."

"He's still resting, sweetie, but I'm sure he'll be up and about really soon."

"His cold must be really bad," Jack reasons aloud. "Can you give him a hug and kiss for me? That always makes *me* feel better."

I laugh softly. "Of course. I'm sure he'll appreciate it."

Jack drags Lily toward her tea party, giving me the chance to dip back inside the house. It's a little strange, getting to see where West lives. The walls are painted a light blue, the wooden floors a stained walnut. Jack's toys are everywhere, not a single surface free from her particular brand of bubbly chaos.

I climb the stairs and make my way to the room at the very end of the carpeted hall, knocking on the door before I enter. West is in bed, propped up on a throne of pillows, a laptop balanced on his belly. He looks up and grins at me.

Diana, who's seated across the room, tosses her newspaper aside. "Thank God you're here," she grumbles. "All he does is complain."

"You said you wanted to make it up to me, remember? You know, for accusing me of being a snitch and putting our lives in danger and—"

"Yes, yes. I get it. I just didn't think you'd have me playing nurse."

I laugh lightly. "When is your flight to New Delhi?"

"Tonight," she replies as she rises from her seat. "I'm . . . excited, I think. It's been a long time since I've seen my family."

"I hope you take this the wrong way, but I hope I never see you again."

Diana grins. "Don't you mean 'I hope you *don't* take this the wrong way'?"

I shake my head and give her a hug. "Not at all."

She kisses my cheek. "Stay out of trouble."

"You, too."

When she leaves, I close the door after her and make my way over to West. I take a seat on the edge of his bed.

"You're making waves online," he says, turning the screen toward me. He has a CNN news article pulled up.

Multimillion-dollar donations given to
World Central Kitchen and Global Fund for
Women by anonymous donor

I set his laptop on the bedside table. "You should be sleeping."

"But I feel fine," he insists.

I pin him with a hard look. "Lift your arms above your head."

West does so but fails to hide a wince. "I'm just tender, that's all."

"Mm-hmm," I reply dryly as I curl up with him beneath the covers. I hug him gingerly and press a kiss to his cheek. "These are from Jack."

West combs his fingers through my hair and hums contentedly. "Who's watching her now?"

"Michael and Lily."

"Do they know how to test her blood-sugar level? What about—"

I press my hand to his chest. "Relax. You went over it with them a hundred times. Jack's in very good hands."

"Right. You're right." He eases against his pillows and takes a deep breath.

"Is it weird?" I ask him. "Seeing Michael with Jack?"

"Not at all. I'm glad that they're together again." He smiles down at me. "And you made that all possible."

"I didn't do anything."

"You got us all out of there alive."

"That's nothing. You took a bullet for me."

West chuckles. "Take the damn compliment."

A comfortable silence falls over us, the distant sounds of Jack, Michael and Lily's laughter filtering in from outside. The air is warm and heavy, nothing but the soft whir of the room's ceiling fan to keep us company. Sunlight streams in through the cracks in the venetian blinds, painting the room in soft, golden hues. When I'm wrapped up in West's arms, all is right with the world. But as I rest my head against his chest and listen to the steady beat of his heart, a question lingers over our heads, one that neither of us seems particularly eager to answer.

"When do you have to go again?" West asks, the first to break the delicate peace we've found.

"Tomorrow afternoon," I whisper. I've been counting the days, dreading every hour that passes us by.

He holds me tighter, breathes me in. I can tell he has a lot on his mind. It's in his eyes, which are brimming with thoughts unsaid. A part of me wonders if he'll ask me to stay. Another part of me wonders if I'll agree to. Our lives were momentarily perpendicular, running alongside one another at the same speed. But now the tracks are diverging, and I'm unsure how or if it's even possible that we'll ever cross paths again.

"I guess we'd better make good use of our time," he murmurs, his hands sliding down to my waist.

I tilt my head up and kiss him deeply, relishing the taste of his lips and the warmth of his body. "I guess we'd better."

We move slowly, taking our time to explore and savor now that victory is ours. I help him out of his shirt, ever mindful of his injury, my eyes sweeping over the canvas of his arms and chest. Greedily drinking in every detail, I dip down to press my lips to the line of his jaw, down the crook of his neck, and then to his collarbone.

My hands sweep over his chest, tracing the outer edges of his bandages. He's healed nicely, and I believe West when he says he feels fine, but that doesn't stop me from being careful. What he did isn't lost on me. If he hadn't thrown himself in front of me, that bullet likely would have found its way directly to my heart. West saved my life, and I don't think there's anything I could ever say to express how grateful I am.

So I show him instead.

Undressing is a sensuous affair, every inch of exposed skin awarded with a give-and-take of reverent kisses. I straddle his lap, memorizing the way his rough palms sweep up my sides, grasping and caressing and mapping out every curve and line available before him. There is nothing quite so thrilling as the sensation of his want between my thighs and the low moan I pull from his lips with the gentle rocking of my hips.

"Je veux te connaître," I murmur against his ear as we approach the crescendo together. "In every sense of the word."

"My darling, you already do."

We fall apart together, these stolen moments belonging to us alone.

CHAPTER FORTY-THREE
Gun-Shy

West

Sacramento International Airport

THE CHOI TWINS need to take a flight from SMF to LAX and *then* they'll be on their way to YVR. I'm not sure why there isn't a direct flight plan offered, but I'm no aviation expert. It probably saves the airline money in some way or another. What I really worry about is how Adelina will fare, dealing with two planes and a hasty transfer.

"This is for you!" Jack says, handing Adelina and Lily handmade bracelets. They both crouch down and accept their gifts, giving her tight hugs.

"These are beautiful," Lily says. "Thank you so much."

"We'll take good care of them," Adelina adds.

We're gathered in front of domestic departures. It's busy today, large groups traveling this way and that with carry-on luggage in tow. The large TV mounted on the wall lists flight information in real time. Adelina and Lily have another hour or so to get through security and arrive at their gate. Traffic on the way here meant they'll be cutting it close.

"Can I talk to you?" I ask her. "Over here."

She nods, leaving Lily behind to chat with Michael. I pretend not to notice the way he takes Lily's hand and kisses the back of it, nor do I question the way her cheeks flush pink. They must be getting along really well, though I have something far more important to focus on right now.

I cup Adelina's cheeks and kiss her. She kisses me back, hugging me tight, seemingly unwilling to let go. *Goodbye* feels too final and *see you later* would only be an empty promise, so instead I say, "I'm really glad you stole from me."

She laughs against my shoulder. Or maybe it's a sob; I can't be sure. "I'm glad I stole from you too."

We cling to each other, neither of us showing any signs of wanting to be the first to part ways. I would keep her here forever, if I could, but that's too much of an ask. No matter how hard I rack my brain, I can't figure out how to make this—*us*—work. She has her life to return to, and I have my family to take care of. I can't ask her to stay, and neither can I go.

"Will I ever see you again?" I ask.

"Keep your eye on the news," she says lightly. "If someone on the *Forbes* billionaire list suddenly comes to financial ruin . . ."

"Probably you?"

"Probably me." Adelina laughs. "Before I go, I have a parting gift."

"You do?"

She holds something up by the strap, a familiar-looking wristwatch. I look down to find my wrist bare. I hadn't even noticed. Talk about an impressive pinch.

"I figured it out," she says with a self-satisfied grin.

Pride swells in my chest. "That's my girl." She tries to hand it back to me, but I shake my head, clasping my hands over hers. "Keep it." *To remember me by* goes unsaid.

Someone clears their throat. Adelina and I both look to find Lily standing there awkwardly, wearing an apologetic smile. "I'm sorry, but we really have to get going. It's going to take us forever to get through security."

My heart stutters. I don't want her to leave, but I don't know what to do that might convince her to stay.

Instead, I kiss her.

I kiss her for as long as I dare, as deeply as I can, because it's the only way I can show her my gratitude. Because of her, my niece is safe, I have my brother back, and I'm free from Berruci's influence for good. Words will never be enough to express my thanks, but this, at the very least, I can manage.

"Have a safe flight," I tell her as I release her, hating how cold the air is on my skin.

"That's literally not up to me," she says with a laugh, making no effort to move away.

It's her sister who has to shepherd her toward the security line. I stay there, watching as she goes, refusing to leave until Adelina is out of sight. A heavy weight bears down on my shoulders, a cold emptiness clawing at my lungs when she's finally gone.

Michael slaps me across the back of the head.

"Ow," I grumble, frowning at him. "What was that for?"

"For being an idiot," Michael says.

Jack gasps. "That's a bad word, Papa."

"My apologies, little bird. I meant to say you're being a big, stinky dummy."

I rub the back of my head. Damn, that smarts. "What are you talking about?"

"Go after her."

"I can't. I have Jack."

"*I* have Jack," Michael says. "Mon petit frère, je suis grave reconnaisant pour tout ce que t'as fait. Mais maintenant, c'est le moment pour toi de vivre ta vie." *My little brother, I am grateful for everything you have done. But now it is time for you to live your life.*

He reaches into his pocket and pulls out a passport. *My* passport. He nods at me as I take it. "We'll be okay. You've found yourself a special woman. Don't let her go. Do what you must to convince her to come home with you."

He's right. What am I doing letting the best thing to ever happen to me walk away? I crouch down and give Jack a big hug and kiss. "You take care of your Papa for me, okay?"

"Are you going on another mission?" she asks.

"Yeah, but I'll be right back. There's just something very important I have to do." I hug my brother next, relief and mania flooding my senses. "Call me if you need anything. I'll message you as soon as we land."

"I will," Michael says. "Hurry. You'll need to charm a last-minute ticket out of the clerk."

I smile wide. Lucky for me, charm is my specialty.

CHAPTER FORTY-FOUR
Partners in Crime

Adelina

I HATE THIS. Not just the fact that I have to endure not one but two flights, but the clawing, cold emptiness in my chest. I already miss West terribly. Strapped into my seat at the very back of the plane, I can't help but replay our final moments together over and over again like some broken line of repeating code.

I should have kissed him longer, hugged him harder. Some small part of me had hoped that . . . I don't know. That I would have been brave enough to ask him to come with me. That maybe he'd ask me to *stay.*

Sinking into my seat, I fiddle with his watch, staring at the delicate second hand as it ticks itself in a circle. He's probably already left the airport and is bounding down the freeway with his brother and niece in the car. I understand why he can't just up and leave. And I . . .

Actually, what *is* there to keep me in Vancouver?

I frown deeply at my own stupidity. "Holy shit."

Lily glances my way. She's ripped into a bag of salted nuts, popping a cashew into her mouth. "What's wrong? If you need to go to the bathroom, you'll have to wait until we're up in the air. They already turned on the seat-belt sign."

"No, it's not that." My heart thuds anxiously against my ribs, a sinking feeling gripping me by the throat. The jet engines on the wings whir to life as the flight attendants begin their final checks. "There's nothing."

My sister blinks at me. "What are you talking about?"

"There's nothing to keep me in Vancouver," I say, my head spinning. "You're moving away. I don't talk to Mom or the rest of the family. I don't have any friends—"

"Loser," Lily snorts, but it lacks any real heat.

"I'm being serious." Tears sting my eyes. Getting on this plane was a colossal mistake. I've never been more aware of just how small the surrounding cabin is. "I want to be with West."

Lily frowns. "Why didn't you figure this out *before* we boarded?"

"I fucked up, okay?"

"Boy, I'll say."

"Not helpful, Lil." I run a clammy hand through my hair. "Shit, am I being crazy about this?"

My sister shakes her head, smiling gently. "Adelina, I've never seen you look at anybody the way you look at West. I think you're crazy for not realizing sooner."

"Why didn't you say anything?"

"Bitch, twin telepathy isn't a thing. What was I supposed to do? Read your mind? I thought you had some reason for leaving."

I suck in a sharp breath, undoing my seat belt to hastily vacate my seat. Lily stands so that I can stumble out into the aisle. "I have to get off this plane."

"Ma'am," snaps the flight attendant. She approaches me with a stern expression, blocking my view of the front of the plane—and my escape. "Ma'am, please sit down. We just closed the doors."

"I'm sorry. I'm so sorry, but this is important—"

"Sit *down*."

People are well and truly staring now, but I don't care. "You don't understand, I—"

"What seems to be the problem here?"

The small hairs on the nape of my neck stand on end. I'd know that voice anywhere. I lean to get a glimpse of the tall blond man standing behind the attendant. He flashes his wallet but quickly puts it away before she gets a good look.

"Air marshal." West lies with such brazen confidence that it's difficult to question him. He turns to Lily and says, "I have a seat in first class. If you'd be so kind as to switch with me, I can keep a better eye on her. Make sure she doesn't cause any more trouble."

Lily's shit-eating grin matches my own. "Oh my God, you two are disgustingly cute."

The flight attendant frowns in understandable confusion. "What?"

"Nothing," my sister says, hastily gathering her carry-on bag. She throws a thumbs-up at me before skedaddling down the aisle.

"I'll take it from here," West tells the attendant. "She won't be an issue. It's just a case of nerves. Isn't that right, ma'am?"

I struggle not to burst into a fit of laughter. "Right. Sorry."

The flight attendant nods, appeased by my answer and West's bravado. We all return to our seats and strap in.

"You know, if you hate turbulence so much, you really shouldn't sit this far back," he says. "You'll feel the wind a lot more because you're further from the center of mass."

A laugh builds in my chest, breathy and disbelieving. "It was the only seat available."

"Knowledge for next time."

"What are you doing here, West? I thought—"

"My brother knocked some sense into me," he says as he takes my hand. "Adelina, you are brilliant in every sense of the word. Ever since you stumbled into my life—"

"Actually, *you* broke into my apartment."

"Please, mon tournesol. I'm trying to have a moment."

I grin. "Sorry. Go on."

West strokes the pad of his thumb over my knuckles just as the plane begins to peel away from the gate. "I never could have imagined finding a more perfect partner in crime. Come home with me. Whatever you need in Vancouver, I'll take care of it. I'll take care of *you.* Just stay with me. I love you, Adelina. Whatever mayhem you have planned next, I want to be a part of it."

"I love you too," I reply with a giggle.

"Want to hold my hand during takeoff?"

I lean across the armrest and kiss him sweetly. "Yes, please."

Acknowledgements

WHEN I WAS still working as a ghostwriter, I pitched the idea of a modern-day Robin Hood–inspired romantic thriller to my client. They said no. I was admittedly a little bummed that I had to put the concept on the back burner, but it's as they say—everything happens for a reason. Fast-forward seven years (eight, by the time this book hits the shelves) and I'm excited to have finally found the opportunity to explore the idea with the help of some of the greatest people in the world.

First and foremost, thank you to my agent, Jim McCarthy at Dystel, Goderich & Bourret. When first we met, I was a fantasy author, so I'm incredibly grateful that you have unshakable faith and enthusiasm in my romantic projects as well. There's nothing I love more than writing across genres and working on my craft, and I can't thank you enough for your support.

None of this would have been possible without the help of my wonderful editor, Amanda Ferreira, at Random House Canada. It must have been fate that we found each other the way we did, and I wouldn't have it any other way. I've been sitting on this idea for so long, and I'm glad I got to nurture it into a full novel with you. Here's to hopefully many more books together! You ask—I'll deliver (even if this means occasionally chili-peppering too close to the sun).

Publishing a book is no small task, so I want to give a huge shout-out to the rest of the team at Random House Canada who made *Thieves* possible: Sue Kuruvilla, Deirdre Molina, Stephanie Alleyne, Evan Klein, Karen Angell, Karen Ma, Mary Giuliano, Lisa Jager, Noah Kahansky, Trina Kehoe, Polly Beel, Megan Costa, Samantha North, Adrienne Tang, Catherine Ryoo, Nicole Brand, Erin Cooper, Natasha Tsakiris, Linda Pruessen, John Sweet, Asher Nehring, Kathleen Jones and Alison Deon.

Thank you to Stephanie, Danielle and FER for enduring the chaotic mess that was my zero draft. Your excitement is contagious and helps me remember that writing for friends is one of the best things about my job. Thank you to my hunny. I wouldn't be here today if you hadn't convinced me to take the leap to follow my dreams.

And last but not least, thank you to you, the reader, for picking up a copy of this book. I hope you enjoyed Adelina and West's misadventure.

That's all for now!

Kat xoxo

Find and support your local food bank at
www.FoodBanking.org

KATRINA KWAN is a Vancouver-based fantasy and contemporary romance author. After graduating from Acadia University in 2017 with a BA in political science with honors, Kwan spent the next six years honing her creative skills as a freelance ghostwriter. With several ghostwritten romance novels under her belt, she's ecstatic to finally be writing books under her own name.

You can find her online at *www.katrinakwan.com.*